I0633493

Copyright © 2023 by KINSLEY ADAMS

All rights reserved.

No part of this book may be reproduced in any form or by any electronic or mechanical means, including information storage and retrieval systems, without written permission from the author, except for the use of brief quotations in a book review.

PROLOGUE

ALMOST DYING REALLY SUCKS. ESPECIALLY THE recovery. But some parts are really nice. Like the snuggling. I can't get enough of it. Probably because I didn't exactly grow up in a hug-it-out type of household. Or, in my case, households. Now, I crave the cuddles. Funny, right? Considering I'm a werewolf and a vampire slayer, I'm supposed to be a legit badass who doesn't need anyone to watch her back.

In all fairness, I used to fit that bill.

Until I met my sister, Lucy. And my mate,

Gabriel. They showed me there's more to life than blood and gore, which is ironic considering Gabriel is the king of all bloodsuckers and Lucy is an alpha werewolf. Their jobs are literally synonymous with blood and death. But they've shown me their softer sides. Something I never thought I would have.

Now, the kicker is, I'm scared to death of losing all this. And the universe has a sick sense of humor because that might just happen. Gabriel, the King of Vampires? Yeah, someone has it in for him. They've tried framing him for murder and bribed the Academy to put a price on his head. When that didn't pan out—thanks to *moi*—they switched it up and dragged witches into the mix.

Witches.

As if having slayers on his tail wasn't bad enough, they had to throw in those crazy spell-casters. I'd never seen a witch before, and I sure as hell don't want to see one again. They're straight-up terrifying. Ever heard of demon summoning?

Yeah, me neither. Until now.

Lesson learned, the painful way.

The damned hellspawn nearly tore my heart out, which is why I'm still in recovery mode. Werewolves might heal faster than humans, but we're far from invincible. Vampires can heal anything short of decapitation, fire, sunlight, or a stake to the heart. Werewolves, not so much. The demon sucker-punched me right through my chest and almost put me six feet under. The healing process has been frustratingly slow. *Agonizingly, torturously* slow.

Believe me, I'm over it.

Like I said, the only upside is the cuddles.

Gotta enjoy them while I can, 'cuz once I'm up and running, it's payback time. That demon almost killed me once. It won't get a second shot.

Let's not kid ourselves. Despite the whole demon-hunting-revenge plan, we're clearly standing on the edge of a precipice. One misstep, one mistake, and it's lights out for us. Just like that. But I refuse to let them—*whoever* is behind all this—win.

Ready or not, here I come.

I LURKED IN THE SHADOWS, MY FOCUS LOCKED ON the tall figure nestled within a small copse of trees. His dark as night, medium-length hair moved in the gentle early spring breeze. The soft moonlight highlighted his sharp features, illuminating his chiseled jawline and otherworldly eyes. Everything about him screamed predator, from his laser focus to the tips of his sharp fangs that peeked out from beneath his lips.

Except tonight, I was the predator. And he was the prey.

Exhilaration jolted through me, and I smirked. My werewolf senses hummed in response to the thrill—something I hadn't felt in the week since the demon had plunged its claws into my chest.

Flexing my muscles, I crept through the trees, my steps silent as I inched toward my mark. Every step was deliberate, every breath measured. My target had sensitive hearing—more sensitive even than mine—and a keen nose, so I had to keep upwind. The main issue was my heart. It pounded in my ears like a war drum. I couldn't get too close, lest he hear it. And if he heard it, I'd fail my mission. I had to be strategic. Had to move fast and take him down before he could react.

I braved another step, then paused and cocked my head.

He seemed completely oblivious, lost in thought. But I knew the slightest sound could alert him to my presence. I had to be silent. Careful. Deliberate.

I took another step.

Then another, meticulously avoiding the fallen leaves and dead vegetation.

Suddenly, my target's head tilted, and my traitorous heartbeat quickened. He turned slightly, his eyes scanning the dark woods surrounding us.

I froze, releasing a breath as quiet as the wind. I

couldn't let him spot me, and I wasn't close enough yet to make my move. Not that it mattered. If he turned his head even a fraction of an inch, he'd see me.

My heart simultaneously pounded and stuttered. One, a symptom of adrenaline. The other, a symptom of my most recent injury, one that had left me comatose for three days. If I was being honest with myself, I'd know that I should be in bed, tucked beneath a swath of blankets, rather than out here, hunting someone in the dark night.

Nah. I refused to quit. I'd already come so far.

My target's gaze swung to the left. Knowing he was about to catch me, I ignored the erratic pounding in my chest and launched myself at him. The look of utter surprise on his face was worth every ache in my body and every ounce of effort I'd put into this attack.

Everyone believed I needed more time to recover, that I was far too weak to join in on their reindeer games. Maybe they were right, but I could still be useful, and I needed to prove that. What better way to do that than to take out the Vampire King himself?

Or as I knew him, my mate.

I slammed into Gabriel, sending us tumbling. For

a moment, we were airborne, and then we were falling.

Gabriel reacted quickly, his muscular arms encircling my waist. His grip tightened around me mid-air, and he grunted when we hit the ground. His back absorbed the impact, but his hold never once loosened.

I chuckled, then rested my arms on his rock-hard chest and stared down at him. "Surprise!"

His expression went through a myriad of emotions from surprise to concern, then relief. After a moment, he loosened his grip and tenderly traced the sunken pit beneath one of my eyes. I'd studied my reflection in the bathroom mirror this morning—I knew how I looked. Even after a week of recuperating, it wasn't pretty. Almost dying did that to a girl. But regardless of my wan complexion and weight loss, I wanted Gabriel and everyone else to know I was still alive and could help.

"You nearly gave me a heart attack," he grumbled in his thick British accent.

A smirk curled my lips. "Can't have a heart attack if your heart doesn't beat."

He rolled his eyes but slowly smiled. "Alright, then you nearly put me back in my grave. Does that work better for you?"

"Not really," I said, laughing. It brought horrific images to mind, ones I didn't want to picture right now. I lowered my head to his chest and snuggled into the crook of his neck. His arms came around my waist and he held me so tightly, as though afraid to let me go. Gabriel had been like this since I'd woken up four days ago. According to him, my three-day *nap* had been the most harrowing time of his hundred-and-seventy-five years of life.

"Sorry," I finally said, lifting my head and meeting his gaze. "I want to prove to everyone that I'm perfectly fine. Lucy and Sam act like I'm made of glass. They won't even let Annabelle or Fynn come to my room, fearing they'll stress me out. And Anna and Vlad treat me like I'm some porcelain doll on the verge of shattering right in front of them."

Gabriel's expression shuttered. He'd been trying so hard to rein in his protective nature, but I could see the struggle on his face.

"You have to understand what it was like for them, Maddie," he said. "What it was like for me. To see you standing there, that demon's hand impaled in your chest." He shuddered. "I never want to see anything like that again. We may be a bit protective of you right now, but we all love you. We want nothing more than to see you well again."

I cringed at the mental image he conjured. It wasn't something I ever wanted to experience again, either. At least we were all in agreement on that.

"I'm—"

"Don't say fine," he argued, his accent thickening. It did that when he became agitated. He fell silent and closed his eyes, his hands moving in soothing circles across my back. I had a feeling it was more to calm himself than it was for me. "You forget, I can hear your heart. It's damaged. You're healing, yes. But you still have a long way to go. I know you're frustrated, but you can't rush this."

It warmed every inch of me to see how much he cared. But I was going a little stir crazy, and I needed him to see that. "Gabriel, I *am* fine. *I am werewolf. Hear me roar,*" I said, butchering the song lyrics.

"Yes, and a fearsome one at that," he said, his tone quite serious. "But you need to be gentle on your body for a little while longer."

I pushed off his chest and rose to my feet. "See? I'm good."

I extended a hand to help him up. His fingers slid through mine, but he didn't use my weight to help him stand.

"I'm better than—"

My words died when the world suddenly

pitched sideways. Gabriel, the trees, and the stars all blurred into a dizzying swirl. I swayed, unable to find my center of balance. My knees buckled, but before I hit the ground, a strong pair of arms encircled my middle, steadying me.

I forced myself to swallow, tamping back the nausea that rose from the pit of my stomach. My heartbeat quickened into a panicked staccato, drowning out everything except the urgent sound of Gabriel's voice.

"Maddie? Maddie, stay with me."

I clung to him, using his touch to ground me. He wasn't swaying like a drunken sailor. I could trust him to keep me standing.

Squeezing my eyes shut, I fisted my hands in his shirt and held on for dear life. "S'okay," I mumbled. "Just need a moment."

So maybe I had overtaxed my body a little.

Gabriel gently stroked my hair, his voice calm and steady despite the situation. "Take your time. I've got you. Breathe."

I pressed my face against him, his chest a firm wall against my cheek, and counted to thirty in my head while slowly breathing in and out.

His scent wrapped around me like a comforting blanket. Gradually, the spinning slowed and the roaring in my ears ebbed, allowing me to gain control of my body. Finally, I managed to pry open my eyes. The trees stood still, and the stars hovered above us, twinkling like beautiful diamonds in the sapphire sky. Everything was back to normal.

I met Gabriel's gaze, his steely eyes shimmering with concern in the moonlight. "You scared me," he murmured, his thumb brushing my cheek.

I offered him a weak smile, hoping to ease some of his concern. "Sorry. Guess I'm still getting my sea legs back," I teased, hoping to lighten the mood. "No big deal."

I hated this. Hated being so vulnerable and weak. I hadn't felt this way in years—not since I'd become a werewolf. Losing the strength I'd gained from that change made me feel weaker than a newborn pup.

Gabriel's eyes never once left mine, as though he feared I'd drop dead if he so much as blinked. He lifted a hand and rested it against my chest, right above my fresh, jagged wounds. The demon had etched the memory of its attack on my body in an imperfect pentagon shape—a permanent reminder I'd carry with me for the rest of my life.

"You have nothing to prove to us, Maddie,"

Gabriel said. "We know you're strong. No one is questioning that."

A weak, breathy chuckle slipped past my lips. "Strong and stubborn, some would say."

One corner of Gabriel's mouth ticked upward. "Can you stand?"

I braced my hands on either side of his waist and slowly straightened. When my knees didn't buckle, he slowly drew his arm back, then lifted his hands to cradle my face. Without a word, he leaned in and pressed his lips to mine in a slow, sweet kiss. In the four days since I woke up from the demon attack, he hadn't done anything more than this. Too afraid to hurt me, I suspected.

Still, I reveled in his kisses, refusing to take a single one for granted. One thing about near-death experiences: they certainly put things into perspective, the things people rarely consider. Who knew how many more kisses we'd get? I hoped a lifetime's worth, but throughout my twenty-seven years, I'd experienced more than my fair share of the universe's sick sense of humor. That which it gave, it could also quickly take away. I'd learned that lesson the hard way.

Leaning into Gabriel's kiss, I grabbed his shirt again, this time for an entirely different reason.

Regardless of my healing injuries, my body craved more than a kiss. But after everything that'd happened in the past few minutes, I knew better than to push myself. Besides, Gabriel had made it quite clear he wouldn't be delving beyond kisses for quite some time. Probably until I could tackle him without fainting.

The kiss ended too soon for my liking, and as Gabriel pulled back, a second wave of dizziness hit me—just to fuck with me a little more. The world blurred and I swayed, but Gabriel was there in an instant, catching me before I could stumble.

"Took your breath away, huh?" Gabriel teased, though his voice didn't quite hit a playful tone. He slipped his arm around my waist again, then helped me lean against the nearest tree, his worry-filled eyes never straying from my face. "Give yourself a moment, alright?"

I nodded, resting my head against his chest. His free hand immediately cupped the back of my neck, and I felt the soft press of a kiss against my head.

"Once you're up for it, we'll get you back to the house and into bed."

Ugh. I hated that bed. Understandably, the doctor had confined me there since waking. And truly, four days wasn't the worst sentencing. But it was the longest I'd ever been bedridden before, and I wasn't handling it all that well.

The stubborn part of me—which, admittedly, was a large part of me—wanted to sprint through the trees and prove I was fine. But the small, rational side of my brain pointed out that I'd barely been able to kiss Gabriel without passing out. Deep down, I knew I had to take it easy and stop pushing myself. Not doing so would only slow my recovery. And that was the last thing I wanted.

"No more stalking me through the woods, okay?" Gabriel said, his voice a soft rumble.

"Aww. And here I thought you'd enjoyed our midnight rendezvous," I said, my voice still a bit weak.

"We can sneak away into the woods any time you want." He held up a hand before I could speak. "*After* you're better."

"Okay," I whispered, hating the word. I was so used to being the one on the front lines protecting everyone else. I was a slayer. It was literally in my job description. Being sidelined felt like a punishment.

Gabriel brushed another gentle kiss against my forehead. "I can't lose you, Maddie. You're far too important to me. To everyone. Promise me you'll take it easy."

Both frustration and warmth filled my chest. I loved having people who cared about me. It was something I never thought I'd find in life. At the same time, I was so used to only caring about myself that I was finding it hard to do things for the sake of others.

"I promise," I finally said. "It just sucks, ya know?"

He gave a soft laugh, his chest vibrating from the sound. "I do know. But this is necessary. For your own good and mine. I don't think I could survive going through this all over again. As you pointed out, I don't have a beating heart, so I need yours to keep beating for the both of us."

The heart in question beat a little faster from his words. I stood straight and lifted my head, smiling when the world didn't sway. "I can do that."

"Good," he said. He leaned down and gave me another kiss, this one even gentler than before, if such a thing was possible. He parted from me and ran a hand down my back.

"Guess we should get back the house," I suggested. "Meredith cleared me to remove the bandages today."

I hadn't yet. The thought of peeling them off made my stomach twist. I'd caught a quick glimpse at the wounds once when Meredith was changing the wrappings. It'd sickened me. But I couldn't hide from them forever.

"She also cleared me for baths and showers again," I continued, my thoughts flashing to the massive Jacuzzi Lucy and Sam had installed in their en suite bathroom. "Maybe I'll take a bath tonight and pamper myself a bit."

A mischievous glint sparked in Gabriel's eyes. "Do you think you'll need some help with that? Because I'm here. You know, to help. To be helpful."

"Oh, I'm sure," I said, chuckling.

"Well, we can't risk you fainting and drowning, now can we?"

"Of course. And that's the only reason you want to watch me bathe, huh? To protect me?"

"Naturally," he said, winking.

I shook my head, laughing. Then I stretched up onto my tiptoes and kissed his stubbled jaw. "Thank you, Gabriel."

His brows rose. "For what?"

"For caring about me," was all I said before taking his hand and slowly leading him back to the house.

GABRIEL AND I MADE OUR WAY BACK TO THE
main house, our pace slow and even for my sake. The
trek felt longer than when I'd first set out tonight,
eager for the chase. Now, it felt endless, like we'd
never escape this labyrinth of trees.

"We're almost there," Gabriel assured me,
reading my fatigue like a pro.

Even I could hear my uneven breaths and the
tired flutter of my heart. I tightened my grip on his
hand, silently reassuring myself that I wasn't alone,
and nodded.

"I could carry you," he suggested, an edge of teasing in his voice.

I shot him a glare that screamed "no way." That was the last thing I wanted. I had a point to prove—to me, to him, and to all my friends. I was no damsel, and I certainly didn't want them to think I was in distress. Hell, I needed to show *myself* that I could go for a simple walk without collapsing.

"Stubborn," Gabriel reiterated.

I merely shrugged, too tired to speak.

Finally, after what felt like an eternity, the dense woodland began to thin, revealing a sprawling estate nestled in the heart of Mississippi's countryside. Lucy and Sam had purchased this place five years ago, after a tragic fire that had devoured their previous home. The house, an imposing yet charming Southern plantation-style abode, offered the privacy our paranormally diverse family demanded.

Lucy had needed a place like this, something large and secluded, where she could hold pack meetings free from nosy neighbors. Here, amid the mossy trees and thick brush, her children could grow up without the ever-present fear of exposing werewolves to the public.

I'd fallen in love with this place the instant I'd

laid eyes on it. Its southern charm was perfect, from the sweeping balconies and the large French windows to the wraparound porch perfect for late-night heart-to-hearts. Lucy and I had spent more than a few late nights out there, idly chatting about our lives. We'd learned so much about each other during those little gab sessions.

Our story was a wee bit of a tangled one. I'd grown up a foster kid with no family history or anyone to care for me. After I'd aged out, I'd used one of those ancestry websites to see if I could track down any long-lost family. My search for roots had taken me on quite the journey. It'd started with Olivia, my late half-sister, who'd taught me all about our family secret and turned me into a werewolf. Then came the twisted family politics—Reginald's death, Olivia's madness, and her power struggle with Lucy. When the dust settled, I'd found myself aligned with Lucy, grateful for a sister who felt like home.

Together, Gabriel and I approached the house. Before we could head up the stairs, the front door swung open, revealing a cherub-faced little girl.

"Mom!" My five-year-old niece, Annalise, shouted, most definitely *not* using her inside voice. "Auntie Maddie's back!"

A second pair of tiny footsteps rushed toward us, and I grinned at the sight of my little nephew. Fynn was almost two and the cutest thing I'd ever seen. He was all about hugs, kisses, and cuddles right now. I stepped inside and chuckled when he stopped in front of me and raised his little arms.

"Up. Up, up, up," he babbled.

"No, little man—" Gabriel started.

I interrupted him by gently lifting Fynn into my arms. Ugh, there was something about baby cuddles that could lift a person's spirits. I tucked him against my side to keep him from rubbing my poor chest, then practically melted when he slung one arm around my neck and laid his head on my shoulder.

Lucy popped around the corner and glared at me. "There you are!" She shook a wooden spoon in my direction, then vanished back into the kitchen.

The smell of Lucy's homemade gumbo instantly made my stomach growl. My injuries had done nothing to curb my wolfish appetite.

Annalise chuckled and poked my belly. "That was loud."

"Well, don't stand there starving," Lucy called out. "Get in here and eat something, would ya? Before it gets cold."

Well, we couldn't have that. Guess my bath would have to wait.

Gabriel placed a gentle hand against my back and guided me toward the kitchen. Fynn hadn't so much as lifted his head, and I silently wondered if he'd fallen asleep. The boy could sleep almost anywhere, but his preference was in someone's arms. It always baffled me to see how easily he could crash. But then, he had no worries in the world. He was a happy little boy with a loving family. The thought brought tears to my eyes, but I blinked them back.

"About time you showed up," Lucy chided with a grin. "I went looking for you earlier to tell you dinner would be ready soon. Imagine my surprise when I couldn't find you."

I smiled sheepishly. "I needed to get some fresh air. Get out of bed, ya'know? Stretch my legs a little."

"Mhmm," she hummed, winking at me. Her brows rose, and she glanced at Gabriel. "I'll bet."

I rolled my eyes. "Listen, just because you're a horn dog—"

She waved her spoon at me again. "Little ears, Maddie."

Right.

Sam strode into the kitchen then, and grabbed a

bunch of dishes. He silently set the table, but I caught the slight smirk on his face.

"Well, I hope you're hungry. I made enough food to feed the entire pack," Lucy said.

Luckily, I was starving. I pointed at Fynn. "Is he asleep?"

Sam strode around me and snuck a peek at his little boy's face. "Oh yeah. Crashed right out."

"Okay. Guess I can eat while holding him."

"You'll do no such thing. He's getting heavy, and you're injured," Lucy scolded. "Sam, can you take him from her and put him to bed? She needs to eat to build her strength back up."

Sam scooped the limp boy from my arms and effortlessly carried him upstairs. The domestic image they painted tugged at my heart. Having a vampire for a mate did complicate matters when it came to having children. But that didn't bother me. For as long as I could remember, I knew I'd prefer to adopt a child in need than have one naturally. So many kids out there needed loving homes and caring parents. I didn't know Gabriel's stance on the matter, but given his own adoption, I had a feeling he wouldn't mind. That conversation could come later, though. When our lives weren't so fraught with peril.

"Maddie?" Lucy asked, drawing my attention back to the present.

I blinked and glanced down to find her offering me a bowl of steaming gumbo. "Thanks, Luce."

"You okay?"

"Just tired," I told her, taking the bowl.

She pursed her lips and studied me, her hands planted on her hips. "Maybe the walk wasn't a good idea?"

Gabriel made a noise deep in his throat, one that told me he agreed with her. I ignored them both and headed for the table, taking the seat next to Annalise. Gabriel, still standing, fetched a glass of water for me and a bottle of O-positive for himself. While he heated his meal, he brought me my drink, then brushed his hand against my back as he left.

I dove into the meal with singular focus, barely stopping for breath. It wasn't until I heard Annalise giggling that I tore my eyes from the steaming soup and glanced up. She was watching me with a wide grin, showcasing the gap where she'd once had two front teeth.

My attention drifted to Lucy and Sam, seated side-by-side. Each held a spoon, but they watched me with open humor. Even Gabriel seemed entertained.

"What?" I asked.

"Hungry?" he teased, pointing at the bowl.

I'd practically drained it, whereas the others looked as though they'd only taken a bite or two.

"Yeah, guess so," I said, laughing. I already felt better than I had a few minutes ago. It certainly helped that Lucy made a mean bowl of gumbo. It'd taken me a year or so to adjust to her cooking—she liked things hot and spicy. But now, I found I craved the stinging heat on my tongue.

"It's always an experience to watch werewolves eat," Gabriel commented, winking at me from across the table. Then he glanced at Annalise, who I swore had gotten more on her clothes than in her mouth. "Especially the young ones."

She giggled again, then dove back into her meal with gusto.

"So, what were you *actually* doing out in the woods?" Lucy asked. Then she flicked her spoon at me. "And please be mindful of the little ears."

Every pair of eyes turned to me. Gabriel, however, seemed content to sit back and sip at his glass.

I shrugged. "I really did go for a walk." That wasn't a lie. I simply didn't include the whole hunting part.

Gabriel smirked behind the rim.

"I got a little tired near the end," I continued. "But it was manageable." I fiddled with my spoon and considered my next words. I had a feeling what I was about to suggest would go over about as well as a fart in church. "I think it's time for me to start training again."

No one moved. It seemed to take a few seconds for my words to sink in. Gabriel leaned forward and placed his glass on the table while Lucy dropped her spoon into the half-eaten bowl of gumbo.

"Maddie...," Gabriel hedged. "You know you were a little more than *just tired* out there."

I scowled at him. "Traitor."

He grimaced and sat back. "I don't mean to betray your confidence, but I need you to look at this objectively. You could barely stand at the end. I almost had to carry you back inside."

A growl rumbled in my throat, one that I swallowed. I couldn't get emotional about this, otherwise I'd never convince them. "That's why I need to start training. I need to build up my stamina again."

Lucy chewed her bottom lip, her eyes flicking between me and Gabriel. "Do you really think this is a good idea? Barely a week has passed since you fought that demon. We're not invincible, hun. We may heal faster than humans, but your injuries were grave. You're lucky you're even alive right now."

I shot Annalise a pointed stare, and Lucy winced.

"Annalise, sweetie, can you take your bowl into the living room, please?" Lucy said. "How about you watch a movie while you eat?"

My niece looked up at me with watery, terrified eyes.

"I'm fine, baby," I said. "I'm alive. And I'm getting better." I leaned down and kissed her forehead. "Go eat your dinner and let me and your mommy talk, okay?"

I waited for Annalise to settle herself in the living room before resuming the conversation. "Look, we all know I need to do this. Need I remind you Gabriel still has a bounty on his head? Jaden and Josh have a plan to expose the corruption, and hopefully that'll result in the Academy calling off the hit. But in the meantime, he's still not safe and—"

"He has his guards," Lucy pointed out.

I huffed. "Yes, I know that. But there's also a demon out there somewhere. Who knows what it's been up to—"

"We've been keeping an eye out," Sam chimed in. "No news yet."

I glared at him, tired of people interrupting me. "There's also the witch coven, and last I remember, they want my head on a silver platter. I can't afford to sit back and wait to heal. I need to get better as fast as possible."

"But rushing it—"

"I don't plan to rush it," I said, this time cutting Lucy off. "I plan to go slow. To take it easy and only do what I'm capable of. But if I can get stronger a little faster, that'd be a good thing, right?"

"What if it makes things worse for you?" Lucy asked.

"Then I'll stop," I said, shrugging. "We won't know until I try. I can't sit around doing nothing anymore."

Everyone fell silent for a moment, the room heavy with deliberation. Then Sam sighed. "She has a point. Do you remember when Corbin stabbed you with a silver blade?"

"Yes, I remember I *rested* for two weeks," Lucy said, scowling. "I took the time I needed to heal. And *then* I started training."

Sam nodded. "Only because you knew you had

time. Maddie doesn't have that luxury. The witches could return tonight, for all we know."

Great. Now I wouldn't be able to sleep at all.

Lucy sighed. "I get it. I do. But I don't like it."

"Me neither," Gabriel grumped.

I reached across the table and took his hand, offering a small squeeze. "I'll be careful. I'll go slow. And I'll stop when I start to feel too weak. It's not like I'm planning to run a marathon tomorrow. I'll start with light runs"—I grimaced at the thought. I *loathed* running—"and maybe some light weight training."

His jaw clenched, but he eventually nodded. "My guards will be here during the day tomorrow. Take one with you if you go out, as a precaution. Please."

I nodded, willing to do whatever it took to soothe his concerns. When everyone returned to their meals, I felt a flicker of triumph, and my sense of purpose renewed. This was a small victory, but it was mine. And it was a step toward the normalcy I craved, toward reclaiming my old self, the one the demon had tried to steal from me.

I wouldn't let that happen again.

I STOOD IN FRONT OF THE BATHROOM MIRROR and stared at my sunken-eyed expression. The three bowls of gumbo I'd gulped down had brightened my complexion and filled out my hollow cheeks a little. But the shadows beneath my eyes remained, betraying my exhaustion and weakness.

Sighing, I slowly removed my shirt, exposing my torso to Gabriel and the unforgiving bathroom lighting. The bandages were white and crisp against my bruised flesh. I'd seen the wounds for the first time two days ago when Meredith changed my bandages. The sight had stolen my breath and brought tears to my eyes. And from the looks of it, things hadn't improved much since then. She'd warned me that they'd take longer to heal than normal, given the extreme amount of damage done, but I'd still hoped for a miracle.

With a deep breath, I reached for the edge of the tape. My fingers trembled, and Gabriel wordlessly took over. His touch was gentle, and the adhesive tugged lightly at my skin as he peeled the strips of tape back, revealing the five raw wounds underneath.

My pulse quickened as I took it all in. The dissolvable stitches were gone and the gashes had sealed, but my skin still looked...*angry*. Red and welted, with bruising that spanned my entire chest.

I glanced up and caught Gabriel's gaze in the mirror. When a tear escaped and slipped down my cheek, he caught my chin and turned my head toward him.

"Hey." His soft voice cut through the silence. He brushed away my tears, then cupped my cheeks. "Scars are a part of our journey. They don't take anything away from you. They add to your story. To your strength. Do you know what I see when I look at you?"

I shook my head.

"I see *all* of you. Your courage, your tenacity, your heart." His hands slipped from my cheeks to my neck. Then he guided me forward until our foreheads touched. "These marks were *done* to you. They don't change who you are. Nor do they change how I feel about you. So they shouldn't change how you feel about yourself. You jumped in front of a *demon* to save me, Maddie. One day, you'll look at these and you'll see them as badges of honor."

A small, fragile smile tugged at my lips as his words washed over me. I absorbed his soothing words, letting them mend the raw emotional wounds left by the demon's claws.

"Thank you," I whispered. I only hoped he was right, and that one day I wouldn't feel such abhorrence when I looked at my chest. I would take it one day at a time.

Gabriel pressed a kiss to my temple. "How about that bath now?"

I nodded. A bath sounded perfect. I wanted nothing more than to sink into the water and forget about all this.

As Gabriel strode to the tub and turned on the taps, I kicked off the rest of my clothes. When the water started to steam, he stepped aside and rifled through the cupboards.

"What are you looking for?" I asked.

"Aha," he replied, pulling out a few candles. "I knew I smelled something fruity."

I smiled and watched as he laid out five candles. For a moment, I wondered if he'd done it purposely to match the five marks on my chest, but I soon realized he'd simply used all the candles Lucy had. He quickly lit them with a small lighter she left in a drawer for this occasion, then gestured me toward the tub.

"Climb in," Gabriel told me.

I lowered myself into the massive whirlpool Jacuzzi tub Lucy had insisted upon when they'd moved in. According to her, Sam had spent two months on renovations to design their ideal bathroom, including this oasis of a tub. Its soft curves let a girl lay back, close her eyes, and float. Even better, the size could accommodate two, including someone as tall as Gabriel—not that we'd had a chance to try it out together yet. Thanks to my injuries, the doctor had sentenced me to sponge baths until now.

Once the water reached my waist, Gabriel turned off the taps, then activated the jets.

A happy moan slipped past my lips, and I laid my head back against the back of the tub. Pure heavenly bliss. My muscles uncoiled as heat seeped into my tired body while the scent of cherry and vanilla candles filled the air.

"Comfortable?" Gabriel asked.

He parked himself on the edge, his gaze attentive, yet casual. Candlelight flickered across his face, highlighting his striking features.

"Why don't you come find out?" I suggested, my tone entirely too innocent.

Gabriel lifted a brow as indecision warred on his face. He wanted to—I could see it in his eyes—but he also feared hurting me.

I sat up and scooted to the middle of the tub, my legs still stretched out. "Come on. Join me."

Apparently I didn't need to tell him a third time.

Gabriel quickly stripped, discarding his clothes next to mine. At the sight of him, a chiseled work of art, my breath caught. He was the epitome of masculine perfection—at least in my eyes. His torso was a canvas of sculpted muscle and taut skin, marred only by the shadows the flickering candles cast, adding to the mystery of his allure. His arms, thick and defined, bore the evidence of years spent mastering the predator within. The sight of him, so powerful and beautiful, made my heart race.

I still couldn't believe he was mine. He was a

force of nature, an entity of strength, speed, and beauty, all wrapped up in one perfect package that I wanted to unwrap with my teeth.

In a display of fluid grace, Gabriel stepped into the bath. The water rippled and sloshed as he lowered behind me, his thighs caging me between his legs.

He settled in, then pulled me back against his chest. The water had risen with his added weight, and it lapped near my chest, but I didn't feel any pain. Instead, a soft sigh escaped my lips as his arms slid around me, enveloping me in a cocoon of warmth and comfort.

I closed my eyes and allowed myself to drift, to exist in this moment of peace and quiet. Gabriel's and my relationship was so new, but moments like this made me feel as though we'd known each other forever. Fate forged the bond between mates, and I felt that connection to the very depths of my soul. The intensity had frightened me initially, seeing as how I had zero experience with intimacy. However, the more I embraced it, the happier I was. I simply had to stop self-sabotaging myself. Yes, that was easier said than done. It was a daily battle, but one I was winning.

"You know, in all my years of foster care, I never

imagined having a moment like this," I said, breaking the silence.

Gabriel started running his fingers up and down my arms, tracing soothing designs into my flesh. "You're not in foster care anymore," he murmured, his voice a calming hum above the jets. "You have people who care about you now."

That simple reassurance, the reminder of how far I'd come, felt like the final ingredient to this peaceful moment.

"Was it really that bad?" Gabriel asked. "You haven't told me much about it."

True. Other than knowing that was how I'd grown up, he knew very little. I'd kept the details to myself, as I did with most people I knew.

"It was rough," I admitted. "Jumping from home to home isn't something anyone wants. I can't even remember how many homes I was in and out of. Most were okay. Some not so much. Of course, in foster care, I never had to fight witches or demons, so..." I shrugged, trying to make light of the conversation.

Gabriel tensed behind me, then slowly relaxed. Guess my joke hadn't been funny.

Interestingly, I found I wanted to open up to him about my past—something I'd never wanted before.

Not even Jaden knew everything. The few times I'd brought it up, her expression had turned pitying, and that was the one thing I hated most.

"Each move, I packed my few belongings into a garbage bag," I told him. "Luggage costs money. But garbage bags are cheap and easily accessible. Someone gave me a suitcase once. It split and fell apart barely ten feet later. I remember feeling..." My voice died.

After a few moments, Gabriel's arms tightened around me. "Feeling what?"

I took a deep breath and decided to take the plunge, to trust him. "I remember feeling like unwanted trash myself. Like I was someone's old, discarded luggage."

Gabriel kissed the side of my head and hugged me close. "You are *not* trash, Maddie."

"I know that now," I whispered. "But when you're young and the whole world is playing hot potato with you, it's hard not to feel unwanted. Just like that piece of crap luggage no one wanted." I shook off my melancholy. "There were some okay moments though. One foster mother I had tried to teach me how to knit. She claimed it was therapeutic and would help with my depression. I never took to it like she did. Couldn't get the damn needles to work right."

Gabriel chuckled lightly.

"But that never mattered to me. All that mattered was she wanted to spend time with me. That she thought I was worthy enough to teach something to. Even now, when things get tough, I pick up the needles and a skein of yarn and try to make that same scarf she tried to teach me all those years ago."

"You didn't stay with her?" Gabriel asked.

My smile fell and I slowly shook my head. "No."

"What happened?"

Despair sank its claws into me, and I stared at the swirling water. "She gave me back, like they all did."

"I'm sorry," Gabriel murmured.

I nodded. "It's probably for the best. I heard a few years later that she died."

"Oh. How?"

"A car accident," I said. "There was another who would take me to the library. I learned to use books as an escape and once she realized that, she'd take me there for a few hours every night. To get some peace and quiet, I think." I chuckled and shook my head. "Do you know what my favorite genre to read was?"

"Hmm. Horror?" Gabriel guessed.

"Paranormal romance," I said, laughing. "I used to love reading books about vampires and werewolves."

Gabriel's whole body shook with laughter. "Now, that's funny."

"Of course, back then, I didn't know they existed. Color me surprised when my sister Olivia told me she was a werewolf."

"How did you get into the slaying business if you loved reading about vampires?" he inquired.

"After my sister turned me into a werewolf, I left her pack. Trust issues, remember? Anyway, I was lone-wolfing it, running through the forest, when I came across my first vampire. He'd attacked a woman and was draining her dry. I didn't even think, I just reacted. I tore his head clean off. Saved her life, killed my first vampire, and disposed of his body. When the cops came, I told them that I'd scared the vampire off. One of the officers told me to look into the Academy. Said I'd make a good candidate. I did what he suggested and never looked back."

"That's when you met your friends?"

My smile returned. "Yeah. Jaden was the first to befriend me. Then Josh and Chris. We busted our asses together to ensure all four of us passed. The friendship continued. They were the first people I ever opened myself up to."

A pang of guilt hit me when I thought of Chris. We hadn't spoken since the night of the demon attack. It wasn't that I couldn't have reached out to him after waking up from my coma, but things were complicated. Revealing my connection to Gabriel had hurt him, especially considering it'd been Chris's job to slay him. Chris saw me choosing to protect my mate—a *vampire*—as a betrayal. Thankfully, Jaden and Josh had stuck by my side. But Chris had branded me a traitor and stormed off. I didn't want to think about that right now though. It hurt too much.

"Then you met Lucy," Gabriel said. He knew a little of my history.

"Olivia finally told me I had another sister, and the little girl within me, the one desperate to find family and make connections, insisted on finding her. I'm glad I did too."

"As am I," he said. "Family is important to you."

Probably the *most* important thing to me. "What about you?"

"Me? You already know everything there is to know."

I doubted that. There were some things I knew for sure. Like how his biological mother had abandoned him in an abbey, only for Genevieve, the former queen of vampires, to find and raise him. His life then took an even darker turn when he had to kill his surrogate mother to save Vlad and Anna. He'd also lost his first mate in that same battle. To add insult to injury, his adoptive father now loathed him for killing his mother. Gabriel's past was nothing short of traumatic. Yet, I knew so little about his brother and sister or the hundred-and-seventy-five years he'd lived prior to these events.

Which raised another question, one I'd been meaning to ask for some time now.

"You're immortal," I commented, leading into my question.

"Well, unless someone kills me."

I shuddered at the thought. "Right. Um. You do know I'm *not* immortal, right?"

Gabriel stilled behind me. "Yes, I gathered that, what with you being a werewolf and all. I'm well aware that your kind lives mortal lives."

"So, how does this work, then?"

"How does what work exactly?"

I rolled my eyes. He was being purposely obtuse. He had to know exactly what I was referring to. "We're mates. But you look to be in your mid-twenties. And I'm almost thirty."

"I hardly see twenty-seven as *almost* thirty."

"*Every* woman sees twenty-seven as 'almost thirty,'" I teased. "My point is, I'm going to keep aging, and you're not. So how does this work? I mean, the day will come when I'll look more like your mother than your lover."

"Blimey," Gabriel said, shuddering. "Perish the thought."

I couldn't help but chuckle. Then I rose on my knees and turned to face him. Gabriel's gaze lingered briefly on my wet breasts before he forced his eyes back up to my face.

"Seriously, though. Have you ever known anyone who's mated with a werewolf before?"

"In fact, I have," he said. He lifted his hand and combed his fingers through my hair, pushing the damp strands back from my face. "Are you sure you're ready for the answer?"

I frowned, but nodded. "How much scarier can it be than picturing myself in my eighties, in love with a man who looks like he's in his twenties?"

Gabriel quirked a smile. His hand cupped my neck and he drew me down. When our lips met, I sighed and sank into the kiss. Somehow, I knew I'd never grow tired of this. Even when I was old and wrinkled.

I parted my mouth and welcomed his tongue, my muscles turning to jelly when Gabriel's kiss turned heated. He stroked my tongue with perfect precision, his thumbs caressing the curve of my breasts. I wanted to climb on top of him right here and now, but I held myself back. I needed to hear this answer, and hopping on his pogo stick wouldn't speed that along.

He broke the kiss and leaned back, staring deep into my eyes. "It's called an eternal kiss and reserved strictly for vampires who mate with mortals."

"Vampires can mate with humans too?"

He nodded. "Of course. The human is always given a choice. Either they can fully transition into a vampire, or they can partake in the eternal kiss. While both processes have similarities, the eternal kiss doesn't require the initial draining of the human's blood. Most humans prefer to become a vampire. It's simpler. But some choose the eternal kiss instead."

Becoming a vampire was simpler? How so? "What does the eternal kiss consist of?"

"You would bite me and drink my blood." Desire flared in Gabriel's eyes. Apparently this was something he very much wanted to do. When he continued, his voice was a touch hoarse. "Doing so stops you from aging and extends your lifespan."

"How often would I need to do that?"

"As often as you like," he replied. "But for necessity, at least a few times a year. It stops your aging and allows us to spend eternity together."

"If humans have this choice, why would they choose to become vampires?"

"Because the eternal kiss ties the mortal's life to their vampire's. If the vampire dies—"

"The mortal dies," I whispered.

He gave a single nod.

"But werewolves can't transition. So my choices are the eternal kiss or...nothing."

Another nod.

Phew, okay. That was a lot to take in. I'd already expressed to him my no-biting rule. And now he was telling me I'd need to drink his blood in order for us to stay together forever.

A week ago, the idea might have disgusted me. But kneeling in front of Gabriel, the tips of my breasts brushing against his chest, his coarse thighs rubbing against my legs, I wasn't sure what I wanted anymore. I'd heard talk of a vampire's bite—that it was the most erotic thing anyone could experience— but I'd always maintained that boundary.

"There's no need to answer right now," Gabriel told me, clearly reading the emotions spiraling within me.

"And if I decide not to?"

Pain flashed across his face, but he quickly masked it. "Then that's your decision. I would never force anything like that on you."

"But I would age and eventually die."

He jerked a nod.

"And you'd be okay with that?" Because I sure as hell wouldn't. I couldn't imagine doing that to him. But I also couldn't see myself drinking his blood.

"Maddie..." Gabriel paused, then kissed me again. "In case you haven't figured it out yet, I'm in this for the long haul. Whatever you decide, I will support."

Had he just admitted he loved me? He hadn't said the words, of course. But the implication was there, right? And why did that make my chest feel so tight? Was that happiness or fear I was feeling? And why couldn't I tell the two apart? Was I so broken that I didn't know the difference?

"Shh," he said, kissing the tip of my nose. "This isn't something you need to decide right this second. Sit. Enjoy the bath. We can discuss this later."

Right. Later.

I sank into the bath and leaned against Gabriel, staring at the swirling bubbles. Though we'd only been in here for half an hour, it felt like I'd stepped into a whole new chapter of my life. A whirlwind of questions circled my mind. If I drank Gabriel's blood, I would live *forever*—or at least as long as he did. And that was a hard concept to wrap my noodle around. Was I even ready for eternity with him?

"I can hear you thinking," Gabriel teased. "Relax, Maddie. The answers will come to you when you're ready."

Relieved he had such faith in me, I did as he suggested and turned my brain off.

These were questions I could mull over in the coming days. First I had to fix our present, then I could sort out our future.

Two restful days later, I took a deep breath and reveled in the cool, pine-scented morning air. Underfoot, the earth was damp but not muddy, and the early spring grass crunched beneath my sneakers as I stretched out my muscles with Josh on my left and Jaden on my right. Yesterday, I'd called them to tell them I needed to start training, and they'd leapt into action, relieved to see me getting back into the swing of things. They'd immediately come over and spent all day beating a one-mile-long track into the trees. It started behind Lucy's house and encircled the woodlands, ending right back here.

Crazy how fast we werewolves healed. It'd only been two days since I'd playfully attacked Gabriel in these woods, but I already felt so much stronger. I wasn't "these hills are alive with the sound of music" better, but certainly much improved. I was dreading this run though. Jaden had set a goal of one mile, and hell, I wasn't even sure I could accomplish that yet.

But I was certainly willing to try.

"Ready?" my best friend asked as she stretched out her quads, clad in full-length running pants and a long-sleeved top.

"No," I chuckled. But that had more to do with my hatred of running than anything else.

These two were the sickening kind of people—the kind that *liked* exercise. But I could tell they were also excited to spend time with me. It'd been a hard week, for sure, with me recuperating and them trying to figure out how to tackle the Academy's corruption. We hadn't had a chance to discuss their progress yet. I figured that conversation was best saved for after the run, when we were all too exhausted to feel any emotions regarding the issue.

Josh finished stretching. He looked...happy. Ugh, I hated running. But these two lived for the "runner's high," they claimed. I'd personally never felt anything but miserable when running.

A fourth figure lurked behind the three of us. Daniel. He was one of Gabriel's human guards. True to my promise, I'd brought him with me. He wouldn't be running with us, but he'd keep an eye on the grounds and be here in case one of us started screaming.

In the meantime, he stood sentinel in the backyard, arms crossed over his chest and his gaze steady. Every time he looked at me, I knew without a doubt that he didn't like me. And I couldn't blame him. I'd kidnapped Gabriel from right beneath his guards' noses. It wasn't a good look for any of the guards—and they hadn't forgiven me yet. But he was here, doing what his king had ordered, because that was his job. I almost felt bad for the guy, forced to guard someone he so clearly loathed.

"Let's do this!" Josh cheered, dragging my thoughts back to my problem at hand.

I snorted a laugh. "Alright, Rocky. Calm down."

Neither gave me a countdown. Instead, they bolted into the woods, running at a pace I *knew* I wouldn't be able to maintain yet. Sighing, I loped after them. It didn't take long—seconds, really—

before the burn set into my leg muscles. Even less time for my thighs to start trembling.

Oh shit. I knew from experience that I could run a mile in three minutes—but that was at top werewolf speeds. Jaden averaged around eight minutes per mile, and Josh around seven. Right now, I'd be lucky to break fifteen. My body felt foreign to me. Old, heavy, stiff.

A couple of tree branches snapped as Jaden and Josh returned to me, their faces barely flushed.

Gritting my teeth, I picked up the pace. If I was going to do this, I had to push harder. I wouldn't improve if I kept things too easy for me.

"Easy does it, Maddie," Jaden cautioned, her eyes tracking the course they'd carved out of Lucy's territory.

"I got this," I puffed, the rhythmic thud of our feet reminding me of my past runs. If I could focus on that, on the body mechanics, on breathing, maybe I would be okay.

I rounded the first curve of our homemade track, the sounds of the awakening forest a soothing backdrop. My breath sawed past my lips, but I kept going, determined to prove myself. Each thump of my heart was a reminder of why we were doing this —to regain the strength stolen from me.

Over halfway into the first lap, my breath turned into ragged gasps, but I gritted my teeth and pushed on until the finish line came into sight. Daniel's expression soured as we approached, but I only used it to fuel my motivation.

"Break," Josh called, slowing his pace as we completed the first lap.

Oh, thank god.

One mile. Jeez, that had been harder than I'd expected. But I'd done it. I hunched over, hands on my knees, as I struggled to fill my lungs with oxygen. Even in the cool morning, sweat beaded my brow. I straightened and stripped my top layer, discarding the long-sleeved jacket on the grass. The T-shirt beneath bared my skin to the dewy morning air, cooling my internal temperature.

"Water?" Josh handed me a bottle.

I snatched it gratefully, my hands shaking as I popped the top and took small sips.

Daniel watched from the sidelines, his expression still as unreadable as ever. I had a feeling I hadn't impressed him. But I'd impressed myself. One mile wasn't much, but to me right now, it felt like I'd scaled Mount Everest.

"Again?" Jaden asked, her voice gentle yet insistent.

"No," Daniel suddenly said, his voice gruff.

My head shot up, surprised at his intervention. "Excuse me?"

"You've done enough today. I don't need you fainting in the middle of the woods," he retorted, his expression hardening. "I'm not carrying your ass out of there."

Fury burned through my stomach. I took a step toward him and chucked my empty water bottle at his head. He snatched it out of the air and threw it to the ground where my jacket still lay discarded.

"Let me be perfectly clear about something," I snapped, fighting hard to keep my breaths even. It wouldn't help me make my case if I could barely breathe. "*I* decide when I'm done. You don't have any say over that. You aren't here to dictate shit to me. You're here to keep watch and that's it."

"Nice way to make friends," Jaden mumbled behind me.

I ignored her retort. "Besides, *if* I passed out, and that's a huge *if*, my *friends* would haul me out of the woods. Not you."

Daniel's jaw clenched, but he didn't say another word. He merely resumed his silent post.

I straightened, meeting Jaden and Josh's gazes, determination simmering in my veins. "Again."

The two stared at me but slowly nodded.

If there was one thing I didn't appreciate, it was being told what to do. The second lap might kill me, but I'd do it to prove a point. Daniel could go suck an egg, for all I cared.

As a group, we set off once more, every step bringing me closer to my goals. No matter how long this took or how hard it was, I wouldn't give up. I was a fighter. I'd always been one. This was no different. A war was heading our way, and I needed to mold myself into something strong and valuable. For me. For Gabriel. For all of us.

The second lap was pure torture. My lungs felt like they were on fire, and my body begged me to stop. I kept repeating the silent mantra in my head, *"You can do this. You're a werewolf. You're strong."* I pushed past the discomfort, focusing wholly on breathing and ignoring the deafening heartbeat drumming in my ears.

I staggered across the finish line and practically collapsed.

"Better?" Jaden asked after I finished guzzling down the water.

I gave her a weak thumbs-up and a forced smile.

"Wanna try for another?" she asked.

"Oh, hell no," I said, wheezing with laughter. "I think a third lap would kill me."

Chuckling, Jaden patted my back. "You got this, girl."

I threw her a weak smile and nodded, all while listening to the awkward stuttering of my heart. It hadn't failed though. And that was all that mattered.

AFTER MY SHOWER, I STOOD IN THE DOORWAY OF Gabriel's and my room, my shoulder braced against the frame. Any moment now, the sun would dip below the horizon and cast the world into darkness, and my sun-averse vampire would wake. This had become my "norm."

Our room was a pitch-black sanctuary, devoid of any hint of sunlight. Seeing as how Lucy and Sam were best friends with two vampires, they'd designed their house accordingly. The guest suite had UV-blocking windows and blackout curtains draped across the entire width of the wall. They'd gone this route so they wouldn't require coffins, something I greatly appreciated. Seeing Gabriel dead on the bed was unnerving enough without adding a coffin into the mix.

Instead, we slept together in a massive king-sized bed, him clad in silk sleeping pants and nothing else. Even from here, I could see the muscled planes of his naked torso, and my mouth went dry.

Clearing my throat, I checked my watch and watched the seconds tick down. At six-ten on the button, Gabriel stirred. Inch by inch, life returned to his body. When his eyes finally opened and found me standing in the doorway, a sleepy smile curved his lips.

"Evening, luv," he said.

I grinned in response, my heart fluttering with anticipation. He'd barely opened his eyes, but he'd known I was here, waiting for him to wake. Without a word, I climbed into bed next to him and snuggled close, relishing in the feel of his arms as they slipped around me. My eyes immediately started to droop, my body exhausted from my day's work. It was a good exhaustion though. The sort that spoke of an accomplished day, as opposed to the injured and half-dead exhaustion I'd been dealing with since coming out of my coma. Unfortunately, I couldn't sleep yet. No matter how comfy I was. We had too much to do.

"How was your day?" Gabriel asked, his voice soft in the darkness.

Excitement bubbled within me and I stretched my body, reveling in every ache and pain. I'd earned them. Pushed myself hard, and accomplished something a couple days ago I wouldn't have thought possible.

"It was good," I told him. "I went for a run with Jaden and Josh. We set out to do one mile but accomplished two."

I didn't tell him that the second lap had taken me twice as long as the first one. Or that I'd only done it out of spite for Daniel. Or that I'd nearly collapsed at the end, and Jaden's arms had been the only thing keeping me vertical.

Gabriel turned his head toward me. Thanks to my heightened senses, I could see the pride shining in his eyes. "Impressive. How do you feel?"

"Sore," I confessed, laughing. "But a good sore, you know? The kind that tells you that you accomplished something."

He leaned in and kissed the side of my head. "I'm glad to hear it. But don't overdo it, okay?"

"I know. Jaden and Josh were there the entire time."

"And my guard?"

I waved a dismissive hand. "He was there too."

Gabriel's deep chuckle echoed in my ear. "Not a fan?"

"He's a jerk."

"I didn't hire him for his personality," Gabriel replied.

Wasn't that the truth. I thought back to his gruff words and unkind expression. "He doesn't like me. I don't think any of your guards do."

"Ah."

When Gabriel didn't say anything else, I stole a peek at his face. "Ah?"

"Well...you did kidnap me," he teased.

"Please, you loved every minute of it."

His smile died. "Not every minute."

Right. "Okay, well, you loved most of it."

Gabriel's arms tightened around me, and I knew he was remembering the demon attack. Every time he did, his face took on this pained expression. Time to change the subject, then. I didn't want to sour his mood this early in the evening.

"Jaden and Josh haven't left yet. They want to chat about their plan for the Academy. And Lucy said Anna called a couple hours ago. She and Vlad are also stopping by tonight with an update."

Gabriel sighed. "It's always work with you. No play."

Was that so? Grinning mischievously, I swung myself over Gabriel's body, capturing his attention as I straddled his waist and pinned his hands above his head. His eyes widened, a playful glimmer dancing within, while a wicked smile curved his lips, revealing the tips of his fangs. Thoughts of our bathtub conversation from the other night rose to mind, but I pushed them aside. I'd think about the "eternal kiss" later.

Releasing his hands, I let my fingers trail along his sides, memorizing the contours and finding the spots that made him squirm and writhe beneath me. The sensation sent a wave of pleasure through my body.

Gabriel swiftly flipped us over, his weight pressing me against the mattress. His tender touch grazed my cheek in a feather-light caress that sent shivers throughout me. A heartbeat later, our lips collided in a passionate kiss, his tongue deftly finding its way past my lips.

I moaned and arched into him, my fingers instinctively digging into his back. Gabriel broke from the kiss and caught my gaze. I saw the silent question within and nodded without hesitation.

Yes, I wanted this.

Yes, I could handle this.

Please, god, yes.

Heat flared in Gabriel's eyes, and he slowly removed my clothes, one piece at a time. His fingers and lips followed in their wake, touching and kissing every inch of bare skin he exposed. Once I lay naked beneath him, he dipped his head, lowering it between my thighs. His tongue was just as skilled down below as it was in my mouth, and soon he had me panting for breath and fisting the sheets. We had to remain quiet due to the many supernatural ears in the house, but honestly, I wasn't sure I could. Pleasure built within me, and I wanted to cry out. Instead, I clamped my mouth shut and squeezed my eyes closed even as Gabriel brought me to climax.

My whole body trembled as wave after wave crashed through me.

"I love how you taste," Gabriel murmured as he climbed back up my body, his lips capturing my mouth. I could taste myself on him and sank into the kiss, hooking my legs around his waist.

Gabriel poised himself above me, then caught my gaze once more. "You okay?"

"I'm fine," I whispered. Still tired, but nothing could stop me from enjoying this moment with him. I might be sore later, but he'd pumped me full of lovely endorphins. Right now, all I felt was bliss and satisfaction.

Gabriel moved forward, the tip of his cock pressing against me. He slid his length up and down, coating himself in me, then he thrust forward.

My head fell back against the pillow and I sighed contentedly. I'd had plenty of sex in my past, but it'd never felt like this. When Gabriel and I were together, it felt like he completed me. Like he was the other half of my soul. That had to be because we were mates. But since I'd never had a mate before, I wasn't sure. Maybe it was just *him*. Truthfully, it didn't matter. I was merely happy to be with him.

Gabriel started to move within me, his motions a bit restrained. I understood why, but I didn't want him restrained. I wanted him wild and forceful. I wanted him to lose himself in me.

Gripping his hips, I flipped us over and took control. For the second time tonight, I pinned his hands to the bed, then I started riding him. Fast. Hard.

The groan that fell from his lips gave me a perverse sense of satisfaction. I wanted to hear it again and again.

A knock echoed through the room.

Gabriel cursed, his wild eyes darting to the door. I didn't stop though. I kept riding him. His hands gripped my hips and for a moment, I thought he might stop me, but his hold only helped keep me upright. No way I was stopping, and it seemed Gabriel was of the same mind.

"Maddie?" came Jaden's voice. "Are you two coming soon?"

I almost laughed at her phrasing. *Soon, my friend. Definitely soon.*

"Be right out," I managed, hoping my voice sounded strong and steady.

"'Kay. Josh and I are in the living room. And Lucy says Anna and Vlad are on their way."

Gabriel's fingers found my clit and I bit back a groan. Instead, I forced myself to say, "Thanks, Jaden."

I listened to the sound of her retreating footsteps and gave a breathless laugh, one that died abruptly when another orgasm slammed into me.

"Gabriel," I moaned, my hips losing a touch of rhythm.

Not that it mattered. Gabriel growled, then gripped my hips as he rode out his own climax. Wet heat filled me, but I kept moving, drawing out every last second of pleasure for him. I finally stopped when Gabriel opened his eyes and gave me a goofy grin.

"I, uh,"—he cleared his throat—"didn't intend for that to happen."

"But I'm glad it did," I said, leaning over to kiss him.

"Everyone's waiting for us."

I chuckled. "They can wait a little longer."

"They can?" he asked, lifting a brow.

I unseated myself, then cuddled beside him. Every muscle felt loosey-goosey now. Exactly what I'd needed after that run. I'd be lucky if I could walk in a few minutes. But we needed to shower and clean ourselves up before heading out into the living room.

"I can't believe you didn't stop when Jaden came to the door," Gabriel said, suddenly laughing.

"Hey," I teased. "I had a mighty fine dick inside me. Not even my sister could have made me stop."

Gabriel choked on his laugh, then leaned over and kissed me. "Let's hurry before they come knocking again."

I grinned. "Yes, and imagine the look on poor Lucy's face if I opened the door in our current state."

Gabriel shook his head. "Get. We have business to deal with."

"Orrrr...we can shower together," I said, winking.

"You know, to save water and time." And more time meant we could have *more* fun.

His eyebrows shot upward as he correctly assumed what I was hinting at. "Again?"

"And again," I repeated.

"You insatiable minx, you," he teased.

I climbed out of bed and raced toward the en suite bathroom. No Jacuzzi in ours, but the standing shower would certainly do. "Only for you, Gabriel."

As Gabriel and I walked into the dining room, every gaze swiveled our way. Those with supernatural hearing all wore expressions with varying degrees of amusement. My cheeks flushed from a mix of embarrassment and sweet satisfaction, but I refused to let their keen observations rain on my post-coital parade. One downside to being supernaturally inclined was our heightened senses. More than once, I'd overheard Lucy and Sam going at it. Now we were returning the favor. Close quarters in shared homes made for some interesting

—and *awkward*—moments. But hey, we were all adults here.

I squeezed Gabriel's hand, then released it so we could take our seats in the remaining two chairs. The other six had seated themselves accordingly at the dining room table. In front of Jaden and Josh lay a stack of documents and a few loose letters. That piqued my curiosity.

"Finally decided to join us, huh?" Lucy joked. "We were starting to wonder if we'd have to send out a search party."

"Oh, har, har," I retorted.

Anna chuckled, nudging Vlad playfully. "They probably got caught up in some 'important' business."

Okay, maybe only a couple of us were adults here.

I blushed deeper, exchanging a sheepish glance with Gabriel. His eyes sparkled with a mix of annoyance and contentment.

"Alright," Sam intoned, his deep voice commanding attention. "Let's get to work, shall we?"

"I think Maddie and Gabriel already did," Lucy quipped.

Jaden shot me a wide-eyed glance.

I rolled my eyes. "Come on, guys."

Laughter filled the room, easing any lingering tension. I leaned back in my chair, a smile tugging at the corners of my lips.

"So, the reason we're here tonight is to share our updates," Sam started, clearly eager to take control of this meeting.

I gave him a grateful nod.

"There's a lot to unpack here," he continued. "I think it'd be best if we tackle each problem individually. After Maddie's injury, we divided and conquered. That method seems to be working. Jaden and Josh agreed to handle the Academy's corruption. Vlad and Anna agreed to look into the person behind Gabriel's contract as well as handle Gabriel's affairs. And Lucy and I agreed to track down the demon and, hopefully, the coven of witches responsible."

Anxiety started to unfold in my gut. That *was* a lot. And all of it rather dangerous. I spoke from experience. Fear had my hands tightening into fists. Without breaking eye contact with Sam, Gabriel reached for my closest hand, pried it open, and massaged my palm with his thumb. My heartbeat slowed, responding to his touch.

"Let's start with me and Lucy since ours is likely the simplest," Sam said. "We've been keeping an ear to the ground, so to speak, but we haven't heard anything about a loose demon in town. If it's still out there, no one has seen it yet. Nor has it harmed anyone. We have a few leads to check out tonight, but so far, all is quiet on the demon front."

That helped soothe my anxiety.

"As for the coven," Lucy chimed in. "We're getting closer to figuring out which one is responsible. When we started digging, we discovered there are more covens in town than we ever expected."

"How many?" Jaden inquired.

"Five that we've found so far. All of which are incredibly insular and refuse to speak to outsiders."

Unhelpful.

"But they're willing to attack them," Sam grumbled, his alpha wolf flaring in his eyes.

"Yes. Hopefully, when we're finished, they'll agree it's in their best interest to be more mindful of what jobs they take." And there was Lucy's alpha wolf.

If I were a coven leader, I'd be afraid to piss off the local werewolf pack. They now spanned over a hundred members, nearly double in size from when Lucy first took over. I didn't know much about witch covens, but I had to imagine the wolf pack was larger.

"In the meantime, we've spread word warning

the witches that if they dare to attack anyone I consider mine again, I'll raze their covens and destroy every last one of their idols."

Whoa. Sometimes I forgot how scary Lucy could be when she set her mind to something.

"Should give them enough reason to reconsider anyone hiring them to come after us," she finished.

I nodded.

Lucy nodded toward Vlad and Anna. "Your turn."

Anna chuckled. "Feels like we're back in school, doesn't it?"

"Except this time, you can't copy my work," Lucy replied.

Anna rolled her eyes. Then nodded to Vlad, who glanced at Gabriel. "Your people are discontent with the information I've been providing to them. Many do not believe you've appointed me as your emissary. I've spoken with the council, and while they believe your life is in danger, they do not agree with the methods you're taking."

"Tough," Gabriel growled, his hand tensing around mine.

"When I mentioned that you brought on your human guards, that appeased them a little. They're highly concerned about your safety, Gabriel."

"I'm perfectly safe," he said, squeezing my hand again.

Vlad's gaze drifted to me, and he nodded. "I know. But Frederick is demanding you make a public appearance."

"Frederick can demand whatever he wants. I'm the king. Not him. Remind him of that for me the next time you speak to him."

Vlad bowed his head. "As for your father... Anna and I have sent word overseas and received confirmation that he remains in England. He hasn't stepped foot off the island. This doesn't mean he isn't responsible for the bounty. It merely means if he is, he's keeping things quiet. Your brother tells us that Adrian has mostly been drowning his sorrows in blood and whores."

I winced at the description, but Gabriel hardly batted an eye.

"That has nothing to do with his sorrows. Those are his hobbies."

Ouch. This time, I squeezed his hand.

"We're still investigating his involvement," Anna added. "Thankfully your brother has agreed to keep an eye on him for us. And he's promised to reach out to us should he need to speak with you about anything. As for your sister, Natalie remains nearby with your father and her caregivers. She's perfectly safe."

Gabriel nodded. "Thank you. I appreciate you checking on her."

All eyes turned to Jaden and Josh, who exchanged a knowing glance, their expressions serious. I clutched Gabriel's hand and leaned forward, my attention now trained solely on them.

"Acting on Anna and Vlad's intel about the Academy, Josh and I did some digging." Jaden's gaze found mine and I saw the heartbreak within. This wasn't going to be good, and I felt her pain down to my bones. "And what we've uncovered is deeply troubling."

My heart sank. The Academy was our home. We revered it. The very organization that had trained us had become a breeding ground for corruption. Anna and Vlad had discovered this prior to the demon attack. But I'd hoped Josh and Jaden had found something—*anything*—that proved Vlad and Anna wrong.

Josh stepped in, his mouth grim as he spoke, "There's a web of corruption within the ranks. Manipulation, abuse of power, and many false contracts."

I rubbed my face, unsure how to accept this.

We'd joined the Academy for one reason: to eliminate rogue vampires who refused to conform to human society and posed a lethal threat. We'd put our faith in the organization, blindly executing anyone they deemed a target. Except now, we'd learned the Academy had sold those contracts for money, turning us into unwitting assassins against innocent vampires.

It sickened me.

They'd turned us into murderers.

Even worse, I'd lost one of our best friends when I brought this information to them. Chris hadn't cared. To him, the only good vampire was a dead vampire. I didn't believe that. And neither did Jaden or Josh. We only wanted to slay the guilty.

"That's not all," Jaden whispered. "It's been difficult to pin down any names. They work in secret and code. They use pseudonyms to hide their identities. But if our intel is accurate, it suggests the academy council has at least one corrupt member."

"It goes that high?" I asked, stunned.

The council led our organization. There were five of them—an uneven number to always keep things fair. They were the ones responsible for everything, the ones who'd brought the Academy into existence. None of us had ever met them, but we'd learned of their existence during our training.

"Which council member?" I asked.

"We don't know yet. Like I said, it's been really difficult to pin down any names. They're exceptionally cautious," Josh replied. "But also, we've had some...problems."

"Like what?"

Josh took a deep breath, his expression hardening with resolve. "Warnings. Little notes that have appeared in our lockers."

My blood ran cold, fear coursing through my veins. "Threats?" I whispered, my voice barely audible.

Neither spoke, their silence answer enough. The gravity of the situation settled heavily on my shoulders.

"From whom? The council?"

"No," Jaden assured me. "From other slayers. We've been asking a lot of questions and word is spreading."

"Oh my god," I muttered, my mind racing with the implication. "You guys need to stop looking into this then. If this is too dangerous, if our own people are threatening you—"

Josh scoffed, anger blazing in his eyes. "I'm not

stopping. No way in hell. The Academy lied to us. They manipulated us. Used us while they sat back and collected their blood money."

His words resonated within me, stirring a vengeful fire in my chest. The Academy had betrayed us all, manipulating us for their own gain. The realization fueled my determination to expose their corruption to the world. To fix the mess the corrupted within had wrought.

"Okay," I murmured, taking a few deep breaths to slow my racing pulse. "I'm with you. We won't let them get away with this."

Josh and Jaden nodded.

"Any ideas on how to move forward?" I asked.

Jaden slid a piece of paper toward me and tapped it. "We recently had a slayer reach out to us. She claims her last few marks begged for their lives and insisted they were innocent."

I shot Gabriel a glance, the weight of Jaden's words piercing my heart. How many innocent marks had we killed in our slaying careers? It terrified me to think of that.

"This slayer let their last target go," Josh continued.

I sucked in a sharp breath. "What?" That went

against our training, but oh, I was so relieved to hear it. "Which slayer?"

"Ginny Hillock."

I knew Ginny. We'd never worked together because slayers often worked alone, but we'd done the typical friendly nod whenever we passed one another in the Academy halls. Ginny was a solid slayer. Reliable. She'd make an excellent ally.

"She said she wanted to help us. She's going to track the vampire down and see if he'll willingly talk to us. If he agrees, she'll call us with a time and place to meet."

"Okay, this is good," I said. "We already know Gabriel is innocent. With Ginny's help, we can *prove* the corruption. Once we do that, surely the council will recognize the corruption within the organization."

Jaden nodded. "That's what we were thinking too. We also need to figure out how many other false contracts there've been."

That might be challenging. As slayers, we rarely let our bounties escape. And if they somehow managed to escape, we continued tracking them until we finally completed the task.

"The more we dig, the more people we'll find willing to join our cause," Josh said. "And the more people we pull to our side, the more the Academy will have to listen."

Okay. This was good. We had a plan. Now, we needed to execute it. "And what about...Chris?"

Josh and Jaden exchanged a solemn look, their expressions reflecting the complexity of that particular situation. I braced myself for their response, knowing that it seemed unlikely that Chris would join our cause.

"We've tried, Maddie," Jaden said, her voice tinged with disappointment. "But Chris's hatred for vampires runs incredibly deep. He's convinced that you betrayed us by saving Gabriel's life."

My shoulders slumped and I ran a hand through my hair. In all fairness, I *had* betrayed them. I could have been open and honest with them from the start, but I'd feared their reactions. Scared they'd slay Gabriel even after hearing everything I had to say. In my defense, Chris had wanted to do exactly that. But what if I'd gone to them from the start? What if I'd explained things before it'd reached that point? Would that have changed things?

Josh added, "He's resistant. He believes you've compromised yourself and strayed from the mission."

Yikes. "He doesn't know I'm a werewolf, does he?"

"No," Jaden assured me. "We wouldn't do that to you. We understand it's a secret."

I gave a crisp nod, then sighed. "We can't give up on him. Chris is our friend. He's like a brother to all of us. We have to find a way to show him that this is wrong. He has to learn that not all vampires are our enemies."

"That might be tough," Jaden said.

"Why?" Lucy suddenly asked.

My focus leapt to her.

"Why does he hate vampires so vehemently?" Lucy continued.

I shared a glance with Josh and Jaden. They both nodded.

Taking a deep breath, I plunged into the explanation. "In my experience, there are three types of people who join the academy." I ticked up one finger. "Those who believe it's the right thing to do— protecting humans from vampires who refuse to obey the law." A second finger. "Those who seek revenge." I lifted my third finger, then winced. "And those who simply enjoy killing vampires."

Anna and Vlad's expressions darkened.

"I joined after I stumbled across a vampire in the middle of feeding on a woman. She was half-dead when I came across her. It certainly was not a situation she'd consented to. I killed the vampire, then joined the Academy's ranks, believing it was the right thing to do." I pointed to my index finger, indicating I fell within the first category.

Anna paled more than I thought possible for a vampire. I offered her a weak smile, knowing my story likely hit close to home for her.

"Jaden joined..." I faced her, my words trailing off.

"I joined when a vampire murdered my fiancé," she continued, her voice quiet. "Jamie was a bartender, and one evening, he never came home. I received a frantic call from one of his colleagues. Jamie had stepped out to take out the trash. They'd found him in the alleyway, lifeless. Two puncture wounds on his neck, his body cold. A vampire had gotten to him. Just like that, my whole world, my future, vanished."

The sorrow in Jaden's eyes was palpable. "I joined the Academy because I didn't want anyone else to suffer the way I did. Or, if they did, I wanted to give them justice."

In a show of support, Josh slung an arm around Jaden's shoulders, giving her a comforting squeeze. Then he faced the group and said, "I joined when a vampire forcibly turned my mother. She hadn't wanted it, and afterward, she'd begged me to give her peace. Which I did."

I sucked in a sharp breath. I hadn't known she'd asked him to.

"I joined with the hope of keeping that from happening to another family. My father didn't handle her death well. Needless to say, he's gone now too."

"Oh, Josh," I murmured. He'd never confessed that part to us before.

He glanced at Jaden, as though taking strength from her.

"Chris...," I sighed. "Chris's story is the most tragic of all of us."

"I didn't think that would be possible," Anna breathed, her face stark.

"A vampire broke into his family's home one night. Tied them all up. Tortured them for fun."

"Oh my god," Anna whispered, ignoring the flinches from the other vampires.

"Before sunrise, after the vamp had finished having its fun, it slaughtered his entire family. Including his baby sister." My voice caught and I had to blink back tears. "She was four years old."

The entire group fell silent. Considering

Annalise was the same age, the depth of the tragedy resonated with us all.

"Somehow Chris managed to escape. He doesn't remember how. I think he's either blocked it out or he did something he chooses not to discuss. Either way, he escaped. And when the Academy opened and started taking recruits, he was one of the first to sign up. He..." I took another deep breath. "He has every reason to hate vampires as much as he does. And it might be impossible to convince him that not all vampires are evil. But he's one of us. He's one of our best friends. I have to try. We don't turn our backs on the people we love," I concluded. "Ever."

Jaden and Josh gave equally determined nods.

Gabriel cupped the far side of my head and pulled me against him. "Your loyalty is admirable. Both to Chris and to me. Knowing what you've all been through, all I can say is how sorry I am. I feel like I need to say more, being that I'm the king and these are my people. But I'm truly speechless."

"All I can say is there's a lot of evil in the world," Anna said, her voice soft. "And it comes in all shapes and sizes. I've been through the same, and it's how I became a vampire. Vlad saved my life. But Lucy has also been through the same, and that was at the hands of a werewolf. Perhaps we can help Chris see *that.* That it isn't *because* they were vampires that they were evil. They were merely evil *and* a vampire."

"We can try," I said, hopeful. "*I* will try. Tonight. If he won't listen to Jaden and Josh, maybe he'll listen to me. I'm the one who broke our relationship. I have to fix it. It's Tuesday, so I think I know where to find him."

"Maddie..." Gabriel shook his head.

"It's okay," I told him. "Chris would never hurt me." And if he did, well, he'd learn the hard way what a pissed-off werewolf was capable of.

"I'll accompany you," Gabriel urged. "You shouldn't be out there alone."

"If Chris catches even the slightest whiff of you, all hell will break loose."

Annoyance flashed in my mate's gaze. He had every intention of arguing with me, but thankfully, Josh saved me by chiming in with, "Jaden and I will go with you."

The spark in Gabriel's eyes faded, and after a moment's pause, he nodded. "Be careful. Call me if you need anything."

"Fine," I agreed. Then I turned to Josh. "But I want to talk to Chris alone. I'm the one he's angry with."

Once everyone was on board, we headed out. If we could get Chris on our side, the Academy would *have* to listen to us. He was the best. And everyone knew how much he hated vampires. Winning him over could change everything.

But first, I had to get him to speak to me, and that would be the toughest battle of all.

It felt like forever since I'd walked the streets of Jackson. A few weeks, at least. Since the night I'd kidnapped Gabriel. Nothing had changed, yet everything felt different. Before Gabriel, I would have spent the night hunting down my bounties. Tonight, I was still hunting, but this time, for a friend. One who didn't want to speak to me.

He may not want to see me, but too bad. And luckily for me, I knew where to find him. Chris had a lot of wonderful qualities, and right now, his reliance on routines was one of them. I knew exactly where to find him this late on a Tuesday night.

Jaden, Josh, and I strolled through the dimly lit streets, the neon signs of various establishments flickering with colorful invitations. The scent of fried food wafted through the air, mingling with the sounds of laughter and music that spilled out from the bars and clubs.

When we reached the entrance of the Last Drop —Chris's favorite Tuesday night hangout—I paused. I merely had to open the door and walk inside, but fear held me hostage, pinning my feet to the concrete. I honestly wasn't sure how Chris would react to seeing me after everything that'd happened. He'd been so angry when he stormed off. So hurt.

I had to try though. Our friendship was far too important to let it wither away in anger and resentment. He was my brother. We'd been through so much together. That had to mean something to him, no matter how furious he was with me.

"Stay out here," I told them.

"Not going anywhere," Josh said.

"Good luck," Jaden offered, squeezing my hand.

I smiled, then stepped inside to a haze of cigarette smoke and the murmur of low conversations. I coughed and waved a hand in front of my face. My eyes scanned the smoky crowd, searching for any glimpse of Chris. The sight of him sitting alone at the far end of the bar, his broad shoulders slumped over an empty glass, tugged at my heart. This wasn't the Chris I was used to seeing. He was usually so happy and playful. Tonight, he looked...lost. And alone.

Taking a deep breath, I pushed through the crowd. The pungent stench of alcohol invaded my senses, and I wrinkled my nose. I'd always hated coming to places like these. They were so cramped and tight.

I pressed onward, closing the distance between me and Chris. Every step brought me closer until I could see the weariness etched on his face. When I reached his side, I hesitated. Maybe I should have done this somewhere private. Somewhere he could yell at me without attracting the attention of other patrons.

His head turned and he stared at me, his eyes hardening into an icy glare. Oh boy. Not a good start.

"Hi," I said, my voice slightly shaky.

His jaw tightened before he raised a hand and signaled the bartender, pointing at his empty glass. "Another."

I took the seat next to him and nodded to the

bartender for one of my own. Alcohol didn't do much to me, thanks to my werewolf metabolism, but Chris didn't know that. Maybe we could drink our miseries away together.

"What do you want?" he demanded in a clipped tone.

The bitterness in his voice jarred me, but I refused to let him scare me off. "To talk to you. To explain everything."

The bartender slid my glass to me, then topped Chris up. He immediately snatched his glass and lifted it to his lips. "What's there to explain?" He tossed his head back and gulped down what I assumed was scotch. He placed the glass down on the bar top, wiped his mouth, then tapped the rim for another.

My eyes widened. Was he trying to drink himself to an early death?

"Chris—"

"You betrayed us, Maddie," he snapped. "Betrayed *me*. There is absolutely nothing for us to discuss."

I swallowed the lump forming in my throat. "I... made a choice. I know it's one you can't understand. But Gabriel is my mate—"

He scoffed, a look of complete and utter disgust

twisting his face. "Your *mate*. You talk like you're one of them." He swung a glare toward me, anger flashing in his eyes. "Are you still even human? Or is he planning to make you into one of *them*?"

I held his gaze, refusing to show how badly his words hurt me. He'd never known me as a human. Olivia had turned me into a werewolf before I'd joined the Academy. But I couldn't reveal that. Josh and Jaden knew, but only because I'd shifted in the middle of the demon attack to save Jaden's life. Chris hadn't been there for that, and he hadn't spoken to me since.

"Gabriel would never—"

"Don't kid yourself," he said, laughing bitterly. "Vampires will do whatever they want, when they want."

Except Gabriel *couldn't* turn me into a vampire. And though he'd told me about the eternal kiss and given me the option to extend my lifespan, he'd told me he wouldn't force that on me. I believed him, too. He wouldn't lie to me about that.

"Chris, please listen to me."

"I have no reason to listen to you," he mocked. "You went behind our backs and broke our trust. We swore we would never do anything to hurt each other. That we were family." He sneered. "But I guess you don't know the definition of that. Makes sense, considering you've never *had* a family."

I sucked in a sharp breath, his words striking a deep, painful chord within me. Anger churned in the pit of my stomach, and without thinking, I lashed out. I ripped his empty glass out of his hand and slammed it down, out of his reach.

Chris's wide eyes shot to me.

"You listen to me, Christopher Thomas," I hissed, fighting to control my inner wolf. She wanted free to tear a strip out of his disrespectful hide. "You, Josh, and Jaden *are* my family. And I sure as hell know what that means. But just because we're family doesn't mean you get to speak to me like that."

He winced, as though regretting his words.

"I did what I did because I *knew* you would never understand," I continued. "I'd only learned Gabriel was my mate three fucking days before you showed us the contract. I hadn't had any time to figure shit out for myself. I was confused and lost. And instead of going to my friends to ask for help, I had to keep them from *killing* the person I'm destined to be with. So I'm sorry you're mad, and I'm sorry you feel betrayed." My voice softened. "But I was afraid and didn't have many choices. Either you'd kill Gabriel or Gabriel would kill you. It wasn't a fun position to be in. Can you honestly tell me that you would have listened if I'd brought this to you at the start?"

Chris scowled.

"No, you wouldn't have. You would have reacted exactly like this. So, yes, I kept a secret. But you know what? You're alive. And Gabriel's alive. I call that a win in my book."

"Just go away, Maddie," Chris breathed, a little of the fight draining out of him.

"No."

He shot me another glare. Shockingly, it wasn't as intimidating as it was before.

"I'll understand if you can't forgive me," I said, the words burning my tongue as I said them. "But you need to face the truth. And soon. The Academy isn't what we thought. Not entirely, anyway. They're taking bribes and using us to kill innocent vampires. Doesn't that piss you off? They manipulated us. We *need* you to help us expose the corruption and make a difference."

He turned away, refusing to meet my gaze. "And if I don't?"

"Then you're a tool," I stated, anger once again rising within me. "And you're letting them control you. That's not the Chris I know."

"You want me to work with vampires," he grumbled, his words slurring a little. Ahh, the scotch was kicking in.

"Yes, we have vampires helping us. Good vampires. I know your past is painful, but not all vampires are evil, Chris."

"I don't know if I can do that, Maddie. My hatred for them runs so deep. I can't just shut that off."

Despair had me slouching over the counter. I hadn't even touched my drink, and I had no desire to drink it now. Not even to drown my misery. I'd really hoped I could convince Chris to join us. I wanted my friend back. But maybe what I'd done had hurt him too much. Vampires were a touchy subject for him, understandably.

After a moment's consideration, I nodded. I'd said my piece, which was exactly what I'd come here to do. He'd heard me. Now, the ball was in his court.

"I understand, Chris. But I hope one day you'll be able to move past your prejudices and join us." I rose from the stool and placed a hand on his shoulder, smiling when he didn't jerk away from me. "I really love you, you know that, right?"

"Yeah," he grunted.

"And I'm sorry that what I did caused this rift between us. I want to mend it, if you'll let me."

He shrugged, dislodging my hand.

"Jaden and Josh miss you too," I murmured.

That made him wince. I couldn't imagine how this must have felt for him. He'd lost everyone he cared about. I would never wish that feeling on anyone. So, I leaned in and gave him a light hug, quickly brushing my lips against his cheek. I needed him to know we still loved him and he still had a place with us.

"Call me if you change your mind, okay?" I said. When he didn't answer, I hugged him a little tighter. Our friendship would likely never be the same, but I refused to give up on him. Refused to let him slip into the darkness all alone.

"Bye, Chris," I whispered.

I straightened and was about to leave when his hand reached out and snagged mine. He didn't look my way when he said, "I miss you too. I miss my dancing partner."

Tears pricked my eyes. After every hunt, we'd go dancing. It was Jaden's way of celebrating life after ending one. And Chris was an exceptional dancer, thanks to the lessons he'd taken prior to his family's death. He'd taught me quite a few moves on the dance floor.

I couldn't resist hugging him again. And this time, when his arms closed around me, I nearly started sobbing.

"Call me tomorrow night when I'm sober," he muttered. "I'll let you know my decision then."

A grin spread across my face. There was a chance he'd turn us down still, but this felt like progress. Like I'd come one step closer to winning my friend back.

I squeezed him tightly, then quickly released him when I heard his breath catch. Sometimes I forgot about my increased strength.

"Talk to you tomorrow," I said.

He nodded, then gestured to the bartender for another drink.

I headed to the door, but before stepping outside, I paused and glanced back at him. If I wasn't mistaken, he sat straighter, and his face seemed brighter somehow. As though the dark cloud surrounding him had lessened.

That gave me hope for tomorrow.

I'D BARELY TAKEN TWO STEPS OUT THE DOOR when I realized something was very, *very* wrong. Instead of the two faces I'd expected to greet me, I spotted seven—five of which did not belong to my friends.

A group of vampire slayers surrounded Josh and Jaden. Anger emanated from their expressions and threatening postures. Tension crackled in the air as the tallest of the mob closed in on Jaden, his hands fisted at his sides.

"If it isn't the little traitors," he crowed, clearly performing for his little posse.

Without hesitation, I rushed to Jaden's side, my protective instincts kicking into high gear. A brief thought flashed through my mind that I wasn't in top fighting shape, but I couldn't stand by and watch a group of people we'd once trusted turn against my friends.

"Hey!" I shouted, my voice cutting through their jeers. I fisted one hand in the leader's shirt and shoved him. "Back the fuck off. Now."

He staggered back a step with a look of complete shock at the strength I displayed. I recognized him then. Bryant, I think his name was. I'd maybe seen him in passing a few times, but not well enough to know anything about him. Or his friends.

All eyes turned to me, the crowd momentarily startled by my presence. Bryant's surprise quickly morphed into pure disgust. "Well, look who we have here. The *vamp*-lover."

My blood ran cold. Did they know about Gabriel? The realization sent a chill down my spine. Jaden's eyes met mine, mirroring my own shock and confusion. Had Chris betrayed my secret? He was the only one who knew besides Josh and Jaden, but I couldn't imagine him doing that to me. Then again, he'd probably thought the same of me.

Bryant raised a hand, brandishing a dagger that glinted in the streetlight. I noted with relief that it wasn't silver, so it posed no immediate threat. I couldn't say the same for Josh and Jaden.

"You're no longer one of us," Bryant spat, fury burning in his eyes. "We kill vamps, we don't rescue them."

Hiding my relief, I squared my shoulders and lifted my chin. "I refuse to kill innocents, whether they're human or vampire."

"Innocents." Bryant laughed, and his followers echoed it. "There's no such thing as an innocent vampire."

Stunned, I scanned the faces of the crowd, disappointment welling within me. The group wasn't large by any means, but it still disappointed me to see so many here who didn't care about right from wrong.

"If the Academy's corruption doesn't bother you, then you're stupider than I thought," I announced to all of them. "Who knows how many innocents you've killed. How many lives you've destroyed in the name of the Academy. How many people you've stolen from loved ones. Families. You hate vampires because they kill humans?" I asked. "Well, now you're no better. So congratulations."

Uneasy murmurs filled the night air. I saw doubt flicker within the eyes of a few, and hoped I'd gotten through to them.

"What's happening isn't right," Jaden continued. "We aren't suggesting we tear down the Academy. We're merely asking the council to step up and purge the corruption. To correct this. We still believe in the system. But it needs to be fair and just."

Before Bryant could respond, the Last Drop's door opened and light spilled onto the street. Everyone glanced up, then froze at the sight of Chris. He stood in the doorway, his dull gaze analyzing the scene in front of him.

I could see the wobbly gears in his head spinning. I had to imagine he was considering his options. Stagger home and fall into a drunken coma. Or stay. If he stayed, whose side would he choose?

Chris took an unsteady step toward the crowd, then scoffed and shook his head.

"Just go home, everyone. Fighting ain't gonna accomplish shit."

He stumbled to the side, his hand pressed against the building for support.

"He's wasted," Jaden said, sighing.

I almost asked, "What gave it away?" but settled for a nod.

Chris took another step, then turned back to face us. He wore a resigned expression, as though he'd given up.

"They're going to expose the corruption, no matter w-what you say or do." He burped. "And if you decide to fight, just know they'll win." He jerked his chin toward us. He babbled something incoherent, then shook his head, as though trying to gather his thoughts. "She's a fuckin' ferocious fighter."

"Who? You or me?" Jaden asked.

I almost laughed. "Let's say both."

"You'll get your asses kicked," Chris mumbled. "And no one wants that. That'd be embarrassing."

"Shit, he's so hammered," Josh muttered.

"We should make sure he gets home alright," Jaden suggested.

I shot Bryant a glance. His mouth twisted, but he jerked a quick nod at his crew, silently dismissing them. Guess the moment had passed. Somehow, drunken Chris had sobered their anger.

"Come on." I nudged Jaden forward. "Let's get him home before he throws up everywhere."

That scattered the crowd a little faster. Seemed no one wanted to watch Chris lose his dinner.

I reached Chris's side first, then grabbed one of his arms and slung it around my shoulders. "Let's go, big guy."

"Maddie? That you?" he slurred. "Where you been? Miss you..."

Man. He was completely wrecked. The booze must have hit a bit harder when he started moving around. A single step later, Chris pitched forward. I caught him easily, silently thanking my strength.

"He's out," I told Jaden. "Josh, can you get the car? I could probably carry him home, but..."

"No one needs to see that," Josh said.

"And you shouldn't be wasting your strength," Jaden added.

I pressed my back against the wall and slid down,

arranging Chris's head in my lap so he could rest while Josh darted back to the car.

Sighing, I combed Chris's hair back from his face.

"He's a mess," Jaden said.

I nodded. "But he's our mess. We'll fix this. We have to."

It was nearing dawn when I trudged through Lucy's front door, my body screaming with exhaustion. The day's events had certainly taken their toll on me, and every muscle ached—a constant reminder of the physical strain I'd put myself through. On the one hand, I wanted nothing more than to collapse into bed and sleep a dreamless sleep, but on the other, I was proud of myself. I'd not only run two miles today, but I'd also finally managed to engage in a little hanky-panky with my hunky vampire king *and* track down Chris. Three days ago, all that would have rendered me comatose. My body was healing, thank goodness. But now, I needed rest.

The house was eerily quiet. The kids were in bed, and Lucy, Sam, Anna, and Vlad were all off tackling their own tasks tonight. Gabriel had remained behind for his own safety, along with a few of his guards. I'd laughed at the thought of Gabriel babysitting, but honestly, he likely hadn't done anything more than keep an ear out in case Annalise or Fynn woke, which they never did.

With heavy steps, I shed my jacket, then dragged myself to the bedroom. Tonight, I was grateful for Gabriel's guards. They provided an extra layer of security that I couldn't provide tonight. I'd made strides in regaining my strength, but clearly not enough yet.

"Maddie?" came Gabriel's voice.

I paused and glanced back. He stood in the hallway, his frame silhouetted by the light.

He swept toward me, his hands hovering near my shoulders. "Are you alright? You look pale."

"Tired," I told him, chuckling. "I did a lot today."

"Perhaps too much?"

"No." I shook my head. "Just the right amount. I'm not going to collapse, but I definitely need some rest."

Without another word, Gabriel cradled my back, then swept his other arm under my legs, picking me up.

"I can walk," I argued, but I didn't fight it.

"Of course you can, but I can also carry you," he said, his voice gentle.

I relaxed into his arms, surrendering to his strength. He carried me effortlessly, his strides steady and confident as he made his way toward our bedroom.

"Mm, a girl could get used to this," I said.

"I bet." He chuckled. "Any time you want me to carry you, just say the word." He gently placed me down on the bed, then slowly undressed me. "Do you want some pajamas?"

I considered his question, then smirked at him and shook my head. "There's still a little time before sunrise. Maybe you should get naked too."

Gabriel's lips curled into a wolfish smile as he considered my suggestion. He'd pulled the curtains back tonight, allowing a bit of the moonlight to spill into the room. He stood in that light while he slowly unbuttoned his shirt, revealing his bare chest and that wonderfully chiseled Adonis belt of his that drew a girl's attention *down*. It did things to me, igniting a familiar fire within. Sadly, while my mind was willing, my body was too weak. But that didn't mean I couldn't enjoy the view.

He discarded his shirt, then moved to his pants. When he popped the button and folded the fly open, I had to bite my lip to keep from groaning. The man was perfection incarnate. The rest of his clothing came off quickly, and I drank in the sight of him. He truly was beautiful.

Closing the distance between us, Gabriel climbed onto the bed, the mattress dipping beneath his weight. I scooted to the side, making room for him to join me. He settled in, his body molding perfectly to mine.

"How did it go with Chris?" he asked, his fingers lightly combing through my hair.

I almost purred, I was so content.

"Better than expected," I admitted. "He didn't throw me on my ass, or kick me out of the bar. I was able to explain myself to him, so that's something. I just hope he remembers it all tomorrow."

"What?"

"He was drinking," I said. "Well, drunk. He passed out and we had to get him home."

"Wanker," Gabriel said, chuckling.

I told him then about the slayers, and how they might have attacked us were it not for Chris. Gabriel stiffened behind me, but didn't say anything until I finished speaking.

"I never thought your people would be a risk to you," he said.

"There's a lot going on. And a lot of mixed emotions. People don't know what to think. So they react. They lash out. They think we're trying to destroy the Academy, which isn't our goal. Hopefully, with time, they'll come to understand that we're trying to fix what's broken."

Gabriel pressed a light kiss against my temple. "And hopefully Chris will come around."

He'd told me to call him tomorrow night. I only hoped he remembered that. And our conversation. I really didn't want to have to go through all that again.

"What are your plans for tomorrow?" Gabriel inquired.

"Strength training, I think. Jaden mentioned something about that."

His laughter reverberated against my back. "She knows you're a werewolf, right?"

"Sure, why?"

He buried his face against my neck and kissed the sensitive spot beneath my ear. I shivered against him.

"Because your idea of strength training is going to be far different from anything she's expecting."

That made me laugh. He was right. It actually made me excited for tomorrow. For years, I'd been hiding my true strength from them. Even today, I hadn't been able to run at *my* top speed. Doubtful I'd be able to lift at my top strength, but surely, I'd be able to lift more than they expected.

"Should be fun," I told him.

Gabriel chuckled again. "I wish I could be there to see their faces."

"I'll record it on my phone for you," I assured him, yawning. "I'll definitely want a video for myself."

"Can't wait to see it. You should go to sleep now," he said. "You'll need your rest for tomorrow."

I nodded, my eyes already closing.

Gabriel pressed a final kiss against the corner of my mouth, then pulled me close. I drifted off with a smile on my lips, excited for what tomorrow might bring.

I BLINKED OPEN MY EYES AND REACHED FOR MY phone. A quick glance told me it was almost ten in the morning. I stared blearily at the time, surprised I'd slept so long. My body had clearly needed the rest.

Rolling onto my back, I stretched, feeling out all my aches and pains. Thanks to my heightened healing, I felt much improved from last night. It was nice to wake up and feel good.

I glanced over at Gabriel and smiled. At some point before sunrise, he'd dressed and positioned himself on the far side of the bed, so as not to alarm me when I woke. I appreciated his efforts, even though they weren't necessary anymore. Something had changed between us, something that didn't frighten me anymore. Originally, the idea of waking to a nude, sleeping vampire had terrified me, but as our relationship developed and evolved, so did my fears.

Slipping out of bed, I crossed the room and opened my dresser drawers. I immediately remembered Jaden's strength training plan today and threw on a pair of yoga pants and a tank top. Then I hurried into the bathroom to take care of my needs. After, I stood in front of the mirror and stared at my chest. The last few days, I'd worn crew neck T-shirts in order to hide my wounds. Today, though, with the tank top, they were partially on display. I wasn't sure how I felt about that. The others had seen the wounds when they'd first happened, so I knew I shouldn't feel self-conscious. But a part of me did. I didn't want people staring at them all day.

I had to get over that.

Eventually, these wounds would turn into scars. And they would always draw people's attention. We lived in Mississippi—there was no way in hell I could forgo tank tops in our summer heat. I was just going to have to adjust.

Pulling back my hair, I threw on a hat, slinging the ponytail through the hole, then made my way into the kitchen, where the overpowering aroma of breakfast greeted me. At first sniff, I picked up on pancakes, waffles, bacon, and coffee. A werewolf's dream come true.

Jaden and Josh sat at the kitchen table with their plates before them.

"Hey, sleepyhead," Jaden greeted me happily. Her gaze immediately dropped to my chest. She could only see the upper part of the wounds, but it was enough. "Oh. Oh wow."

"What?" Josh asked, lifting his head. He turned my way, his own eyes widening when he caught sight of them.

"Pretty gnarly, huh?" I asked.

Jaden nodded. "Do they hurt?"

"A little now and then. Sometimes they catch the fabric of my clothes. I really am feeling a lot better though."

She winced sympathetically.

"But they're healing fast. I bet within a week, they'll be scars."

"That soon?" Josh said.

"I think? Honestly, I'm just guessing here. I've never had wounds like this before and—"

Jaden coughed into her hand, then cocked her head to the side, her gaze directed at something I couldn't see from where I stood. I stepped forward and glanced around the refrigerator. Chris stood there, leaning against the counter, a mug of coffee clasped between his hands.

My eyes widened and I shot Jaden a quick glance, shocked I hadn't known he was here. Guess my nose had been more focused on the breakfast buffet.

"He decided to join us today," Jaden informed me.

How was he even vertical after last night?

"Chris," I said, surprise lacing my voice.

He lifted his mug, then froze when his attention landed on my chest. Something akin to anger flashed in his face. "What the hell happened to you? Did your *vampire* do that?" He shoved his mug onto the counter, then stalked toward me, fury rippling beneath the surface.

"What? No, of course not," I snapped. Had no one told him about the demon? "What are you doing here?"

If I'd known to expect him, I would have covered up. No human could survive what I'd been through. Not to mention, I was healing faster than a human. Chris was going to have a lot of questions, and to be perfectly frank, I wasn't sure how I wanted to answer. He clearly didn't trust anything non-human. My betrayal had hit him hard. How much harder would it hit him when he learned I wasn't human? I was afraid to find out.

"Forget what I'm doing here. Tell me what the fuck happened to you." He reached out as though he meant to touch the wounds, then thought better of it. Thank goodness. Healed or not, I certainly didn't want people *touching* them.

He whistled under his breath. "Maddie. What the fuck?"

A good question. I glanced at Jaden. "How much does he know?"

She shrugged, then returned to her coffee. "Only

what you've told him."

Great. So he knew nothing about the witches, the demon, or...me.

"Let's have a seat," I told him.

He shot Josh a confused look, then followed me to the kitchen table. I grabbed a plate and loaded it up with five pancakes. Jaden had very quickly learned that my appetite rivaled even the hungriest college boy's.

Once I sat, I glanced up to find Chris staring at my plate. "You're going to eat all that?"

I considered my answer, then finally nodded. I refused to hide from them anymore. It wasn't fair to keep a secret from Chris, but not Jaden and Josh. It would not only put a strain on Chris's and my relationship, but on his friendship with them too.

Chris lowered into the chair across from me, unable to tear his eyes off my chest. I might have found it flattering, except I knew he wasn't ogling my breasts—he was staring at the wounds. Chris had never shown any interest in me beyond friendship, nor I him. And we were both perfectly okay with that.

"Where to start..." I drummed my fingers against the table, then picked up a pancake and gobbled it down.

He briefly tore his attention away from the wounds to watch me wolf down my first pancake. "Um." He eyed my plate, then shook his head and gestured at my chest. "How about you tell me what did that to you?"

I swallowed, then reached for a second pancake. "A demon."

Chris gave a slow blink and his mouth hung agape. It took a few moments for him to recuperate from that. "A demon?"

I nodded. "Whoever is behind the contract on Gabriel's life didn't appreciate it when I abducted and hid him away in the cabin. Once they realized they couldn't rely on the Academy to fulfill the contract, they hired witches."

Chris's eyelids fluttered, as though he was struggling to take this all in. "Witches."

I engulfed half of the second pancake and nodded. "Witches. They magically tracked Gabriel. When they found him, they also found me. They attacked. I won. The second time they attacked, they were better prepared. They sent more witches and a demon. They still lost."

"Looks like you almost lost too," he murmured.

Was it me, or did he seem a little pale? I probably would have been too. The Academy taught us about vampires. They'd never even mentioned the other paranormal species.

"Yeah, I nearly bit the dust during the battle," I admitted.

"She would have been fine if she hadn't jumped in front of the damn thing when it was trying to kill her mate," Josh grumbled.

Yeah, he and Jaden were still a little sore with me about that. Like Gabriel, they thought what I'd done was reckless. I thought of it more as heroic. Tomato, tomahto.

"It nearly ripped your heart out," Chris commented, his gaze tracing the five jagged cuts.

I nodded. "Nearly."

He finally tore his focus away and stared me deep in the eyes. "How did you survive that?" His eyes flicked to the pancakes, which clued me into his inner thoughts.

"I'm not a vampire," I told him.

"I figured. It's daylight and you're eating."

"But I'm not..."

I drew a deep breath, my stomach suddenly knotted and threatening to spew up everything I'd eaten. Last night, I hadn't been sure I'd ever be ready to confess this to him, and here I was, not twelve hours later, about to spill the tea.

If he was back for good, then I had no choice. My accelerated healing, my strength, my speed—I'd kept all that hidden from them in the past. But it'd been simpler times then.

"You're not what?" he pressed.

I caught Jaden's eye. She gave me an encouraging nod. Right. I could do this. If he rejected me, I'd survive. I had others. He wasn't the only important person in my life. But he *was* important, so I hoped he listened.

"I'm not"—I drew another deep breath, then took the plunge—"human."

Chris jerked in his seat, his eyes flaring wide. "What?"

Oh boy, not a promising start. "Um, I'm a werewolf."

He surged to his feet so fast, the chair fell. Jaden, Josh, and I sucked in a collective breath. The atmosphere in the kitchen shifted to something more tenuous. I knew my confession would be a lot for him to process, and I needed to give him time to do that.

"You're a..." Chris stammered, his voice filled with shock and disbelief. He cleared his throat and tried again. "You're telling me you're a werewolf? That's not possible. Werewolves aren't real."

I might have laughed if he hadn't looked so alarmed.

"That's what everyone thought about vampires before they came out, remember?" I rose to my feet. "But it's the truth. I didn't tell you guys earlier because it's forbidden. We aren't allowed to reveal our existence to humans." Technically, Olivia had broken the law when she'd told me what she was. But Olivia had lived by her own rules.

"A werewolf," he repeated, as though testing out the word. "And you were born one?"

"No." I didn't bother diving into that. He didn't need those gory details right this second.

He released a low, disbelieving laugh, then turned to Jaden and Josh. "And you two knew?"

"We only just learned about this ourselves," Jaden confessed. "Maddie shifted during the fight with the demon to save my life."

I hadn't realized Josh had told her that part. She gave me an appreciative smile.

Her words seemed to calm Chris, as though it made it easier for him to accept knowing they'd only recently learned about this.

"It's not something I can go around telling people," I said. "You guys shouldn't even know now. If the alphas find out—"

"Alphas," Chris repeated.

I nodded. "Werewolves live in packs. Or most do. I joined Lucy's pack for a while, but found I prefer to lone-wolf it."

He laughed. "Do you know how this sounds?"

Sighing, I stepped out from behind the table. I wondered if I'd need to shift in order to make him believe. Jaden hadn't seen me in wolf form. Or at least, not that she remembered. She actually had seen me once, before all this happened. But Gabriel had compelled her to forget, for her protection.

Understanding seemed to dawn on Chris's face. "That's why you call him your mate." He shook his head. "I thought you were just using his words, but no, it's because you also aren't human."

I winced. What he said was true, but it still stung.

"Christ, Maddie. Every time we talk, it's like you have more secrets."

"I know. But I just explained why I couldn't tell you."

"And that's how you survived the demon attack? Because you're a werewolf?"

"Yeah," I said.

"Jesus." He spun around and ran a hand through his hair. "I...I have no idea what to make of all this."

"I'm still the same person," I told him. "You just didn't know that I turn furry and howl at the moon."

When he snorted a laugh, I felt a bit of the weight rise from my shoulders.

He turned back to face me, an inquisitive glint in his eyes. "You're a werewolf?"

"Um, didn't we already establish that?"

That glint turned hard. Whatever thoughts were going through his head, I had a feeling I wouldn't like them.

"Prove it," Chris said. "Show me."

Jaden's head swung in my direction, excitement dancing in her eyes. Josh had seen me once before, but even he looked intrigued.

"Seriously?" I asked.

Chris planted his hands on his hips and stared me down. "I wanna see this."

"Me too!" Jaden squealed.

Chris blinked at her. "You're enjoying this?"

"Yeah! I can't believe you aren't. One of our best friends is a freaking werewolf. That's exciting."

Shaking my head, I snarfed down the last three pancakes, knowing I'd need the energy. They wanted a show? Fine. I'd give them one. I owed them that much.

I PULLED OPEN THE SLIDING BACK DOOR AND LED my friends outside into Lucy's spacious backyard. With every step, my palms grew clammier, and my throat grew tighter. As we walked, my mind raced. Would Chris still accept me after he saw me shift? Would this be the thing that tore us apart? God, I hoped not. I truly hoped he accepted me. I wasn't worried about Josh and Jaden, considering they were still here even after learning what I was. But out of the four of us, I was the odd man out. The non-human. For the first time since becoming a werewolf,

I found myself wishing I'd turned Olivia's offer down. Of course, if I had, I never would have joined the Academy and met my friends in the first place.

As we strolled across the yard, I noticed someone had already set up a series of dumbbells for us to use. Jaden, Josh, and Chris must have been here for some time before I woke up. The sizes made me laugh—the highest was a fifty pounder. I could lift that with my pinky toe. Hmm. Maybe me shifting into wolf form would be a good thing. They needed to understand what I was capable of. Fifty pounds didn't even begin to touch upon that.

We'd just reached the tree line when a sound caught my attention. I turned to find Daniel skulking out of the house, his face just as grim and annoyed as the day before. Maybe he only had the one expression.

Rolling my eyes, I said, "There's four of us here. And all of us are vampire slayers. I think we're quite capable of protecting ourselves."

He merely glowered, then took up his mantel leaning against the house, his arms and legs crossed. His favorite position, apparently.

Whatever. If he could ignore me, then I could ignore him. I only hoped he didn't shit himself when he saw me shift.

I turned back to my friends. Jaden's grin and twinkling eyes made me chuckle. Josh looked intrigued, but not quite as excited as Jaden. Considering he'd seen me in wolf form before, I wondered if he was feeling a little apprehensive. Chris, on the other hand, stood with his arms crossed, as though he didn't believe a word I'd said inside. Funny how a vampire slayer could be such a skeptic.

"Well?" Chris asked. "Gonna show us your wild side now?"

Wild side. That was one way of looking at it. I wasn't sure what he was expecting, but I knew he was in for a world of surprise. No one quite understood the magic behind shifting. All we knew was that a woman like me—five-foot-five and a hundred and twenty pounds—could turn into a beast who reached five feet at the shoulder on four legs and gained an additional hundred pounds.

"You guys ready?" I asked.

Chris just rolled his eyes, but Jaden bounced on her toes, her dark curls bobbing at her chin.

I chuckled, then reached for the hem of my tank top. The second I started lifting it, I paused and glanced at Josh and Chris. "This requires me getting naked so I don't destroy my clothes. Is that a problem?"

Both guffawed.

Jaden laughed, then grabbed Josh by the shoulders and spun him around. "No offense, Maddie. But I'm the only person he gets to see naked now."

Josh laughed before pressing a quick kiss against Jaden's cheek.

Chris, however, doubled down, his stare hardening, as though he suspected this was some sort of trick. I merely shrugged. Werewolves rarely cared about stripping naked in front of others. It came with the territory. And it was something I'd had to quickly overcome after becoming one.

"Alright," I said. "Just remember I warned you."

He scoffed. "I've seen a naked woman before."

I was sure he had. I quickly shucked my clothes, biting back a laugh when Chris's cheeks reddened. Behind him, I caught the sound of Daniel anxiously shifting his weight against the house. Yeah, I bet he hadn't expected to see his king's mate stark naked today.

Men. They cared so much about nudity. It was just flesh. Everyone had all the same parts. But they all got so flustered at the sight of bare skin.

I tipped my head back and let the familiar tingling sensation sweep through me. My wolf came to life and pressed toward the front of my mind. I hadn't let her out since the night of the demon attack. Shifting took strength and energy—two things I'd lacked since waking up. Almost dying certainly sucked all the life out of someone, and I was only starting to recover. But I had enough energy to spare for this. Plus, I needed it. Needed to feel the earth beneath my four paws. The wolf was part of me, and it gave me joy to let her run free.

Closing my eyes, I embraced the transformation, allowing the power to surge through my veins. When my first bone snapped, I heard my friends gasp. Understandable. Witnessing someone shift forms for the first time was a memorable—and jarring—moment. And we still had a ways to go.

Bones shifted, muscles stretched, and fur sprouted from my every pore. I dropped to the ground, then rose before them as a massive, tawny-colored werewolf.

I shook myself out, then opened my eyes to find Jaden staring at me in awe, her hands covering her mouth. Josh, on the other hand, wore a knowing smile, his admiration evident.

Chris pulled my attention away from the other

two. He stood statue still, his eyes locked on me. He'd uncrossed his arms and now they hung at his sides, but his fingers had curled into fists. That didn't bode well. He didn't say a word, but I could hear his elevated pulse.

"Wow, Maddie," Jaden said. She stepped forward, her hand held out. Before she reached me, she stopped and cocked her head. "Can I touch you? You won't bite me or anything, right? You're really you in there? Not a *real* wolf?"

I chuffed a laugh, then ducked my head.

She snickered as she placed her palm between my ears and scratched my fur. Normally, I wasn't a fan of someone *petting* me since I wasn't really an animal. But if it helped her come to grips with this, I'd happily make the sacrifice.

Josh braved a step toward me, coming flush with my side. "When I first saw you shift on the field, I thought a vampire had knocked me into next week. I didn't even believe it was you, not until after, when you shifted back. Things were so chaotic I wasn't able to process anything then. But I remember. You saved Jaden's life. If you hadn't shifted, you wouldn't have made it in time to stop that vampire."

I ducked my head in a nod.

"I'll never be able to repay you for that," Josh said.

"I don't think I ever had a chance to thank you either," Jaden said. She smoothed her palm down my neck and over my back. "You're, like, the size of a horse!"

Not quite. Horses were much taller.

Chris cleared his throat then, and all three of us glanced at him.

"Damn. I really didn't believe you when you said you were a werewolf."

I chuffed a small laugh. I mean, his disbelief had been pretty obvious.

He took a slow step toward me, his gaze raking over my form. "Jesus, you're huge."

I straightened my back and lengthened my neck, showing him that our heads were level with each other. Chris's eyes widened and he whistled.

"And there's more of you? An entire pack?" he asked.

I bobbed a nod. Maybe one day I'd explain that there was a pack in almost every state. Not to mention, even more across the world. We weren't few, we were many. But he probably wasn't ready to hear that today.

Chris reached out, his hand hovering by my

cheek. When he paused, clearly unsure whether he wanted to touch me, I pressed my face against his palm. He jumped but didn't pull back. Instead, he explored my features, even going so far as to ask me to open my mouth so he could see my teeth. At the sight of my monstrous fangs, he took an instinctive step back. I understood his reaction. Werewolf teeth were far larger than any other creature's. Vampires had sharp canines for piercing flesh, but werewolf fangs crushed throats. Ours were longer and thicker.

"Are you going to be okay with this?" Jaden eventually demanded, asking Chris the one question we were all dying to know.

Chris glanced at her, his teeth raking over his bottom lip. "I won't lie. This is a lot to take in. And I'm... I'm hurt, Maddie, that you never told us this. We've known you for almost six years. We shared our lives with you. We never held anything back. And in the span of two weeks, we learn that you're a werewolf and mated to the vampire king, the same vampire I'm supposed to kill. You went behind our backs and hid him from me. I mean, what else are you hiding? How can we trust you again?"

"I trust her," Jaden said. She stood next to my side and placed her hand on my back. "We could point out your failings too, Chris. When she came to us with the truth, you bailed. You weren't there when the vampires and witches attacked. And you weren't there when we had to face a demon. You were off, what, getting drunk?"

My eyes widened. Jaden hadn't once expressed any unhappiness with Chris, so this shocked me. And from the looks of it, Josh too.

"If not for Maddie, I would have died. Maddie almost *did* die." She leaned her weight against my side. "So, I trust her. She kept something from us, but from what she told us, she wasn't *allowed* to tell us she's a werewolf. I respect that. We all understand hierarchy and taking orders. Some orders we may not like, but that doesn't mean we disobey them."

"And Gabriel?" Chris asked Josh and Jaden. "Aren't you angry about that?"

"I was at first," Josh said. "But then I saw them together. There's a connection there, Chris. One we can't possibly understand. You weren't there when Maddie almost died. I wondered if Gabriel would die with her."

I sucked in a sharp breath and swung my head toward Josh.

He gave me a sad nod. "He didn't handle it well, Maddie. And I don't mean he was going to lose control of himself. I mean, he was sad. Angry. Hurt.

Upset. Desperate. If you died—and it was hit-and-miss there for a bit—I wondered how he would react. What he would do. He clearly loves you."

Tears pricked my eyes, but I blinked them back. Gabriel and I hadn't admitted we loved each other, not yet. But it was undoubtedly the direction our relationship was heading. We were mates—love seemed inevitable. It was different hearing someone say it out loud though.

"The way we see it"—Jaden stepped forward—"is you either choose to forgive her or you walk away. But you should know, Josh and I aren't going anywhere. Maddie has proven time and time again that she loves us. She's fought and nearly died for us. That kind of loyalty can survive a few secrets."

Chris's gaze shifted between the three of us, standing united. He chewed his bottom lip as he contemplated Josh and Jaden's words. A mix of emotions played across his face, and I braced myself for his response, not sure what to expect.

He took a deep breath, then said, "Okay. I hear you. And Maddie, I accept your apology. I can't promise that I'll work well with vampires. I certainly can't fathom befriending one. But I can promise not to kill your *mate*." He struggled with the last word. "Or your other two vampire friends.

And, yes, I'll help you guys with the Academy. If there are people within the organization taking bribes, like you said, then we need to root them out. The Academy is too important to all of us to let it fail."

Relief washed over me. With a happy yip, I pranced forward and knocked Chris to the ground. Before he landed, I hovered over him and licked his face from chin to forehead.

"Oh, gross, Maddie!" Chris exclaimed.

But Josh and Jaden laughed, only egging me on. I licked him once more, then stepped back, grinning.

Chris climbed to his feet, rubbing his face with his sleeve. "I may forgive you, but *never* do that again."

I gave the equivalent of a shrug, then pranced around my circle of friends. Happiness bubbled within me, and before I could stop myself, I tipped my head back and unleashed a delighted howl. My three friends all jumped in unison, their eyes equally wide as they stared at me.

"Guess that means she's happy?" Jaden said.

"Happy or not, shut it," Daniel bit out near the house. "Wanna alert every vampire in the area of our location?"

Since I couldn't snap back at him, Jaden did it for

me. "It's daytime, idiot. What vampires do you know of that are awake?"

Daniel closed his mouth with a click. I turned to him and winked, which only seemed to enrage him further.

"Hey!" came a shout from the back porch.

My head snapped up and I found Lucy standing in the kitchen on the other side of the sliding door. She planted her hands on her hips and wore what I called her *alpha stare*.

"What the hell are you doing?" she snapped. She stalked onto the porch. "Maddie, you know better! You can't just—" She waved a hand at me and my friends. Exasperated, she dropped her hands to her sides and groaned. "The alphas are going to kill me for this, do you know that? You told *another* human about us?"

"I won't tell anyone," Chris said, his voice humble. "Your secret is safe with me."

Her burning gaze turned to him. "It better be. And on a personal note, you hurt my sister, and I'll rip you into small pieces and feed you to my children. Got it?"

My eyes widened. *Holy shit, Luce.*

"Uh. Got it," Chris repeated, his face paling.

"Good." Her scowl morphed into a grin. A

psychotic grin that made my blood run cold. Lucy had really grown into her alpha position over the years. With a final glare in my direction, she slammed the door shut and disappeared back inside the house. I hadn't even heard them come home. They must have heard my howl and come to investigate. Whoops.

"Alright, shift back," Jaden said. She marched over to the weights and perused the selection. "Time for strength training. We need to get you back into fighting shape because I want to see what you can *really* do. No more pulling punches. Time to unleash the beast."

I huffed a laugh, shifted, and quickly dressed.

Once in human form and dressed, Chris came toward me and pulled me into a hug. I didn't usually like hugs, but after everything Chris and I had gone through this week, I decided to make an exception. I had my friend back. Nothing else mattered.

"Come on, Maddie!" Jaden called. "Show us what the big bad wolf is capable of."

Chuckling, I stepped out of Chris's embrace and strolled into the woods.

"Hey! Where are you going?"

"To get something heavier!" I called back.

9

"*Underworld?*" Chris asked, his gaze fixed on me.

"Seen it," I admitted with a rueful grin. What I didn't admit was that it was one of my favorite series. Even before I'd met Gabriel, the whole epic werewolf-vampire romance had called to me. I'd never stopped to consider that before. "I'm surprised you've watched it, considering everything."

Chris shrugged. "I like the action, I guess. And can't complain about a woman in leather."

Oh god. I laughed and rolled my eyes. Typical male response.

"*Teen Wolf*," Jaden interjected.

"The show or the movie?"

"Either. Both?" she said, laughing.

"I've seen the movie. Not the show. Teenage dramas aren't really my thing."

"Oh, you have to watch the show." She feigned swooning on the couch. "I don't watch for the plot."

The room erupted with laughter. This felt good. To have all four of us together again. I hadn't realized just how much I'd missed this. Chris's absence had left quite the hole, and I was glad to see it repaired.

I leaned back in my chair and stretched out my muscles. We'd spent the entire afternoon strength training. My friends had kept challenging me to lift anything and everything in sight just to test my limits. And I'd indulged them because, for once, I didn't feel like a fragile little flower about to snap in half. Meredith had told me I'd heal fast once my body started recuperating, and she hadn't been wrong. I was bursting with energy and ready to take on the world.

Or a demon.

More than once, I'd spotted a calculative gleam in Chris's eye. He was probably wondering if he could beat me in a fight now that I'd promised to stop holding back. He didn't stand a chance of course. But there was no harm in letting him wonder.

Jaden, Josh, and Chris kept the conversation flowing, chatting about the many different werewolf movies out there and comparing them to me. Partway through discussing the merits of *An American Werewolf in London*, Jaden's phone rang.

She fished her cell out of her pocket, then gave a small gasp. "It's Ginny!"

"Who's Ginny?" Chris immediately asked.

I waved a dismissive hand, then gestured for Jaden to answer the phone.

She did so with a huge grin. "Ginny, hi!"

"Hey, Jaden. Sorry it took me so long to get back to you. Tracking down this vamp has taken all my free time. He isn't making it easy," Ginny said, her words easy for me to hear. Josh and Chris weren't so lucky.

"Oh, no. Were you able to find him?"

"Find who?" Chris whispered.

I waved my hand again, this time more dramatically.

"Yes. Finally." Ginny released an exasperated sigh I was sure even Josh and Chris could hear. *"It took a bit of convincing, but Benjamin's agreed to meet with you guys. Provided I'm there."* She gave a

141

bitter laugh. *"Guess he thinks I'm his friend or something."*

Jaden snickered at Ginny. "Okay. When do you want to meet and where?"

I preemptively held up my hand to stop Chris from asking yet another question.

"I need tonight and tomorrow night to check out a few things regarding his alibi and tie up some loose ends, but I think I should be good to meet the night after that. Benjamin wants to meet somewhere public. He suggested Shade Pub. Do you know it?"

"No, but that's fine. We'll find it."

"Great. Let's aim for around ten p.m. See you then."

Jaden ended the call, then sat back with a pleased grin.

"Okay, can someone please tell me what's going on?" Chris asked.

Chuckling, I pointed at Josh. "You two fill him in. I'll be right back."

I rose to my feet and glanced toward the hallway. Sunset was approaching—I could feel it in my bones. Almost like my wolf could sense it now. Gabriel was about to wake, and I wanted to be there when he did, if only to explain that Chris was here. Gabriel would figure it out quickly, of course. But I wanted to prepare him for it.

"Where are you going?" Chris asked.

Right. Gabriel wasn't the only one who needed preparation. I released a slow breath, then turned to face him. "It's almost sunset."

Understanding dawned on my friends' faces, and the sharp scent of both fear and anger permeated the room. It didn't take long for me to realize it came from Chris, but I didn't comment on it. His emotions were for him to deal with. He didn't need me sticking my nose in. Though, I'd always suspected his hatred had stemmed from fear.

"Gabriel's going to wake in a few minutes," I continued. "But he may not be the only vampire here tonight. Anna and Vlad sometimes make an appearance an hour or so after sunrise. Are you going to be okay with that? Being amongst vampires?"

Chris leaned forward on the couch and dangled his hands between his legs. The initial disdain on his face transformed into a flicker of concern. The only vampires Chris had been near were ones he'd staked. He'd never had to be friendly with one before.

"You said we can trust them," Chris said.

I nodded. I had said that. And I'd meant it.

"Then let's do this. I promised I'd try."

"Thank you," I whispered.

As I made my way down the hallway toward Gabriel's and my room, I passed the two guards stationed at the door—neither of which were Daniel, thank goodness. His shift usually ended about an hour before sunset.

I gave the guards a smile, then stepped into the pitch black bedroom. Gabriel didn't stir, and he wouldn't for another few minutes. I only hoped he woke in a good mood—not that he'd ever woken in a grumpy one, other than our first night together in the cabin. But I'd had a wonderful day with my friends and hoped that continued throughout the night. I wasn't in the mood to clean up spilled blood. It all depended on Chris and Gabriel. More so the former.

I eased onto the edge of the bed and watched, waiting for Gabriel to wake. He seemed so peaceful when asleep. Enough so that it nearly convinced me to crawl in next to him. But before I could, the sun dipped below the horizon, and a slight shift in the air rippled over me.

Gabriel stirred, his eyes fluttering open, revealing the mesmerizing stormy depths that drew me in time and time again. I couldn't help but smile when our gazes met.

"Hi," I whispered, my voice filled with warmth and affection.

After an entire day of waiting for him to wake, I finally felt complete. Even while hanging out with my friends, something had been missing. And now, I realized what—or rather, *who*—it was.

"Evening, luv," Gabriel replied. He reached up and gently brushed my cheek, his gaze searching mine. "You're looking positively radiant tonight."

I leaned into his touch, my smile widening. "I feel really good tonight. I'm definitely improving. I feel stronger than I have in days."

"That's wonderful." He flashed me a smile, the tips of his fangs peeking out from beneath his lips. The sight had once startled me, but I'd grown used to it now. They were a part of him. As much as my wolf was me. I had fangs part of the time too.

Gabriel pushed onto his elbows and leaned in to kiss me.

I stopped him with a hand on his chest, though heat warmed my cheeks. "Jaden and Josh are in the living room waiting for us. And so is..." I paused, my teeth raking over my bottom lip before I finished with, "Chris."

One of Gabriel's dark eyebrows shot upward. "Chris?"

"He was already here this morning when I woke up. He came with Josh and Jaden. We had a pretty in-depth conversation about everything that's happened, and I finally told him about my wolfier side. Of course, they made me shift in front of them," I said, chuckling.

Gabriel's eyes widened. "That's an eventful day."

"It is. But he agreed to forgive me, and he's also agreed to be friendly with you."

"How noble of him," Gabriel intoned.

"He's trying, Gabe."

That crooked grin returned. "I love when you call me Gabe."

I couldn't help but smile.

"Fine. I'll be friendly too," Gabriel conceded. "But only if I can have that kiss now."

"You're such a charmer," I murmured as I leaned in.

I brushed my lips against his. I'd meant to keep it chaste. Just a quick peck before dragging his tush out of bed and into the living room. But the second our mouths met, I wanted more. So much more. My lips parted and I eagerly welcomed his tongue.

Groaning, Gabriel threaded his hand through my hair and cupped my cheek, holding me steady as he thoroughly kissed me. If this was how we spent every sunset, sign me up. His kisses were addicting, and I never wanted to stop. Even better—thanks to his vampire-ness—no morning breath. That'd always been a pet peeve of mine with previous lovers, but it was a part of the "vampire magic." They awoke every evening in pristine condition, no matter their state at sunrise.

I'd watched the whole process with Anna once. After a slight scuffle with another vampire that had left her looking like she'd gone three rounds with a pit bull, she'd climbed into bed and succumbed to sleep. During the day, I'd watched as the magic gave her a vampiric makeover. It'd fixed her hair, cleansed her skin, healed her bruises and cuts, even corrected her makeup. For the first time ever, I'd found myself a wee bit jealous of bloodsuckers. It took me hours of effort to look as good as Anna did when she woke.

Once we parted, Gabriel swung his legs over the side of the bed and stood. He quickly dressed—a show I most definitely enjoyed watching—then strolled out into the hallway, pausing briefly to greet his guards and discuss the upcoming shift change.

His ever-changing human guard made me nervous, but Gabriel assured me that none were permitted to enter the house without first being interrogated to ensure they had nothing to do with recent events. And thanks to Gabriel's power of compulsion, his guards couldn't lie. I trusted Gabriel's power, but I also knew compulsion didn't work on the strong-minded. Deep in the back of mind, I constantly asked, "What if?" What if one of his guards was involved? What if they'd successfully fooled him? What if they were just waiting for the right moment to strike? Thankfully, so far, none had proved untrustworthy. And I was grateful for that.

Taking Gabriel's hand, I led him through the hallway, then paused right before we turned the corner.

"Ready for this?" I asked.

"I will be a delight," Gabriel assured me, winking.

"Just be yourself."

"That's what I said," he teased.

Chuckling, I took point and led Gabriel into the living room.

The second we stepped into view, Josh reached for the remote and turned off the television. An eerie hush fell over the room, one that prickled the back of my neck. Josh and Jaden stared intently at Chris, as though they expected him to attack Gabriel. When he didn't so much as twitch, they relaxed.

I, however, did not.

I wanted to trust Chris, but we were dealing with decades of hatred for vampires. Chris wouldn't easily overcome that in a single night. Nor did I expect him to. What'd happened to him and his family was heart-wrenching. I couldn't expect him to overcome his biases that easily. I just hoped he gave Gabriel a chance.

Clearly sensing the rising tension in the room, Jaden offered Gabriel a friendly wave, then purposely set her sights on her phone while Josh merely greeted Gabriel with a manly nod.

Chris moved to the edge of the couch, his glare locked onto the vampire standing in front of him. Gabriel, on the other hand, exuded a calm and confident air, as though he faced this sort of problem every single night. Perhaps he did. He was a king, after all. Doubtful every single subject loved him. I had to imagine he had experience facing people who hated him.

"So..." I cleared my throat, breaking the silence. "Chris, this is Gabriel. My mate."

Gabriel's hand brushed my back, then he stepped forward and extended his hand. "It's a pleasure to finally meet you."

Chris's eyes flicked between Gabriel's

outstretched hand and his face. The room seemed caught in a suspenseful stillness, waiting for Chris's response. Hell, I felt like I was hovering on the edge of a precipice, waiting for *someone* to do something. I held my breath as I watched Chris's every move. If he so much as reached for anything other than Gabriel's hand, I would be there in an instant.

Finally, Chris reluctantly reached out, gripping Gabriel's hand in what I assumed was supposed to be a crushing handshake. Unfortunately, Chris was human. It probably felt more like a playful puppy trying to nip at Gabriel's hand.

Chris pushed to his feet, his hand still clasped within Gabriel's. "So, you're him."

"And you're him," Gabriel retorted. "I know how much you mean to Maddie. Therefore, I'd like you to know how important you are to me."

Chris's jaw tightened, his one eye twitching as he fought to control his baser instincts. When he spoke, it was with clear, crisp words. "I hope you understand, vampire, that the only reason I haven't buried a stake in your chest is because of her. She's my family. And if you *ever* hurt her, I won't hesitate to end you."

My shoulders tensed, and I fought the urge to rush forward and tuck Gabriel behind me.

"I assure you, Chris. I cherish Maddie. Her happiness and safety are my utmost priority. I would never purposely cause her harm. But let's be clear about something. If I ever *did* hurt Maddie, she'd likely kill me herself." Gabriel glanced over his shoulder at me with half a smile.

"Damn straight," I said, grinning.

Jaden kept her eyes on her phone, but I saw her smirk.

Chris still clutched Gabriel's hand, his knuckles white from the pressure. After what seemed like an eternity, Chris's rigid posture softened, and he released Gabriel's hand. "Fine."

Gabriel inclined his head, then returned to me. He leaned down and pressed a kiss against my temple—one of his favorite ways to show affection.

"I have some needs to attend to," he murmured in my ear.

Meaning he needed to feed. Vampires drank blood, I understood that. But he'd chosen not to broadcast it to Chris, Jaden, and Josh. I appreciated his discretion. I wasn't sure how far Chris was willing to go tonight, and I didn't want to push him. Granted, Gabriel only drank from a bottle, but I didn't feel like getting into that discussion with my friends tonight.

This time, I gripped his hand and gave it an appreciative squeeze. "Thank you."

Gabriel gazed down at me and smiled. "Anything for you."

As he disappeared into the kitchen, I turned my attention back to my friends, aware of Chris's lingering tension. Of all the ways I'd imagined this, that'd certainly been the best-case scenario. No one was bleeding, no one was dead—what more could a girl ask for when her mate was the king of vampires, and her friends vampire slayers?

"So, that's him," Chris stated once we were alone. I didn't bother pointing out that Gabriel could hear everything we said. Chris already knew and likely didn't care.

"Yup."

"You know, for a king, he doesn't seem very..." Chris let his sentence hang.

"Very what?"

"Kingly. I mean, all anyone ever talks about is how powerful and well-protected he is. And yet, he's here with no people, no guards—"

"There are two guards in the hallway," I told him.

Chris shrugged. "We were told he kept dozens of guards with him at all times, that he didn't go unprotected. We had to infiltrate the hotel just to catch a glimpse of him. Yet, here he is. Playing homemaker with you."

I honestly wasn't sure how to take that comment.

Jaden chuckled. "He's more than a king, Chris."

"Oh?" He turned to face her. "And what else is he?"

She placed her phone on the coffee table and lifted her head to meet Chris's stare. "He's strong. Both physically and mentally. I caught a few glimpses of him fighting. He knows how to take care of himself. And he has the power of compulsion."

I flinched—I hadn't wanted Chris to learn that. Knowing him, he'd assume Gabriel compelled me to care for him. And from the look in his eyes right now, the thought was there.

"But he's also compassionate, protective, and fiercely loyal," Jaden continued, as though she felt the need to defend him. I appreciated her words. They'd mean more coming from her, seeing as how she wasn't his mate. "He has a depth to him that goes beyond his vampiric nature. Josh and I witnessed all this firsthand while he was sitting at Maddie's bedside."

Josh nodded. "For a vampire, he's a good guy, Chris. He might surprise you."

"And before you ask, no, he didn't compel me into caring about him," I said.

Chris's eyes widened.

"Please, it's written all over your face."

He wiped his expression clean. "And how would you know if he had?"

"Maddie's too stubborn to be compelled," Gabriel called from the kitchen, proving that he could hear us.

I chuckled and shook my head. "Thanks for that."

But what surprised me more was the sound of Chris's laughter. My head whipped back and I stared wide-eyed at him.

"What?" Chris asked, shrugging. "He's not wrong. You are stubborn."

Pushing off the couch, Chris meandered toward the kitchen. I cursed and trailed after him, afraid of his reaction when he found Gabriel standing there with a glass of blood. I wouldn't hide him or pretend he didn't drink blood. I just wasn't sure how Chris would respond to the sight.

"So, vampire, if you're so much more than a king, tell me. What do you do in your free time?" Chris rounded the corner and came to a sharp stop when he caught sight of Gabriel in the kitchen.

I poked my head around the corner to find Gabriel leaning against the counter, a wine glass full of what I was sure was O-positive in his hand.

Chris's gaze locked on the glass, but he seemed to shrug it off. "Besides being all regal and stuff."

My body relaxed. Catastrophe number two evaded.

Gabriel chuckled, the sound rich and melodic. From the sight of Chris's shudder, I wasn't the only one affected by it.

"Free time is a luxury I rarely have. In fact, this is the quietest my life has been in ages."

"The quietest?" I said, chuckling. "Someone's actively trying to kill you. In the last two weeks, we've fought witches, vampires, and a demon. But *this* is the quiet life for you?"

Gabriel turned an affectionate smile my way, one that made me a wee bit weak in the knees.

"Usually, my nights are full of politics, meetings, and speeches. But when I do find some downtime, I enjoy art and literature. I have a passion for history and I enjoy exploring the intricacies of the human experience through paint."

I had no idea what that even meant. That he liked art?

Chris, however, seemed impressed. "You don't strike me as the artistic type."

Gabriel's smile widened, and Chris tensed at the sight of his fangs.

"Appearances can be deceiving. Immortality allows us to pursue many passions, and I wasn't always a king. In fact, despite being alive for a hundred-and-seventy-five years, my time as king has been a brief six years—a mere drop in the bucket of my existence."

"You aren't alive," Chris stated, though there wasn't any bitterness in his voice.

"Forgive my choice of words," Gabriel responded in a measured voice. "It was merely an expression."

"Maddie doesn't like art and literature," Chris suddenly stated.

Ah. And now I saw why he'd begun exploring this line of conversation.

"Maddie likes movies and fiction, hunting and fighting. She likes—"

"I'm aware of what Maddie enjoys," Gabriel stated. "As I said, immortality allows us to pursue many passions. I'm sure she and I will find many things to enjoy together throughout the course of our lives."

"Your lives," Chris repeated.

But before he could dive deeper into that, the front door ripped open and two tiny little monsters came plowing inside, the larger of the two chattering loudly about what she wanted to eat for dessert.

Phew. Saved by the children.

I pushed off the wall just in time to hear Annalise scream, "Auntie!" and launch herself into my arms. I heaved her up and listened as she animatedly told me about her day.

When Lucy staggered through the front door, laden with bags, everyone moved to assist.

"Wow, full house tonight," she commented as the door swung closed behind her.

"Where's Sam?" I asked.

Something flashed in her eyes as she handed the bags to Gabriel. She told the kids to go play in their rooms, and once they bolted down the hallway, she turned and faced me.

"One of my pack mates called. They came across an unknown creature attacking a human. It didn't sound like a vampire, werewolf, or witch. In fact, it sounded like…"

Fear shredded my insides. "The demon?"

She jerked a nod. "Sam went to investigate."

"Alone?"

"He'll be fine, Maddie. He took a few of the pack

members with him. We'll wait here for an update."

I could tell from her perplexed expression that she didn't like waiting any more than I did. But they had kids now—a family that depended on them. They couldn't both rush headfirst into battle.

I could, though.

Yes, Gabriel was my mate, but he didn't rely on me like Lucy's children relied on her.

Gabriel came up behind me and placed a comforting hand on my back.

"Everything's going to be fine," Lucy assured me, likely sensing my dislike for this situation. "Sam will find the demon and destroy it, okay?"

No. Not okay. The demon was stronger than Sam. I'd seen the truth of that in its psychotic eyes while it listened to my dying heartbeat.

Lucy would *not* lose her husband tonight. Hell no.

Marching into Gabriel's and my bedroom, I grabbed the leather harness Anna had designed and given me the night of the demon attack. I changed clothes into something more appropriate, then slid it on. Once buckled in, I armed myself to the teeth, filling every single slot, sheath, and scabbard with a myriad of stakes, daggers, and my sword.

"Maddie?" came Gabriel's voice from the

doorway. "What on earth are you doing?"

"I'm going out there," I told him. "I refuse to let that thing kill Sam or anyone else."

"Hey." Gabriel stepped into the room and touched my chin, lifting it until our gazes met. "You're not ready. I know you're feeling stronger, but—"

"I'm going. I'll call you with updates. But I can't just sit here and wait."

"You can't—"

"Gabriel," I snapped, immediately regretting my tone.

He blinked, then nodded. "Fine. Then I will be with you every step of the way."

"Okay," I said.

"We'll go with you too," Chris murmured from the hallway. He poked his head inside and shrugged. "I wasn't there last time. But I'm here now. I'd like to help."

"Thank you," I said to both of them. "Thank you for understanding how important this is to me."

That creature had almost killed me once. I wouldn't let it take anyone else. Especially not my sister's husband.

I slid my last dagger home. "Let's go demon hunting."

THANKS TO LUCY'S INSTRUCTIONS, IT DIDN'T take us long to find Sam. Or the small pack of werewolves he'd chosen to hunt the demon with. Relief blasted through me at the sight of my sister's perfectly healthy husband. It would have killed me if we hadn't arrived in time. Sam seemed surprised to see us but quickly accepted our help. The more the merrier when it came to hunting demons.

He and Jaden quickly put their heads together and came up with a plan. They decided it would be best to split our group of fifteen into three parties.

Sam, Cole—Lucy's second in command—and I were each given a group to lead. My group consisted of the usual suspects: Gabriel, Chris, Josh, Jaden, and myself. Afterward, each group chose a grid within the search area. Then we primed our cell phones with each other's numbers to call the second we spotted the demon, and off we went.

Now, we just had to track the evil bastard down, which was proving more difficult than I expected.

It was a demon, for crying out loud. How hard could it be?

"Maddie?" came Jaden's voice from behind.

I angled my head until she was in my periphery. She stood behind me, armed to the teeth with stakes and daggers—not that stakes would do anything against the demon, but better safe than sorry. The last time we'd faced the demon, it'd had an entire witch coven plus a few vampires fighting alongside it. Who knew what it was traveling with this time?

"Which way?" Jaden asked, pointing to the intersection in front of us. We'd all agreed that my nose was likely the most sensitive among the five of us and were relying on it to track the bastard down. The one upside to demons was that they stunk. Or at least, this one did. I would *never* forget the acrid stench it'd put off. Almost like sulfur—which made sense when one thought about it. I had no idea if hell truly existed or if that was where one summoned a demon from, but if so, the concept of sulfur and demons went hand in hand.

I lifted my chin and scented the air. So far, I hadn't had any luck in picking up its horrifically distinct stench. But if I wasn't mistaken, the air did seem a bit stinkier to the left. I gestured in that direction, and together, the five of us plodded on.

About a mile later, I drew another deep breath, then winced.

"Oh," I muttered, holding a fist to my mouth. "Either someone cooked some incredibly rotten eggs or our demon is that way." I pointed in the direction of the scent.

My team followed my pointed finger.

Because, of course, the demon was hiding in a desolate alley that looked like the setting from every horror movie ever made. Knowing our luck, the second we entered the alley, a trench coat-clad man with a hook for a hand would pop up behind us.

Gabriel and I exchanged a wary glance. I knew very little about demons to date—other than how to almost die at one's hands—but if I had to guess, I'd wager that a demon would love to hang out in a dark, creepy alley similar to this one.

"Down there?" Chris asked.

"Down there," I repeated.

Yeah, not a single one of us wanted to venture into the pitch-black alley. Our primordial instincts had kicked in, telling us to run in the *other* direction. Not that we would.

My poor heart was beating double-time, and fear flooded my veins. Given my history with the demon, my body's reaction seemed entirely reasonable, if not a tad bit inconvenient.

"Easy, Maddie," Gabriel said, his hand a comforting presence against my back. "You aren't alone."

I knew that. But that didn't help slow my pulse. I hadn't been alone last time either, and my mind took complete pleasure in reminding me of that. Along with the demon's sickening grin and the crazed light in its eyes as it plunged its freaking hand into my chest, impaling me on its claws. My chest ached just thinking about it. Somehow I knew if I looked down, I'd see that exact hand skewering me right this second. Fear had a funny way of playing mind games with someone.

"Let me take the lead," Gabriel urged.

I shook my head. "I should take the lead. My sense of smell is stronger than yours."

"You can direct me," he said. His fingers wrapped around my wrist. "Please, Maddie."

I shot him a glance, then softened at the sight of fear in his eyes. I wasn't the only one struggling here. Gabriel had his own nightmares. Ones that involved watching his mate nearly die right in front of his eyes. It wasn't just for my sanity that he'd offered to take the lead. He truly didn't want me anywhere near this demon. A desire I completely understood. I didn't want him anywhere near it either.

"Okay," I whispered.

Relief lightened his stormy expression. With a gentle hand, he guided me behind him before he entered the alleyway. We passed by a series of fences, gates, and garbage bins. But even the bins couldn't mask the stench that grew stronger and stronger with every step until I damn near gagged with every breath.

"Oh, sweet lord," Jaden grunted behind me. "That's quite the stench."

She'd been unconscious when we'd last faced the demon, so she hadn't had the pleasure of smelling it. Tonight, she wasn't quite as lucky.

"It's close," I whispered.

Fear ratcheted my pulse, but I refused to let that hold me back. We had an obligation to destroy this thing before it could hurt anyone else. An obligation I refused to fail to uphold. The witches had summoned the demon to kill me and Gabriel. That made it our responsibility to kill it. Before it hurt anyone. Surely, with the five of us working together, we would accomplish that.

Of course, my mind took that moment to remind me that there'd been more than five of us last time, and we'd failed then.

Shut up, brain.

Something rustled in the near distance. I nearly jumped out of my damn skin. Only at the last second did I remind myself to calm the eff-train down and breathe. Not that breathing was particularly easy right now.

"I hear it. I'll update the other teams," Josh murmured.

I nodded, then replied with, "Two houses up. Right-hand side." I pointed at a dilapidated wooden fence that looked like it'd seen better days.

Then came a pained moan. Weak. Like they couldn't find the strength to raise their voice.

Shit! Had the demon hurt someone?

My instincts screamed at me to run toward the sound, to protect whoever the demon had harmed.

But Gabriel's cool hand snatched mine, holding me back and grounding me in the moment.

"No heroics, Maddie," he murmured, his eyes burning with a preternatural glow. "We need to stick together and be strategic. This demon is dangerous, and we can't afford to let it catch us off guard."

Right. I knew that. I was just so used to hunting alone, exactly how the Academy trained me. But I had to remember, things hadn't gone so well the last time I faced this demon.

Nodding, I swallowed the lump in my throat. Gabriel was right. As much as I wanted to rush in and save the day, doing so would only get me killed.

"Whoever it is has survived this long," Chris continued. It shocked me that he agreed with Gabriel. "They can wait thirty more seconds while we come up with a plan."

"Right," I whispered.

"Okay. The yards are fenced, but we can jump them," Chris relayed, fixing his grip on his crossbow. "I propose we split into two groups. Gabriel, you, and I will lure the demon out. Josh and Jaden will circle around to the front of the house and catch it from behind by surprise."

I unsheathed my sword and watched as Jaden and Josh each grabbed a pair of daggers.

"We'll try to herd the demon away from the victim," Chris continued. "Josh and Jaden, it's on you to kill it."

A part of me wanted to reverse the roles. Gabriel and I weren't human, after all. We should be the ones making the kill. But I quickly saw the intelligence in Chris's plan. Gabriel and I would be the ones fighting the demon off, with Chris backing us up. With luck, it wouldn't expect Josh and Jaden, and hopefully, they'd kill it before it even realized what was happening. No fighting required on their end.

The only part of the plan I wanted to change was shifting. My fangs were likely better suited than any weapon. But shifting required me to remove the harness and strip, and I couldn't communicate with anyone here post-shift. That left me feeling more vulnerable than I liked, so I ignored the urge and nodded, agreeing to Chris's plan.

Gabriel, Chris, and I positioned ourselves between two houses, hiding in the shadows, while Jaden and Josh circled around back. I wasn't sure how sensitive a demon's senses were, if it'd heard our plan or could hear Jaden and Josh moving through the grass. From the smell of it, though, the demon hadn't left. A good sign.

Biting my lip, I leaned around the corner of the house and stole a quick glance. A path ran between the two houses, flowers growing on either side. The flowers had wilted, their stems and petals blackened. A side effect of the demon's presence?

At the back, near a side door, I caught sight of a hunched figure. Possibly a young woman. She sat curled in a ball, her arms tucked over her knees. I frowned and braved a step out from behind the house. She was human. And I didn't see a demon anywhere nearby. Had it left?

"Maddie." Gabriel reached for me.

I slipped out of his grasp and took another step down the path.

"Hey," I called out, trying not to startle the woman. Had the demon heard us and fled? "Are you okay?"

The woman's head shot up, her eyes wide with terror. She scuttled backward, hiding in the shadows. I could still see her, thanks to my wolf's heightened vision, but her features seemed obscured somehow. It wasn't until she turned her head to me, her lips stretched in an unnaturally wide grin, that I nearly shat myself.

I staggered back a step. Was she possessed? Could demons do that? She looked nothing like the demon I'd faced a few weeks ago. Could there be more than one? Please, God, no.

Jaden and Josh appeared at the bottom of the path, their expressions equally confused. The overwhelming scent of sulfur had led us here, but I couldn't actually see the creature. Had the demon tricked us somehow?

After another quick glance around to ensure we weren't about to be attacked, I started back toward the woman. "Are you hurt? We can help you."

High pitched, manic laughter spilled past her lips—lips spread far too wide to be natural.

Oh. Oh, hell no. That wasn't natural.

I had to force myself not to run. But sweet lord, every hair on my body stood on end. I had no idea what was happening here. I just knew we couldn't leave her here like this. The demon must have done something. Or, and this was far more terrifying to think about, the demon could change shape, and we were staring at the monster right now.

I nearly screamed when she rose from the ground. Most people, when they stood, pushed up from the ground, fighting gravity every step of the way. But this woman moved from the top down, as though controlled by marionette strings.

Fear wormed through my stomach, and I

clutched the hilt of my sword until my knuckles turned white.

Whatever had happened to this woman, I couldn't leave her like this.

"Demon," she suddenly hissed, her voice guttural and deep. A voice that was no longer her own. That sinister grin spread across her face, and she pointed at me. "It wants you. It'll take you."

Hands snatched my hips and pulled me backward, shielding me behind a broad back. Gabriel stood before me, his every muscle primed and ready.

"What are you?" Gabriel demanded.

I stepped out from behind him, refusing to hide. If we faced this thing, it would be together.

The woman cocked her head, a sheen of red rolling over her eyes. "Demon. Wants. Her." She tilted her head in the other direction and studied me. "Tasty little wolf." Her head twitched upright. She reminded me of a puppet. Someone who had no control over her body. Something flashed over her face, a brief flicker of fear before the darkness consumed it. "It comes."

What comes? I opened my mouth to ask when suddenly, Chris's voice rang out, "Behind you!"

I spun around just in time to see the true demon, its monstrous form emerging from the shadows. Its eyes glowed red with malevolent hunger, and its claws curled with lethal intent. That sinister gaze locked on me, and next came the grin, flashing its many fanged teeth. A mouthful of nightmares. When its bisected tongue flicked past its lips, tasting the air, I knew it recognized me.

The demon lunged at me, its speed and ferocity catching me off guard. Gabriel reacted instantly, pushing me out of the way, but he couldn't avoid the demon's attack in time. Its scythe-like claws sliced through the air, ripping through Gabriel's shoulder.

"Gabriel!" I cried out, fury and panic seizing me.

But Gabriel didn't so much as pause. He countered the demon's assault with a fierce blow of his own, striking the demon in the head. It staggered backward toward Chris, who shot it with his crossbow. The bolt pierced the creature's chest but hardly slowed him. I made a mental note that either the demon's heart wasn't in its chest or it could survive without it. Neither thought was encouraging.

The demon was relentless. Its every attack seemingly centered on trying to reach me. It dodged Gabriel's attacks with uncanny ability, its gaze firmly locked on me. There was no doubt who the target was here. Guess the demon wanted another taste of me.

Well, too damn bad.

"Stay back, Maddie!" Chris shouted as he reloaded his crossbow.

Jaden and Josh joined the fray, slashing their daggers across the demon's back.

The four of them had edged me out, as though they had a silent understanding to keep me away from the demon. But I couldn't stay back. I couldn't watch my friends risk their lives for me while the demon slowly whittled them down. Even surrounded as it was, they'd barely hurt it.

I took a deep breath, gripped my sword, and then, with a burst of preternatural speed, I lunged at the demon. I didn't aim for the chest or gut, the two largest targets. Instead, I went for the neck. If I could separate its head from its body, surely it would die.

The demon grinned in surprise, pleased by my willingness to join the fight. I swung out with my sword, the blade catching its throat, but it danced away before I could do any real damage. It watched me while it dodged Gabriel's attacks, an intelligence to its gaze that more than rattled me.

Then it darted to the side and grabbed Jaden, crushing her to its chest as it pinned her arms to her sides. The demon walked backward, pressing its back against a wall so no one could sneak up behind it. Her scream when the demon placed its mouth to her throat froze me.

"I kill her," it said, its chapped lips pressed to her skin.

"Touch her and I'll fucking end you," Josh snarled.

"Tasty little wolf. Come to me."

I felt something roll over me, a sudden need to go to the demon. Its eyes locked on mine, its mouth brushing oh so gently over Jaden's throat. She struggled against its hold, fighting with every fiber of her being to free herself from its grip.

"Here, little wolf. Come to me."

I swayed and before I could stop myself, I took a step toward the demon.

"Compulsion, Maddie!" I heard someone shout. "Fight it."

"Little wolf," the demon crooned. "Tasty little wolf." It pressed its open mouth against Jaden's throat, its fangs scraping her skin.

She cried out, struggling helplessly against the demon's hold.

"Come to me, little wolf. Friend live if wolf feed me."

I slowly blinked, barely aware of someone

shaking me by the shoulders. Fingers clicked in front of my face. I took another step. Then another.

Something sharp stung my face and my head whipped back. It wasn't until Chris's face swam in my vision that I realized he'd hit me.

"Wake up, Maddie!" he screamed, his words dim.

"Someone kill this fucking thing already!" came another shriek.

"Here, little wolf," the loudest of the voices crooned in my head. "Come to me."

"Madison, listen to me. You are stronger than this demon. Compulsion can only have power over you if you allow it. Do you hear me? You are stronger than this! You're too stubborn to let a demon sway you. Now, *focus!*"

Those words. Gabriel's voice. He sounded so scared. And there was so much yelling. Crying. Shouting. I blinked again in an attempt to force the voice out of my head.

I was stronger than the demon. I was. I knew that. I shook my head and cleared my thoughts.

"Little wolf?" the voice was quieter now. Less compelling.

Clamping my eyes shut, I gritted my teeth and tuned the voice out. It almost hurt to do it. Felt like

I'd fried every synapse in my brain. But the world came screaming back in full clarity. My eyes popped open and I stared at the demon.

"Stay. The. Fuck. Out of my head."

The demon jerked, as though shocked I'd broken free of its hold.

Then its eyes darted around the yard just in time to see Sam and his team of wolves join the battle. They rushed into the backyard, all in human form, but eyes blazing with the power of their wolves.

"Maddie!" Sam shouted.

The demon stepped back, clearly debating the odds of survival now that our numbers had flourished. Taking advantage of its distraction, Jaden drove her elbow into the demon's gut, stomped down on its foot, and threw her head back, smashing her skull into its nose. The demon barely gasped in pain as Jaden tore free of its grip. Instead, it...*vanished*.

Just like that.

Gone.

"No!" I shouted, spinning in circles. Where'd it go? Was it still here? Was it planning another sneak attack?

The woman behind us cried out and dropped to the ground, clutching her head. "It's gone," she whispered frantically. "It's gone. It's gone."

I did another circle, my eyes scanning the darkness for any sign of movement whatsoever. Had the demon actually left? Was it even possible for something to vanish like that? It'd done something similar when fighting Gabriel back at the cabin, but I'd assumed that trick was for short distances only.

Guess I was wrong.

"It's gone," the woman whimpered a few more times before dissolving into hysterical tears.

"Jaden?" I shouted.

"I'm fine. I'm okay. It didn't even hurt me," she called back.

Relief had me lowering my sword, then slowly walking toward the woman, who was now surrounded by a large crowd of werewolves. She lay crumpled in a ball on the ground, face buried in her hands as she sobbed, and utterly oblivious to the many eyes staring at her.

I had absolutely *no* idea what had just happened. I only knew this wasn't over. Not by a long shot.

11

"THAT WAS FUCKING WILD," CHRIS MUTTERED AS we hurried through the streets toward our vehicles.

A few blocks back, Sam had broken away from us, eager to return to his car and get home. The fight with the demon had unsettled him. He'd assured me he was fine, but I'd seen him reaching for his phone the second we parted ways. As for the other pack members, they'd dispersed from the scene as quickly and quietly as possible, hoping not to attract any unwanted attention.

"I've never seen anything like that before," Chris continued.

Josh offered a subdued hum in agreement. My usual lively group seemed sapped of its signature banter and jokes. Instead, we were understandably a mix of anger, concern, and disappointment. The damn demon had slipped right through our fingers. It'd just *poofed* out of existence. Gone in the blink of an eye. Gabriel had described that particular ability to me after I'd woken from my injuries, and I'd witnessed it a few times when the demon and Gabriel had been fighting, but seeing it again still rendered me speechless. The creature wasn't just moving so quickly it *seemed* to teleport. No, it was *actually* teleporting.

I'd also never seen anything like that. Vampires moved fast, but I could still track their movements. The more important question was where had it gone? Back to hell? Did hell even exist? Or had it returned to the coven responsible for summoning it? Did the witches control it? And if so, had they been the ones to send the demon after that woman tonight? If so, why? Or had the demon somehow broken free of its witchy shackles?

Cripes, that was a terrifying notion.

I had so many questions and absolutely no

answers. Which did *not* make me happy. Nor did I have any means of accessing these answers. Few knew of demons, and my Google searches had revealed very little other than biblical references—which I had a feeling didn't apply in this situation—and horror flicks.

The only people I could think to ask were the witches who summoned it. But I had a feeling the coven had no desire to talk to me since I'd killed quite a few of their sisters. They only had themselves to blame for that. They'd been the ones to hunt down Gabriel and try to kill me. I'd merely defended us.

"I can't get over that woman," Jaden commented as she kicked a small pebble out of her path. "It was like one moment she was possessed. Then the next, she was perfectly fine. Traumatized, sure. But physically fine. No more terrifying grins or red eyes. No horrifying messages about demons wanting to eat you. Just back to normal."

"Yeah," Josh said. "That was something else. Do you think she'll be okay?"

Who knew? We'd done all we could for her. According to her frantic husband, one moment she'd been cooking them dinner, the next, gone. He'd heard a strange noise in the kitchen, and when he investigated it, he'd found their meal burning on the stovetop and the porch door left wide open—his wife gone. He'd called the authorities, but they hadn't been too interested in the situation, stating that she'd likely gone to the grocery store and would return home soon. All his poor wife remembered was hearing a strange voice in her head commanding her to obey and come outside.

The way she'd described the demon's voice in her head—I was intimately familiar with it. I'd heard the same thing when the demon had ordered me to come to it. It seemed entirely unfair. These things were terrifying enough without the added power of compulsion.

What I wanted to know was why it'd chosen *that* specific woman? Considering it reached her mind from outside the house, how extensive was its power? Was it like a vampire and unable to enter the house without permission? That might give me a measure of relief.

Gabriel had informed us that he needed to maintain eye contact while compelling someone. Clearly, the demon didn't. Unless it *had* ventured inside and the woman just didn't remember.

There were so many unknowns. I didn't like it one bit.

"She should be fine," Gabriel said, his words drawing me out of my thoughts.

"Unless the demon returns for her," I commented, my voice barely above a whisper. I wouldn't be able to sleep tonight, no doubt about it, worrying about this woman.

"We left your number with her husband in case anything strange happens," Gabriel reminded me. "We've done all we can for them. Our focus now needs to be on tracking this demon down and keeping you safe."

I halted in my tracks, stopping across the street from our vehicles. "Me? Why me?"

"Uh, did you not notice how that demon reacted to you?" Chris chimed in. "The second it laid its eyes on you, it lit up like a kid in a candy store. In case you've forgotten, the demon literally tried to compel you to go to it so it could eat you. *Eat. You.* Maddie, that's just..." He shuddered, unable to finish his sentence.

Yeah, spoken like that, it sounded a little kooky. Did demons have a food preference? And if so, was it werewolves? Surely not. Unless...were there werewolves in the demon dimension? Or, and this thought was far more disturbing, had the demon merely gotten a taste of me during our last encounter and enjoyed it enough that it wanted more?

Okay, Chris wasn't the only one shivering now.

"There are so many things we don't know about this creature," I said to my friends. "Does anyone else feel like it might be a good idea to learn more about it before we try fighting it again?"

Josh, Jaden, and Chris immediately shot their hands up like school children eager to answer a teacher's question.

"Might be wise," Gabriel replied, his usually cheerful voice deep with worry. "We don't know anything about these things. Other than its physical appearance."

"And that it can compel people and teleport," I added. "The problem is, I haven't been able to find anything online. I mean, other than what you'd expect to find. Nothing on *real* demons. My experience with them consists of *The Exorcist* or *Evil Dead*. And I really don't think those are trustworthy resources."

"Hey, no dissing Bruce Campbell," Chris called out. "The man is a legend."

I snickered, well aware of Chris's man-crush on poor Bruce. "I'm just saying this demon isn't playing by any of the rules we know."

"Well, maybe it's time we go old school then," Jaden suggested. "Jackson *does* have a local library, you know. They might have something. Old legends, myths, ancient tomes, manuscripts. Something we wouldn't necessarily find online. Maybe demons predate the internet?"

I mean...it was an idea. And since I couldn't think of anything remotely better, it seemed like an idea worth entertaining.

"Well, it's a thought," Chris said. "And you never know. Maybe they have like a 'Demon 101' book or something. Hey!" He whirled around and faced Jaden. "Aren't there university classes that involve demons?"

Hmm. My mind took off with that thought. Jaden was literally a student at Belhaven University. Despite everything that was going on—the witches, the demon, the Academy, the contract on Gabriel's head—she still had a connection to the university, even though she had taken some time off classes. And perhaps, our way in.

"Like a religious studies class," I said. Then I turned to Jaden with a wicked grin. "At Belhaven, perhaps?"

"Oh, no, no, no," Jaden said, hands in the air.

"Do not suggest what I think you're going to suggest."

I grinned at her.

"No, Maddie. Come on," she whined pitifully. "I don't wanna seek out the religious studies professor and ask for a one-on-one lesson about demons."

"Sure you do!" I chirped.

Her expression shuttered, and she unleashed a glare on me. "You're serious, aren't you?"

"Yup! It won't take long, I'm sure. In fact..." I dug out my phone, opened the web browser, and searched "religious studies" and "Belhaven University." Results instantly populated. "Oh, would you look at that? Professor Noel Gaymes teaches Introduction to Biblical Theology." I clicked the professor's name and read his profile on the university website. "Says here his office hours are Monday, Wednesday, and Friday, from one to two p.m." I tapped my chin playfully. "If I'm not mistaken, tomorrow is Wednesday."

"I hate you," Jaden growled.

I grinned. "No, you don't."

At the look of dismay on her face, I killed my grin and said, "Look, you don't have to if you don't want to, but..."

"Yeah, yeah, yeah, I get it. What other options do we have?"

"The library," I said. "It was a good idea. And I can take Josh and Chris there tomorrow afternoon, hopefully while you're chatting with some smart professor about demons."

"You realize he's going to relate it back to religion, right? That's literally his job."

Gabriel's soft snort had me shooting him a playful glare.

I turned my focus back to Jaden. "But maybe we'll learn something helpful. Either way, it can't hurt, right?"

She grumbled, then stomped toward her vehicle. Josh and Chris followed close behind since she was their ride. Gabriel and I had brought my car.

Once she reached the driver's side door, she spun back around and faced me. "Fine. But in the meantime, we need to all agree that we aren't going to go after this demon again. Not until we have more answers. Okay?"

I nodded my agreement. "If anything, going in blind has made matters worse. If that demon had managed to compel me tonight..." My words ran dry. I couldn't bear to even contemplate those repercussions. Thankfully, Gabriel and my friends had been there to help snap me out of it.

"Yeah," Chris said as he leaned on the passenger-side back door. "I'm all for playing the role of the brave knight, but it seems foolish to do it when we're outmatched and, sadly, clueless. And while I'm usually okay with learning on the job, I think we could do with a little bit of studying beforehand this time."

"Well, would you look at that," Josh teased. "I never thought I'd see the day when you made a wise decision. Usually you're the leap first, ask questions later sort."

Chris grinned, then flipped Josh the bird.

I couldn't help but laugh. Of the four of us, they often saw Chris and me as the impulsive ones, while Jaden and Josh tended to be more restrained and careful.

"What about everyone else?" Josh asked. "Should we put the word out to all the other paranormals? Warn them about the demon and to keep an eye out for it?"

I could see that either working in our favor or creating a complete disaster. I turned to Gabriel to get his take on this.

He pondered the question with a serious air

and took a few moments before answering. "The werewolves are already in the know. And obviously, the witches. The only ones in the dark are the vampires. If we *don't* pass this information along, it might seem like a delinquency in my ability to lead. It's my responsibility, after all, to protect my people." He took another moment. "Perhaps it'd be best to send out a general warning to the entire paranormal community, along with the instructions not to engage unless given no other option."

"Really? Why not ask for help with killing this thing?" I asked.

"Your view of vampires may be a bit skewed due to your connections. Myself, Vlad, Anna, we're the exception, not the rule. Most vampires have little to no combat training. They're former humans who now have heightened senses, increased strength, and a hunger for blood. They lack all understanding of battle tactics or fighting techniques. Against a civilian human, yes, the vampire would win. Against a demon, however—"

"They'd be massacred," I finished, recalling the demon's strength and abilities.

"But I thought every vampire possessed a power?" Josh said. "Like Vlad can see the future,

Anna can speak with animals, you have the power of compulsion."

"These gifts take centuries to develop. Again, you've encountered the exception, such as Anna. Anna's abilities progressed faster than any vampire I'd ever seen because she drank ancient blood. However, a mutual friend taught her how to fight. Vampires aren't like werewolves, who train to fight since infancy. We're solitary creatures, and with all the new laws in place, we hardly hunt anymore. Those who do are put down. Slaughtering a demon is far from their wheelhouse."

"Alright. So warn them, but inform them to keep their distance. What about the humans? Should we warn the authorities?"

"Oh. I don't think that's a good idea at all," Jaden said. "Imagine how they'd respond? They'd probably launch a manhunt, and the demon would slaughter them. Which would result in the government's involvement. Then martial law. Just complete chaos."

I blinked. "Okay, I don't think it'd be *that* bad."

She shrugged, then glanced at Josh and Chris, who seemed just as on the fence.

"Sadly, I could see it happening exactly like that," Josh said.

"There'd be city-wide panic," Chris added. "But the real frightening thought is the repercussions."

"What do you mean?" I asked.

"Imagine afterward. Let's say we kill this demon. What's to stop someone else from summoning another? I mean, right now, witches are the only ones who summon demons. Probably because humans don't know about them. But if we brought the existence of true demons to light, *of course* someone would summon one. Just think—how many people would love to summon a demon to say...kill their cheating wife? Or their wretched boss? Or to find all the riches in the world?"

"Again, you're describing a genie," I said.

"Sure, but demons can accomplish at least two of those things. And come on, we all know someone who would likely summon a demon to demand riches. People do stupid shit when they get greedy."

I considered everything Chris said and slowly nodded. "Yeah, ignorance might be best in this case."

"And if the demon goes on a killing spree and slaughters a bunch of humans?" Josh asked.

I winced. That was certainly a scenario playing out in my head right now. "We'll just have to track this thing down and kill it before that happens."

"I don't love the idea of keeping the authorities in

the dark," Josh said. "But if you guys think it's for the best, I'm willing to go along."

Well, we sort of had a plan then.

I strode toward my car, my keys jingling in my hands. Once I reached the driver's side door, I paused and faced Jaden. "Be careful when you speak to the professor. Model all your questions in an academic research type of way. Last thing we need is to clue some professor in about what's going on and kick-start a witch hunt, figuratively and literally. We want information, not chaos."

"Gotcha," Jaden said. "A grad student researching the merits of theoretical demons."

"Hey, that actually sounds pretty good," I said, laughing. I unlocked my car door, then pulled it open. "Alright. Library and university tomorrow. Meet at Lucy's mid-afternoon?"

I watched my friends file into Jaden's car, then gave them a small wave, one they matched before they pulled onto the street and headed home for the night.

"Your friends truly care for you," Gabriel said as he rounded my car and climbed into the passenger seat. I slipped inside and started the engine. "The four of you share a deep bond."

I couldn't help but smile. "They mean the world to me."

He placed a hand on my thigh and gave a gentle squeeze. "As you do to them. And to me."

I shot him a glance, my stomach warming at the sight of his tender smile.

"Promise me you won't do anything rash," Gabriel urged. "I know you're desperate to kill this demon. But we really shouldn't go after it again until we know more."

That was an easy promise to make. Eager to soothe his worries, I nodded and curled my fingers around his, holding tight. "I promise."

12

GABRIEL AND I RETURNED TO LUCY'S HOUSE TO
find Annalise and Fynn parked in front of the
television, wearing their pajamas. I glanced at the
clock with raised brows. It was after eleven p.m.
What on earth were the kiddos doing up this time of
night? Before I could ask, voices rose from the hall,
drawing my attention.

"Thank you, Mom. I really appreciate this,"
Lucy said.

Barbara was here? Over the years, I'd visited
with Lucy's parents quite a few times—but our *first*

introduction had been what one might call colorful. I may have—*ahem*—broken into Lucy's home and held her mother at stake-point in order to force Lucy to talk to me. Prior to that moment, neither had even known I existed. But that was five years ago. I'd grown up a wee bit since then.

Barbara's story, like many others, was rather traumatic. In an effort to save her life after Olivia's werewolves attacked her and her husband, Lucy had forced Anna to turn her into a vampire. Richard had been luckier, and his wounds less grave. A year later, he'd decided to fully transition alongside his wife so that they could continue to share their lives together.

Romantic, right?

I certainly thought so. It wasn't lost on me that I was facing a similar decision of my own now. I couldn't become a vampire but I could extend my lifespan by drinking Gabriel's blood. With everything that was going on, I hadn't had the time to give it much thought. I didn't see any other option, though. If I didn't drink his blood, I would continue to age, and that didn't seem like a pleasant option. But if I took this step, I would tie my life to Gabriel's. Meaning, if the day came when he died, so would I. He was approaching two hundred years, so I didn't see that day coming anytime soon. I had to imagine it *would* happen eventually. Death was inevitable for all creatures. If drinking his blood allowed us to spend more time together, that was a good thing, right?

"It's no problem, darlin'. Your father and I can take the kids. Just until this all dies down."

I froze in my tracks. Then I glanced at the kids to find Annalise staring at me with a sad smile and tears shimmering in her eyes. Oh, hell. I strode to her side and plopped down next to her.

"What are you watching?" I asked quietly.

She shrugged. "A show."

Ah. Super helpful. I glanced at the television, but I didn't recognize the cartoon.

"Mom's sending us away," she whispered.

"Yeah, that's what it sounds like," I replied. Cupping her head, I slung an arm around her shoulder and pulled her close. "But maybe it's for the best."

"Sam?" came Lucy's voice from the back of the house. "Do you have their toiletries?"

"Almost," he replied in a gruff tone.

I shot Fynn, who looked just as miserable as his sister, a glance. "I don't wanna go."

Opening my other arm, I welcomed my nephew into my lap and held them both. It didn't take a genius to figure out what was going on. Sam and Lucy clearly wanted the kids out of the way while we hunted the demon. I'd seen the look on Sam's face after the demon had vanished, the concern shining in his eyes. He'd hurried away so quickly, his phone already in his hand. He must have arranged this immediately after the fight. And I understood why. The demon wanted me. And I currently lived here, under the same roof as his children.

I didn't disagree. These were dangerous times. And not just because of the demon. We had witches to contend with too. The kids would be safer elsewhere.

I looked down at my niece and nephew, both still wrapped in my arms. Their shoulders shook with silent tears and it broke my heart. Clearly, they didn't want to leave their parents.

"Hey, it'll be okay," I told them. "You're gonna go with Grammy and Grampy and have a wonderful time."

"That's right," came a deeper voice. I lifted my head to find Lucy's father striding toward us, a soft smile on his face. "And do you know who else is going to be there?"

Annalise shook her head.

"Grandma Elena. She's very excited to see you two."

Sam's mother? But she didn't live in Jackson. "You're taking them to New Orleans?" I asked.

"To Perish," Richard said. "Elena is going to meet us there. Along with Auntie Sophie and Auntie Aimee. They'll watch you during the day when Grammy and Grampy are sleeping. You guys are going to have so much fun."

Alarm tore through me. Three werewolves and two vampires? Wasn't that a little overkill? Of course, these were Sam's parents' first grandkids. I suppose that tended to make werewolves feel a little territorial.

Lucy hurried into the room, looking a little more than haggard, with Sam hot on her heels. Guilt ricocheted in my chest. They were sending the kids away for their own safety. Because of me.

"Auntie Sophia wants to show you how to bake astronaut muffins," Lucy said. "And Grandma Elena wants to take you for a midnight run. You're going to have so much fun, you won't even miss us."

Lucy dumped her armload of toys on the couch, then hurried out of the living room. When she returned a minute later, she had two pieces of luggage in hand. One adorned with *Paw Patrol*, the other with stars and moons. She quickly filled the bags with books and toys.

"The other bags with their clothes and toiletries are by the door," Lucy said.

Barbara nodded. "Good. Then we should get moving if we're going to make it to Perish before sunrise."

Lucy gave a jerky nod, and a momentary flash of pain streaked across her face.

"It's okay, darlin'. We'll take great care of them."

"I know you will, Mom. I'm just going to miss them." But Lucy buttoned up that bottom lip before her kids spotted her weakness. The last thing we needed was for them to break down at the sight of their mother crying.

Barbara and Richard stood, and each took a bag. Sam scooped up Annalise while Lucy picked up Fynn. Gabriel and I grabbed the additional bags. Then, together, as a large troop, we filed outside and loaded everything in Barbara and Richard's car.

The goodbyes were tear-filled and lengthy, but eventually, the doors closed and Barbara and Richard backed out of the driveway. As we all returned to the house, I reached out and took Lucy's hand, squeezing it.

"I'm so sorry," I whispered to her and Sam. "This is my fault—"

"Do *not* blame yourself," Lucy interrupted. "You did nothing wrong. It's not your fault the demon's taken an interest in you. That fault lies on the shoulders of the witches that summoned it. And the blame for that rests with whoever wants Gabriel dead." She squeezed my hand back. "We'll figure this out. And once we do, we'll kill them. Simple as that."

I slowly nodded, ever so grateful to have her in my life. I glanced at Sam, who nodded. I couldn't imagine this was easy for either of them.

Sam clapped a hand on my shoulder, then disappeared deeper into the house.

"Oh, Gabriel," Lucy said. "Here. Vlad dropped by earlier tonight with a message for you, but you were out demon hunting." She handed him a sticky note, then left, likely in search of Sam.

I chuckled at the sight of Vlad's perfect scrawl on a freaking sticky note. Who knew Dracula had become so progressive?

Gabriel took the note. "It's from Elias."

Elias. I knew that name. But where had I heard it before?

"Your brother?" I finally asked, recalling Anna

and Vlad mentioning him a few days ago. According to them, he'd been keeping an eye on Adrian for us.

"Apparently, Elias wants me to call him at my earliest convenience," Gabriel said.

"If you call him, he'll have your phone number," I told Gabriel. "Meaning he'll be able to track you. Can we trust him? Remember, you still need to stay in hiding until we resolve all this. And we still don't know for sure who wants you dead."

Gabriel shot me a glance, a hint of surprise crossing his features. "Of course. He's my brother. Elias and I have always been close."

"One could say that about your father as well," I argued.

Gabriel shook his head. "Elias and I never let anything come between us."

"But didn't the council choose you over him for the throne? Even though he was the heir?" I pressed, recalling everything everyone had told me over the years. Gabriel had petitioned the council to bypass Elias and place Gabriel on the throne instead. Politically, Gabriel had staged a coup. Surely, that would create some animosity between the two brothers?

Gabriel considered my words for a few moments, then shook his head. "The thing to understand about

Elias is that he's always been more relaxed about things. Politics, power...these aren't his cup of tea. He merely did what my mother told him to do. He has other interests and hobbies. It's more likely I'd find him in a pub, passionately debating the merits of Oasis over Blur."

I had no idea what that meant. "Sounds...very British of him?"

Gabriel grinned. "Precisely. And since he prefers listening to 'Champagne Supernova' over discussing crown affairs, I think it's safe to say we can trust him. He's never shown any resentment toward me. He respected the council's choice. Was a bit relieved, in fact. He laughed, clapped my shoulder, and said 'Thank all things bloody.' He's never been anything but supportive."

That certainly eased the knot in my gut.

"Elias cares more about family than anything else," Gabriel added. "If he's reaching out, it would be wise to find out why. He may genuinely have something helpful to contribute. Besides, I recall him once complaining about how there was too much sitting involved in the council meetings."

Okay, that made me laugh. It definitely didn't sound like we had anything to worry about. "Sounds like a good guy," I said, wrapping my arms around

Gabriel. "It's just hard to know who to trust these days. The person who wants you dead could literally be anyone."

"I know. We'll figure this out, I promise," Gabriel said. He hugged me tight and kissed the top of my head. "Trust me, though. I know my brother. Now, let's give him a ring and see what he has to say about our dear ole dad. It should be around six a.m. in England. So we'll have a little bit of time to chat before sunrise."

Gabriel fished his phone out of his back pocket, then punched in the number and waited. He placed the call on speaker even though I could hear the conversation without it. After a few rings, a jovial voice came through.

"Hello?"

"Hello, brother," Gabriel replied, a slight chuckle in his voice.

A beat of silence, and then Elias started chattering, his voice dripping with classic British charm. *"Gabriel! Long time, old chap. Heard you've been dodging quite a few arrows lately."*

"Understatement of the century. Since when did you get so caught up in family gossip?"

"Oh, you know, ever since the local pub ran out of the good blood, and I needed new entertainment,"

Elias replied, the sound of his chuckle echoing through the open phone line. *"I've had quite an earful about it all from this side of the pond. But if there's one thing I know, it's that you've got the tenacity of a bulldog when pushed into a corner. Not to mention, rumor has it you haven't been navigating this mess alone. Something about a fierce young lady turning things on their head and kidnapping you?"*

Gabriel rolled his eyes, but the playful smile on his lips spoke volumes. "Yes, that would be Maddie. My mate."

Silence filled the line for a heartbeat. Then, *"Your mate?"*

Ah, so he hadn't heard that part.

Gabriel nudged me, then gestured to the phone. Time for introductions, I suppose. "Hi, Elias," I said, my cheeks burning. "It's nice to meet you, so to speak."

"And you," he said. *"To think my dear brother has found another mate. I truly didn't know that was possible."*

I swallowed and diverted the topic away from Gabriel's first—and deceased—mate. "I've heard a lot about you. Especially about your love of something called Oasis? Care to tell me what that is?"

Boisterous laughter boomed through the line. *"A*

British rock band, luv. Gabriel, what have you been teaching her?"

"She's American, Elias. She thinks fish and chips is a card game and *Doctor Who* is a medical inquiry."

The three of us laughed.

Gabriel moved the phone closer to him. "Elias, your letter mentioned you have some concerns about Adrian. Can you shed some light?"

"Right. Yes. I've recently come across some intel that suggests Adrian has been forming new alliances. And sadly, not with vampires. According to my sources, he's been mingling with some formidable witches."

Gabriel's grip on the phone tightened, and my stomach dropped. I'd suspected Adrian for so long. But hearing this confirmation, learning that others knew he was conspiring with witches, left me with no doubts. He was clearly the one behind all this.

"Any specifics?" Gabriel asked. "Names?"

"The details are still fuzzy, but one name that keeps popping up is a witch named Elara. She's apparently a rather powerful force and has garnered quite the reputation in a brief span. Rumor has it she excels in demon summoning."

Gabriel and I stared at each other, his expression

a mask of horror. That sounded exactly like our little problem.

"*I haven't many specifics yet. But I do intend to keep digging. If our father is planning to dabble in black magic, we must do something about it. Could you imagine the scandal?*"

"I'm afraid our dear father has already been dealing with black magic," Gabriel said. "We've tussled with a few of the witches already. And we're quite familiar with the demon they've summoned."

Elias went silent. Then came a rushed breath. "*You're serious?*"

"Deadly. We've been trying to track down which coven the witches belonged to, but it's been challenging. These witches are rather secretive. But now we have a name. And that'll help immensely. Thank you, brother."

"*Yes, yes, of course. Do be careful. We may have our differences, but I care for your well-being. Give the devil my regards, will you?*"

"Stay safe, Elias. Don't bring any attention to yourself."

"*Course not, dear boy. That would be foolish, and I am anything but.*"

Once the call ended, Lucy reappeared, her face

wan. Thanks to her supernatural hearing, she'd likely heard the entire conversation.

"It has to be Adrian," I told her. "If he's dealing with witches…"

She nodded. "And now that we have a name, I can pin down which coven we're dealing with."

"Really? You think you can track her down?" I asked.

"Absolutely," Lucy replied. "The only reason the witches have let us be is because they know attacking you or any of us will start a war between my pack and the covens. They don't want that. I can use that leverage to learn which coven she belongs to. Once we have that information, we can arrange a meeting and discuss the lovely demon they summoned. Perhaps I can even convince them to stop dealing with Adrian. That would certainly weaken him," Lucy continued.

She stepped away, bringing her phone to her ear. When she started speaking to Cole, I tuned her out and faced Gabriel.

He sighed, running a hand through his already disheveled hair. "You know, I never thought I'd see the day when our family affairs turned into something out of a spy novel. Political intrigue is one thing, but adding demons and witches into the mix is madness."

"At least life with you won't ever be boring," I said, laughing.

He shot me a wry smile and pulled me close. "You have a peculiar sense of adventure, luv."

I tucked my head against his chest, my thoughts spinning. Maybe it was for the best that Sam and Lucy had sent the kids away. It hurt to do it, but they *would* be safer. Safer than here, anyway.

"Alright," Lucy said after ending her call. "My people are going to look into this Elara. See what they can find out about her. Once we figure out which of the five covens she belongs to, I'll request an audience with her high priestess. Regardless of how crafty they are, I highly doubt any coven wants to go up against a pack of pissed off werewolves. They'll agree to meet."

"And if they don't?" I asked.

"Then we take matters into our own hands," Lucy replied. "Jackson belongs to me. I will *not* allow demon-summoning witches to reside in the same city as my children. It's as simple as that. If I have to eradicate the entire coven, so be it."

THE NEXT DAY, CHRIS, JOSH, AND I FOLLOWED through with the plan and visited our local library while Jaden was off meeting with the religious studies professor at the university. It'd been quite the adventure for the three of us, slogging through the shelves to find anything and everything remotely demonic related. The librarian eventually clucked her tongue and reminded us we could only borrow five books each. And now, Josh, Chris, and I were back at Lucy's, surrounded by a chaotic mess of books. Some were purely academic and/or religious, while others looked like we had plucked them from the "Adult Paranormal Romance" section. We'd gathered a range of research from tomes on demonology to stacks of novels featuring shirtless demon love interests. We were casting a wide net, hoping that something—*anything*—might shed light on what we were truly up against.

Lucy leaned over my shoulder, her finger tracing the muscular abs of a demon with soulful eyes on one of the romance novel covers. "Do you think there are any demons that look like this? Asking for a friend, of course."

I snorted back a laugh. "Don't let Sam overhear you asking that." Thankfully, Sam had gone out in search of sustenance for us all. I'd never gone to college, but I had to imagine I was living the experience now. Studying required food, right? Specifically pizza. Mm. Here was hoping he brought back something covered in yummy, gooey cheese.

Josh, having just put down a detailed illustration similar to the nightmarish creatures we'd seen, shot us an amused glance. "After what we've seen? If they do exist, they're definitely keeping a low profile."

"Or maybe they're just in high demand in the demon modeling industry," Chris suggested, chuckling.

Josh smirked. "Yeah, I've heard hell's version of *America's Next Top Model* is killer."

Our small group chuckled.

"Alright, let's try to focus, please?" I asked. "We need to find something that can help us." Then I muttered, "*Anything* that can help us."

"We definitely need to filter out fact from fiction," Lucy continued. "This book claims that negative energy attracts demons and salt repels them."

"That's better than mine," Josh commented. "Mine says to place black tourmaline at your windows to ward your home against demons." He slapped the book closed. "I highly doubt crystals will repel these things."

"Mine says..." Chris muttered as his gaze raked the pages. He sighed and slumped in his chair. "Demons are misunderstood spirits who love cats."

"Cats?" I repeated.

"Cats." He held his hands a foot apart. "Big, fluffy cats."

Josh, having reached for another book, laughed and shook his head. "This one says demons grant wishes."

"Pretty sure that's a genie," Lucy commented.

"Ugh!" I dropped my head down onto my own

book and sighed. "This is useless. What *do* we know?"

"You mean other than what they look like?" Chris asked.

"Yeah, other than that," I mumbled to my book cover.

"Nada," Chris said.

"Squat," Josh retorted.

"Zilch," Lucy added.

"You three are hilarious," I deadpanned.

Plucking my resolve, I snatched the next book out of the pile and marveled at the title: *Celestial and Infernal Beings: A Comprehensive Examination of Paranormal Entities in Myth, Legend, and Contemporary Accounts.* Well, at least that sounded more academic than swoon-worthy. I flipped to the table of contents and thumbed through the list, tapping the word demon. I turned to page one-hundred-and-thirty-five and began reading.

Within the realm of paranormal studies, demons occupy a particularly intricate space. These beings, inherently tethered to the hellish dimension, present themselves as monstrous figures—often described with crimson glowing eyes, scaled bodies, scythe-like talons, and a voracious mouth filled with sharp fangs designed for the macabre act of tearing asunder any prey. Their tails, uniformly barbed, serve as yet another testament to their nightmarish origins. It is widely accepted within the academic community that these creatures can only access our earthly dimension through the direct intervention of witches, who have the power to summon and control them.

I straightened in my chair, my eyes widening on the text. This sounded promising! Closer than anything else we had found yet. The description matched the creature we'd met exactly. I waved at my friends, then read the same paragraph aloud before continuing onward.

"The exact mechanisms of these summonings remain somewhat elusive, but certain established norms have emerged from both anecdotal accounts and scholarly investigation. Once summoned, a demon is bound to the will of the invoking witch, adhering strictly to their commands. However, once released from this bondage, the demon is no longer restricted, thus leading to potentially catastrophic outcomes as they run amok, free from any form of control.

"The broader implications of demon summoning are even more profound. There exists a prevailing theory within the academic circle that every act of summoning creates a rift between our earthly dimension and the hellish plane from which these creatures emerge. Though empirical evidence remains scant, the consensus is that with each subsequent summoning, the rift widens, making the act of summoning progressively easier. This continual tearing of the dimensional fabric is believed to compromise the stability of our realm.

"While the vast majority of witches, understanding the potential consequences, typically refrain from engaging in demon summonings, there are those who, driven by personal motives or sheer malevolence, disregard the potential peril posed to the broader earthly realm. It is this minority that often finds themselves at the epicenter of debates surrounding the ethics and ramifications of meddling with entities beyond our comprehension."

The tome continued, but I paused, staring at my friends. This was *exactly* what we were facing.

"That doesn't sound good at all," Josh mused. "What do you think it means by 'every act of summoning creates a rift between our earthy dimension and the hellish plane from which these creatures emerge'?"

Yeah, that sounded pretty awful. I leaned back and stared at the ceiling as though it might provide me with all the answers. "I think it's like poking holes in a sheet. The more holes you poke, the weaker and more transparent it becomes. So maybe every time a witch summons a demon, they're poking another hole between our world and hell."

Josh raked a hand through his hair. "So, eventually, if you keep poking holes, the sheet just... disintegrates?"

"I had a sweater that happened to once," Lucy said, chuckling.

I shook my head, ignoring her jibe. "Basically, the witches have the power to bring down the veil between the dimensions."

"And turn our world into a B&B for demons," Chris surmised. "Welcome to Earth. Would you prefer a city or ocean view with a side of chaos and destruction with your stay?"

Josh snorted. "House rules: No tormenting any souls before ten a.m. And if you could avoid scaring the neighbors, that'd be swell."

"Guys," I admonished. I understood that they used humor to hide their fear but now wasn't the time. "This is scary. And serious. If every summoning rips the veil between our worlds a little more, how many summonings would it take before, you know, hell literally breaks loose?"

Josh and Chris sobered and fell into a heavy

silence. This was unchartered territory for us, and I felt completely unprepared to tackle it. And unfortunately, the book didn't provide a step-by-step guide on how to keep any of this from happening.

Lucy broke the silence. "Okay, let's focus on one problem at a time. As far as we know, the coven has only summoned one demon. Let's just worry about killing that demon and then I can have a chat with all the covens about their extracurricular activities."

"Is there anything in that book about killing demons?" Chris asked, leaning over my shoulder to take a gander at the text-heavy pages.

I sat up and started reading.

"Or even just some general vulnerabilities," Josh chimed in. "You know, like how vampires are allergic to garlic and a good suntan?"

I chuckled. "Sadly, no mention of garlic here." I kept skimming the pages, then paused when the subtitle *On the Extermination of Demonic Entities: A Comprehensive Analysis* caught my eye. Tapping the page, I started to read aloud.

"Throughout supernatural history, demons have been classified among the most resilient of entities, exhibiting a capacity for endurance that often surpasses that of most creatures on the earthly plane. To comprehend the intricacies of dispatching such a formidable foe, one must first familiarize oneself with the nature and origins of these beings.

"Hailing from a dimension that is, in many ways, antithetical to our own, demons inherently possess attributes that render many traditional means of extermination ineffective. For instance, given their presumed origin from infernal realms, it is unsurprising that fire, which would be lethal to many creatures, proves ineffectual against them. Their native habitat, rife with intense heat and flames, has imbued them with a natural immunity to such elemental forces.

"A particularly vexing characteristic exhibited by these creatures is their ability to teleport over short distances. This capability allows them a swift evasion from threats, making direct confrontation even more challenging.

"Compounding that challenge is the demon's innate power of compulsion. This ability allows it to exert significant influence over the will of other beings, complicating efforts to engage or confront it directly. Precautions must be taken to safeguard oneself from this manipulative power, else the demon will turn one's own strengths and weapons against them.

"However, despite their formidable defenses and

capabilities, demons are not without vulnerabilities. Through extensive research and documentation, it has been deduced that the most effective means of exterminating a demon lies in severing its head. Beheading, as brutal as it may sound to the layperson, disrupts the vital energies that sustain the demon, leading to its rapid demise. The act requires significant force and precision, given the demon's prodigious strength and agility."

"Damn," Chris said, laughing. "I don't think I understood most of that. Why can't these academic sorts write simply?"

I rubbed my temples, where a headache had started to throb. I had to agree with Chris. Why couldn't they just say, "behead the bastards" and be done with it? Why all the academic speak?

"Well, I understood one thing," Josh said. "Cut its head off. I like it. Simple. Effective."

"It won't be that simple," I told them. "Do you think the demon is going to give us that opportunity? We've faced it twice, outnumbered it both times and barely injured it. It isn't going to just stand there and let us chop its head off."

"Killjoy," Chris muttered.

"Be that as it may," Josh said, "that's the only plan we currently have."

"I just wish there was something we could do to weaken it first and improve our odds," I said. "But I don't see any mention of actual vulnerabilities on this page."

"They're demons for a reason," Lucy said.

"The only thing I can think of is us taking as many numbers as possible, overwhelming it, and beheading it."

"Except the damn thing can vanish," I reminded them. "How do we keep it still long enough to chop its head off?"

No one offered an answer for a few moments.

"Maybe it's not about keeping it still," Lucy finally mused, tilting her head as she thought. "Maybe it's about predicting its movements. We know it can teleport short distances. Perhaps it has a pattern or limit."

Chris raised an eyebrow. "You're suggesting we learn its habits, get into its head?"

Lucy shrugged. "If we understand how it thinks, maybe we can anticipate its next move. Make it play into our hands."

Josh smirked. "Oh, sure. I'll just grab a cup of coffee with it, have a chat about its favorite teleportation spots. Shouldn't be too hard."

I laughed despite the situation. "You do that. Let us know how it goes."

Josh winked. "Will do. Maybe it's a latte kind of demon."

"It would also help if we could disrupt its ability to use compulsion," Chris added. "We'd stand a better chance if we're not constantly fighting off its influence."

All eyes turned to face me.

"You broke its compulsion last time," Chris said. "How'd you do it?"

"Gabriel mentioned once that compulsion is weaker against strong-willed minds. I heard the demon's voice in my head, but I knew it wasn't my thoughts telling me to walk to it. It was controlling me. I was able to take back control of my mind when I heard Gabriel calling to me."

"Well, I think we're all strong-minded here," Lucy said. "So, maybe that'll play in our favor."

"Maybe. But I also think it'll help if we're all together. You guys helped keep me centered and focused."

"Good to know," Josh said.

Sighing, Chris glanced back at the stack of books. "Any volunteers for another academic deep dive?

Maybe there's another long-winded section on demonic mind tricks and how to resist them."

"I'll join you," Lucy volunteered, her gaze wandering to the sexy, half-naked demon on the front of one novel.

I was about to offer the same when Jaden suddenly came breezing through the front door. "Oh my god," she stated loudly before dropping into the nearest chair and glaring at me. "Next time, *you're* the one who gets to talk to the professor."

Chuckling, I pulled up a seat next to her. "That good, huh?"

She dove into her purse and pulled out a notebook, one she slapped down on the table in front of us. "Would you like to hear how demons are the minions of Satan? Or how they can differ depending on which religion we're studying? Or era of human civilization?" She groaned and tipped her head back. "I don't think I learned *anything* useful there today."

"That's unfortunate."

Jaden lifted her head and stared at me. "That's *unfortunate*? That's the response I get?"

"Well, would you like me to offer you a cookie?"

"Yes!" she exclaimed, though she was grinning. "A damn big cookie too. I deserve one. I just sat through an hour of endless prattle that wasn't helpful to us whatsoever."

"Okay, one cookie coming right up," I told her. "In the meantime, would you like to hear what *we* learned?"

Jaden's focus jumped to the books, her gaze taking in the many, *many* covers. "Wait, did you actually learn something from these books? My suggestion worked?"

I couldn't help but smile. "Yeah, your suggestion kicked ass. Who knew the library would actually have a useful book on demons?"

Jaden fist-pumped the air and let out a whoop. "Okay, now I deserve two cookies."

Snickering, I rose from my seat and headed off into the kitchen in search of a whole damn bag.

AFTER CHOWING DOWN ON TWO SIZABLE BAGS OF cookies and going through what felt like a mountain of sandwiches between the five of us—two of whom were werewolves—we finally settled down to share everything we'd learned about the demon with Jaden. When I reached the part about decapitation being its only weakness, Jaden's face drained of all color.

"It sounds simple when you put it like that," she said, "but the only time we've gotten remotely close to this thing is when it's on the offensive. Any other time? It's lightning quick, always teleporting just out of our grasp."

The memory of its claws embedded in my chest surfaced. I winced, then shut my eyes and focused on steadying my heartbeat.

Jaden had a point. The demon only risked getting close when it was confident of a kill.

Which brought an idea to mind, one that was incredibly dangerous. But it might be the only way. To get it to come to us, we needed to make it believe it had the upper hand. The challenge, however, would be getting everyone on board with the plan. Especially Gabriel. And I needed him awake before I pitched my idea to the rest of the group. He had every right to weigh in on this crucial decision.

Sunset, though, wasn't for another two hours.

Which was how I found myself sitting in the living room, watching *Hotel Transylvania* of all movies. At first I'd questioned my friends' motives. But it'd all made sense fairly quickly once the wolfman came on screen. Vlad was lucky enough not to be here to witness the Dracula representation, but Lucy and I weren't so lucky. I could only imagine how the Count would feel about *this* movie. Last I'd heard, he hated all films that centered on anything remotely Dracula related.

Thankfully, the movie was amusing enough to pass the time. And a few hours later, I found myself perched on the edge of the bed that Gabriel and I shared, fidgeting with the delicate duvet cover. I suspected this conversation wouldn't go well. After everything we'd all been through over the past few weeks, no one would be happy with my plan. But I honestly couldn't see any other way to kill the demon. It was too clever, and unfortunately for us, far too powerful to tackle head-on. Its powers gave it a distinct advantage. The only way we'd win this fight was by being sneaky and outsmarting the hell-beast. We could handle that, right? I had to believe we were smarter than a freaking demon.

I didn't have to wait long for Gabriel to wake, and soon, movement caught my attention.

Gabriel blinked open his eyes, and when he caught sight of me, a warm smile spread across his face.

"Hi," he murmured, his voice rich with affection.

"Hey, Sleeping Beauty," I greeted, returning his smile with one of my own. I slid in next to him and curled into his side, resting my head on his arm.

His arms immediately closed around me and pulled me closer. "I must say, I do love waking up this way."

"Me too," I murmured, knowing his mood would change in a few minutes.

Gabriel leaned over and kissed me, his lips soft against mine. I reveled in the feel of his tongue stroking mine, of his hands curling around my hips, of his thigh slipping between my legs. For a moment, I debated throwing caution to the wind and jumping his undead bones right here and now. Unfortunately, I couldn't. I'd told the others we wouldn't be more than a few moments, and I didn't want to do anything that might distract Gabriel from our pending conversation. No matter how good he felt pressed against me.

Obviously sensing my hesitation, Gabriel pulled back. "What's wrong?" Then he frowned. "Your heart is racing. What's got you all flustered this early in the evening?"

I couldn't help but smirk as I poked him lightly in the ribs. "You always get my heart racing."

Gabriel's laughter, a sound that never failed to make my heart skip a beat, filled the room. "Well, that's definitely a good thing. But this is different. I can tell. You look...troubled."

I forced another smile, if only to soothe him. Strange how easily he could read me, considering we'd only been in each other's lives for a few weeks now. I wanted to blame the mating bond for that, but I think that was just Gabriel. He was far more observant than most gave him credit for.

"There is something we need to discuss," I told him. "But it's a conversation we all need to have together. Not just you and me."

"Alright. Should I be worried?"

I didn't want to lie to him, but I also didn't want to make things seem more dire than they were. It was a fine line to walk.

"Nah," I told him. "Just everyday stuff. But we should head out into the living room. The others are waiting for us. Vlad and Anna will be here in an hour or so, but we can have this conversation without them. We can fill them in when they arrive."

His eyes narrowed playfully, and I found myself grateful that mind-reading wasn't one of his powers. The way my thoughts constantly strayed to naughtier things when in his presence, imagine how awkward that would be.

"Do I have time to eat before we have this very serious discussion?" he asked in a husky tone.

"Vampires don't eat, silly," I said, chuckling.

He feigned surprise. "Wait, we don't?"

Laughing, I gently swatted his arm. Gabriel snagged my hand and lifted it to his lips, placing a light kiss against the tips of my fingers. His eyes turned sultry as his other hand ran up my inner thigh. "I wasn't referring to a meal."

Oh.

Oh!

Shit, my whole body started trembling. The effect he had on me was baffling. One sentence, and I was practically jelly in his arms.

"Who needs to talk when there are *other* things we could be doing instead?" he continued.

"We do," I said breathlessly. "We need to talk."

"That's a shame." Gabriel slid one of my fingers into his mouth, his fangs scraping my flesh.

Fuck. That shouldn't have turned me on. But it did. We had a strict no-biting policy. One he obeyed to the letter of the law. He liked to tease me sometimes. Show me what I was missing. And I had to admit, it was working. For a brief moment, I wondered how it would feel if I let him sink his fangs into me.

"Maddie?" he murmured, his voice like liquid honey.

I released a tremulous breath and stared at him, at a loss for words. He nipped my finger pad and my whole body jolted as though struck by lightning.

"Madison?" he said, his accent drawing out my name.

When I didn't pull back, he slid his other hand down past my waist until he could cup my bottom. He scooped me closer until our mouths were a hair's breadth apart.

"Your heart is racing again," he murmured, his warm breath brushing my skin. "Though I suspect for a completely different reason this time."

I swallowed, my throat suddenly drier than the Sahara Desert.

"What naughty thoughts are playing out in that head of yours?" he asked, his fingers kneading my ass cheeks.

I still couldn't speak. This close to him, my focus dropped to his mouth, and the two pearly white fangs within. I couldn't believe I was entertaining this thought. When I'd finally agreed to be his mate, I'd made *no biting* my number one rule. And here I was, contemplating it. Something had to be wrong with me.

"Maddie?" Josh called from the hallway.

It snapped me out of my reverie, and I jerked away from Gabriel. "We're coming!"

"Hmm. No, we aren't. But we could be," Gabriel whispered in my ear. "Just say the word."

Sweet baby Zeus, my mate was pure temptation. I turned my head, fully intending to order Gabriel out into the living room. Except, he took that moment to kiss me. *Truly* kiss me. This wasn't a peck on the lips or a quick smooch. This was possession. Hot, needy possession. He pressed me back onto the bed, his mouth ravaging mine, his hands sliding beneath my shirt.

I arched my back, then plunged my fingers into his hair, anchoring him against me.

How on earth could I resist when the man could kiss like *this*?

"Hurry up, you two," Josh called back.

I wrenched away from Gabriel with a gasp. He didn't pull away though. Instead, he nuzzled the side of my neck, his fangs gently marking my skin.

My fingers instinctively tightened in his hair. "Gabriel, we have to—"

Another scrape of his fangs.

Every synapse in my brain fired at the same time. My fingers went lax and I released his head, giving him permission to continue. I panted for breath, my chest heaving against his. I'd never felt this way before. So mindless with need. I wanted him to sink his fangs—and cock—into me.

What the hell was wrong with me?

Nothing. Nothing was wrong with me. I just happened to have a mate who was the walking embodiment of sex. And that made it incredibly difficult to get out of bed and do things.

Like kill a demon.

That thought sobered me.

Gasping, I cupped his cheeks and lifted his head until our eyes met. His blazed with two kinds of hunger, and I wasn't sure which one turned me on more.

"Living room," I rasped. "We can't do this right now."

"You sure, luv?" he retorted, his voice edging a growl.

I nodded, though it killed me to do so.

I watched him struggle to rein himself in, and fuck, that was just as sexy to watch as him ravaging me.

"You good?" I asked after a moment.

He nodded. "You?"

"Not in the least," I admitted with a breathless laugh.

"Good. Me neither." He raked a hand through his hair, then forced himself off the bed.

I slid out of bed and stood next to him, my legs shaking. All I wanted was to tumble back into bed with him. And from the look on his face, he wanted the same.

With a quiet groan, Gabriel leaned in and kissed me again. "How do you expect me to go out there with you looking like this?"

"Looking like what?" I asked.

He brushed his mouth against mine. "Sexy. Rumpled." He pressed his lips against my ear. "Delicious."

I choked on a breath.

"I would never bite you without your consent," he continued, his words so low I could barely hear them. "But I think that day is soon coming."

I didn't argue. It seemed silly to deny a truth I was coming to realize myself.

He straightened and took my hand. "Shall we?"

I gave a shaky nod. I'd simply come into the room to greet him when he woke. And now, it felt like my entire world had shifted on its axis. Surely, I wasn't *actually* considering letting him bite me, right?

Except I was.

My whole body lit up when I thought about it.

Shaking that thought from my head, I followed Gabriel out of our bedroom, past his guards, and into the living room.

Jaden, Chris, and Josh sat on the couches, once

again flipping through Lucy's streaming services in search of something to watch. I feared their next choice. As for Lucy and Sam, they sat at the dining room table, still combing through the plethora of demon books we'd hauled home. Sam leaned back in a chair with a thoughtful frown on his face as he read the same words we'd gone over earlier today.

"Well, well, look who decided to join the land of the living," Jaden teased, breaking the silence.

Thankfully, no one seemed aware of everything that had just passed between Gabriel and me. Relieved, I glanced at the TV and this time, caught sight of Moana prancing against the screen. Chuckling, I shot Josh a glance, who shrugged and said, "I like Maui."

Sam closed his book and placed it back on the table, then reached for another—the same one Lucy had been ogling earlier. I bit my lip to silence my laughter, then shared a covert glance with Lucy, who hid her blushing face behind another book. When Sam lifted his head to scan the room, she ducked behind the book and pretended to look studious.

Gabriel's gaze drifted toward the pile of books and he quirked a brow. "Anything useful?"

"Actually, yes. There's one book where the author clearly had experience with *real* demons. We learned beheading is the only known way to kill a demon. Which is made challenging due to their compulsion and teleportation abilities."

Another nod.

"Which actually leads me to the discussion I wanted to have with all of you." I drew a deep breath. "I have a plan."

Everyone's attention settled on me.

"As we all know, the demon is fixated on me. We agreed we would hold off until we learned more about it. Well, that day has arrived." I drew a deep breath, then dropped the bomb I knew no one wanted to hear. "I think using me as bait is our best option here."

As expected, a chorus of protests erupted around the room. The only one who remained silent was Sam, who watched me with a calculative stare. I forced a weak smile, then lifted my hand and silenced the room.

"I understand you guys don't want me near this thing. I'm not suggesting we dangle me in front of it. I'm suggesting we use me to lure it into a trap. I won't be alone out there. You'll all be nearby, waiting in the shadows. The demon can teleport. That's our main concern here. We need to strike fast and hard. Surprise it. If its focus is on me, that'll give the rest of you the chance to overwhelm and kill it before it has a chance to vanish. We know its strengths now. We also know how badly it wants me. With luck, if we combine our resources, the demon won't so much as lay a finger on me. I lure it somewhere secluded, make it think I'm trapped, then we launch our attack. Go for the throat. Sever its head before it even has a chance to look around."

Gabriel released my hand, and just like that, the heat from a few moments earlier fizzled out. Talk about a mood killer.

"You can't expect me—*us*—to agree to this," Gabriel growled.

"I don't see any other option," I continued, hoping I could make him see reason. "This thing is too powerful. We need to strike hard and fast before it even realizes what's going on."

"And if it vanishes before we can take off its head?"

I shrugged. "That could happen. But does anyone have any other ideas?" When no one offered another suggestion, I continued, "With all of you there, I won't be in danger. And if we can lure the demon somewhere alone, it'll be all of us against it. One strike, that's all we need." I turned to Gabriel, wincing at the anger darkening his eyes. "And it has to be you."

"Me?" he growled.

"You're the fastest one here. Sam, Lucy, and I are strong, but we don't have vamp speed. You're the only one that can rush in and sever its head before it even realizes what's happening."

Chris sighed, running a hand through his hair. "Are we seriously considering this?"

"If anyone has any other ideas, I'm willing to hear them," I repeated.

No one spoke.

"Promise me," Gabriel demanded. "Promise me you won't sacrifice yourself to save someone. I can't go through that again."

I forced myself to swallow, overwhelmed by the flood of emotion rushing through me. I still found it astounding that I had people who cared about me. I gave a small smile and said, "I promise."

His lip curled, expressing his unhappiness with this idea, but he finally said, "Fine. But we're waiting for Anna and Vlad first. I'm not going after this thing without them." Then he sighed and pulled me into his arms. "You're going to be the death of me."

I chuckled and rested my head against his chest.

"You're already dead. So you can't blame me for that."

Quiet laughter came from everyone else.

"When do you want to do this?" Chris asked.

"The sooner, the better. Tonight."

Jaden whistled under her breath. "Not a lot of prep time."

"There's nothing really to prep," I told her. "We give Gabriel the biggest sword we have, arm the rest of you, and a-hunting we go. Aim for its heart, eyes, brain, you name it. Anything that might weaken it enough to keep it from teleporting *if*, for some reason, Gabriel isn't able to behead it."

"Oh, I'll cut the bugger's damn head off," my mate announced, his voice low and deadly. "It's never laying another finger on you again."

15

"HAVE I MENTIONED HOW MUCH I DISLIKE this?" Gabriel's voice crackled in my ear via a sleek Bluetooth headset tucked discreetly in my ear.

"Only every two minutes or so, like clockwork. But hey, who's counting?" I replied in a near-whisper. Interestingly, the book on demons hadn't ventured into their senses, so I had no idea if they were as sensitive as mine. I had to assume they were, being that the creature was demonic.

Earlier, after arming ourselves at Lucy's place, Gabriel had unilaterally decided that we needed to make a pit stop at an electronics store for a tech upgrade. I'd laughed. This coming from an old vampire who didn't even like carrying a cell phone. But if it made him happy, who was I to disagree? The look on Jaden's face when Gabriel handed her his no-limit black credit card was meme-worthy. One stealthy upgrade later, and we were all sporting military-grade communication earpieces. Now, I was strolling aimlessly through the dark streets, flaunting myself as bait, while my team yammered nonstop in my ear.

"See anything suspicious yet?" I asked. "Or am I just getting my steps in for the night?"

"All's quiet still," Gabriel replied.

For some reason, I couldn't scent the demon nearby either. The last time we'd hunted it down, its horrific scent had led us right to its intended victim—and the demon itself. Tonight, though, bupkis. Because of course. The one time we *wanted* to bump into an actual demon...

Ambient noise carried over the line, but no one else spoke. The point of this was for me to play bait, to look like a victim. But for that to work, we had to actually attract said demon. Maybe it was smarter than we gave it credit for. Maybe it recognized that this was a trap. We were screwed, if that was the case. Our whole plan hinged on this thing coming after me.

So where was it?

Perhaps it didn't have free rein like we'd assumed. The witches might have taken control of it after it attacked that woman. We truly had no way of knowing. And I didn't love the idea of wandering the *entire* city in search of it tonight. Jackson wasn't small by any means.

After another thirty minutes of pointless wandering, I gave up and came to a stop in front of a house in the middle of a random residential street. I truthfully had no idea where I was.

"Try looking more...vulnerable?" Sam's voice cut in. "I don't know. Drop a shoe or something."

Drop a shoe? Was he serious? "What in the name of Jiminy Cricket would that accomplish?"

"Okay, drop your bag then," Anna chimed in.

My bag. Good lord. Who put these people in charge?

"Maybe it's just waiting until you're good and distracted," Jaden said.

So *everyone* wanted me to just drop my stuff? I shook my head, then fished my cell out of my pocket. If the demon wanted me distracted, I could do that. But that didn't require me taking my shoes off or throwing my bag down. Instead, I started flicking through my phone and pretended to type out a text message.

After a few moments, in which I considered ditching this entire plan and going home to binge-watch Dracula movies all night, a familiar nauseating scent hit me. Something like rotten eggs with a side of despair.

My heartbeat quickened, an involuntary reaction to the imminent threat. I couldn't help it. My body remembered what it was like to face this thing, and my nervous system kicked into gear, preparing me for a fight.

Gripping my phone tightly, I forced myself to stand still and focus on my cell, hoping I gave off a distracted air.

"It's here," I whispered, my every muscle tensing. *Play it cool*, I told myself. Keep the demon focused on me so it didn't sense my team coming in from behind. I had to play the part, make it think it was the hunter, not the hunted.

The streetlights chose that moment to start flickering, plunging the streets in and out of darkness, while an eerie wind picked up, sending a shiver down my spine.

"Can you lead it away from the residential area?"

Lucy asked, her voice crisp and clear through the earpiece. "The last thing we need is someone seeing it."

I pretended to scowl at the streetlights, then resumed walking at a steady pace. But inside, I felt cold. Its eyes were on me, tracking me. My skin puckered with goosebumps and the hair on the back of my neck stood on end.

"Good, Maddie," Vlad murmured. "Keep going. Just a little further. There's a park at the end of the street. It's empty."

"We're close. Keep moving," Gabriel said.

I nodded—not that anyone could see that—and hurried toward the park.

"It isn't following her," came Jaden's voice. "It's hanging back."

Cursing inwardly, I slowed my pace. A few steps later, Sam's suggestion from earlier came to my mind. Make myself look vulnerable. The demon had only come out into the open when I'd appeared distracted.

We needed this to work. I needed to lure the creature to the park where Gabriel could sneak up on it.

God, this had better work.

I quickened my pace, then with a muffled gasp,

forced myself to stumble. My bag slipped from my shoulder and its contents scattered across the cold ground. Okay, maybe I performed that a little too well. It'd take more than a minute to clean this up—and I really didn't love the idea of playing the role of sitting duck for that long.

"Poor little wolf," came the creature's sinister voice. It slithered through the darkness and echoed in my head.

I froze like a deer caught in the headlights. Unfortunately for me, my ploy had worked. I'd lured it out into the open. But too soon. I was crouched on the street in front of the abandoned school, not in the park, like Sam had hoped.

It laughed, a sound that made my skin crawl. "Found you, little wolf. Sweet, delicious, little wolf."

Still playing my role, I gathered my scattered belongings, then forced my legs to move, bolting for the presumed safety of the park. The demon's mocking tones pursued me, every word ramping my erratic heartbeat.

"Maddie?" Gabriel's voice rang in my ear. "You with us, luv?"

"Hurry," was all I whispered.

The demon's voice grew threateningly playful. "All alone now, little wolf. All mine."

My shoes hammered the pavement as I ran. The park wasn't far now. A few more seconds.

"Where are your friends, little wolf?"

I'd almost reached the park, the open space promising safety. But as quickly as hope swelled, it died when a shadow whipped by me. I slammed on the brakes, screeching to a stop when the demon suddenly materialized in front of me.

Shit. *Shit!* This wasn't the plan. I wasn't supposed to get *this* close and personal with it again.

Well, time to improvise.

I stared the demon down, its sinister eyes drilling into mine. It didn't matter that my damn knees were quaking or my hands trembling. I had a job to do here: distract it. Every second counted, and I had to buy Gabriel and the others time to position themselves. We only had one chance at this.

"Nice to see you again," I commented wryly.

The demon's lips peeled back into a snarl, revealing a mouth more terrifying than a Great White Shark's. I took a step back and infused my voice with every bit of strength I possessed. "You know, there's this minty thing we have here on Earth. It's called toothpaste. You might want to look into it. Because your breath would scare off a skunk."

It cocked its head, its barbed tail flicking irritably

behind it. If I had to guess, it had no idea what I was talking about. Instead, it stepped forward, and its wicked three-inch claws caught the moonlight. Yeah, I still had nightmares about those things.

"Keep those bad boys to yourself," I said, pointing at its hands. "Who knows where they've been and I don't fancy going another round with them."

Another swish of its tail.

Somewhere in the distance, a twig snapped. I sucked in a sharp breath but kept my attention solely on the creature in front of me.

"While we're talking about hygiene habits, may I also suggest a shower?" I stole another step back, hoping to place a little more distance between us. "I mean, the rotten egg smell is a little much, don't you think?"

The demon snarled. "Stop talking, little wolf. Come to me."

Its words tugged at me, echoing in my head. I almost took a step toward it. Oh, no, not this again.

"I'm already here," I told it, gritting my teeth to fight the compulsion trying to take root within me. "Why are you so interested in me anyway? In case you haven't noticed, this city is full of werewolves. We aren't exactly a rarity."

I inched another step back.

The demon tensed, prepared to attack. But before it could lunge, a blur of movement whipped through the darkness. Gabriel charged out of the shadows, wielding the sword Anna had recently given me. He swiped at the demon, the blade shimmering in the moonlight, but the demon was faster. It sidestepped the attack, then retaliated, lashing its tail at Gabriel.

Proving again that he was the fastest vampire on the block, Gabriel leapt back, the demon's barbs narrowly missing his face. With a menacing growl, he engaged the demon in a brutal battle, one I could barely follow with my own eyes. The way they moved around each other, their strikes landing one after another. The scent of blood perfumed the air, but I wasn't sure who was winning.

Vlad, Anna, Sam, Lucy, Jaden, Josh, and Chris melted out of the shadows, but I held up a hand, ordering them back. If the demon spotted them, it would vanish before we had a chance to kill it. We had to let it think it could win this fight.

"Stay back," I whispered into my headset, hoping the demon didn't hear me.

Gabriel spun in a tight circle, his jacket whipping out at the sides, and appeared at the demon's back. Before it could turn, Gabriel hacked at the demon's back. Three long cuts appeared, one at the base of its neck, one across the middle of its back, and one at the waist.

The demon roared, clearly unimpressed by this turn of events. Guess Gabriel had touched a nerve—or three.

Enraged, the demon whirled around and sliced at the air near Gabriel's face. Except he wasn't there. He kept moving, staying ahead of the demon's attacks. Gabriel orchestrated another attack, one that drew blood from the demon's shoulder and another from its chest.

It wasn't enough.

Gabriel could keep cutting it, but it wouldn't bleed out. And if he damaged it enough, the demon would just disappear. Right now, the only reason the demon hadn't teleported away was because it believed it still stood a chance. If Gabriel continued hacking it to pieces, though, it would bail.

"Kill it, Gabriel!" I hissed. "Cut off its head!"

The demon whirled around to face me, its lips pulled back over its whetted teeth. It hissed at me— legit, *hissed*—then spun back to Gabriel in time to deflect the killing blow. Its hand shot out and gripped Gabriel's arm midair. A quick snap and it bent Gabriel's arm backward.

With a groan, Gabriel fell to one knee. The demon twisted his arm again, forcing Gabriel to open his hand and drop his sword. He could have easily broken the demon's hold, but it's back was to me, and Gabriel's sword lay on the ground in front of me. Gabriel flicked a glance at the blade, then to me. And I understood. He'd faked the fall to create this perfect opportunity. The demon had completely forgotten about me.

Grinning, I dashed in, knowing this was our chance to end this fight right here and now. The demon was too busy laughing at Gabriel, thinking it'd won. The only thing it'd won was a one-way trip back to hell.

The second my fingers closed around the sword's hilt, time seemed to slow. The demon whirled to face me, a triumphant look in its eyes. But surprise, sucker! With my own glorious yell, I swung the blade with every bit of strength I possessed and severed the demon's head clean off its shoulders.

Time wasn't just slow anymore. It stopped.

I stared at the demon. It stared at me. Then, it started to fall. Slowly at first. Eventually, momentum caught up and its entire body crumpled to the ground like a marionette with its strings cut. A second later, the head landed with a thud, its eyes still faintly glowing before they flickered out like a cheap light bulb.

I stood there, panting, sword still gripped in my hand. Fuck, that felt *good*. So, so good.

Gabriel picked himself up and stared at me, pride shining in his eyes.

"Have I ever told you how damn sexy you are?" he asked.

I chuckled and closed the distance between us. He pulled me in, our bodies flush against each other.

"So, do we kiss now? Or after we get rid of its putrid corpse?" I asked.

Gabriel leaned down. "Why not both?"

I had to agree. Today was certainly a day to celebrate. We'd killed the demon and knocked one task off our ever-growing to-do list. Productivity was so hot.

16

GABRIEL KICKED THE BEDROOM DOOR SHUT behind us, his eyes filled with an intensity that sent shivers down my spine. In one fluid movement, he scooped me up and pressed me against the wall, his lips finding mine as though drawn by some magnetic force.

"You were incredible tonight," he murmured between kisses. "Do you have any idea how it felt watching you behead that demon?"

I reached between us and palmed him through his pants. "I'm having an inkling."

He laughed, his body vibrating against mine. His mouth found mine again as my hands found their way into his hair. God, I loved his hair. So silky and soft, and just the right length to grip.

"You did a great job too," I told him. "Faking that fall so I could kill it."

He ground his hips against mine. "We make a good team."

"Hell yeah," I replied before capturing his lips again. I was done talking now. Surprising, I know.

I climbed down Gabriel's body, then placed my palms against his chest and shoved him down onto the bed. He happily dropped onto the mattress, his charming grin kicking my pulse into overdrive. I dropped onto the bed with him, then straddled his hips.

I wanted him naked. Now. A desire I made come true with one solid yank. Buttons flew like bullets across the room, but I didn't care. And from the looks of it, neither did Gabriel. His pants went next, tossed aside without a second glance, followed instantly by his boxer briefs. The second he was naked, I slid down his body and took him into my mouth.

Gabriel choked on an unnecessary breath, his hips bucking upward. I hadn't had the chance to explore his body quite like this yet. The focus had always been on me. But it was time to return the favor.

I took my time, enjoying his contours and planes. I used my tongue to map out the curve of his head and the slight ridge beneath. He was larger than any partner I'd had before, enough so that I had to use my hand at the same time. Not that he complained.

"Maddie," he whispered, his voice a touch hoarse.

I grinned before resuming the lord's work, sucking a little harder and moving a bit faster. Gabriel groaned, the sound almost animalistic. Then his hands gripped my shoulders and he flipped us over, his weight pinning me against the mattress.

"I knew that mouth of yours was wicked," he teased, a wild light in his eyes. "If you kept that up, we'd be finished sooner than I'd like."

"Hmm," I mused. I loved the idea of bringing him to completion with just my mouth. It gave me a nice little ego boost. But he was right. Neither of us was ready to end the night just yet. Mind you, he *was* a vampire, and it wouldn't take much to rev him back up again. A little nip of blood, and he'd be raring to go.

Blood I'd told him I wouldn't share.

A decree I was now second-guessing.

But that was a question for another time. When happy little endorphins weren't flooding my brain.

"Fine, if you insist on prolonging the experience, who am I to argue?" I said, grinning up at him.

Gabriel laughed, a rich sound that filled the room. He dipped low and kissed me, his tongue giving mine a single stroke before he broke away and moved south, stripping me as he went. His lips marked every inch of me, likely committing my every curve to his memory, as I had done to him. After tossing aside my pants and thong, he came to a stop between my legs and grinned at me, his fangs flashing in the dim light.

My breath caught at the sight of them. That shouldn't turn me on, but lord help me, it did. What was going on with me? I'd been adamant when I said his fangs would never pierce my flesh. But lately, that was all I could think about. My whole body yearned to feel them breach my most sensitive areas.

"Maddie?" Gabriel whispered, a slight frown wrinkling his brow.

I pushed those thoughts away and smiled. "Sorry."

A knowing grin crossed his face. "Don't be sorry. It's okay to be curious. It's also okay to never experience a vampire's bite. It doesn't bother me either way."

"It doesn't?"

"Of course not," he murmured. He leaned down and brushed a gentle kiss against my stomach. Without another word, he shifted his weight down and settled between my legs. The second his lips found their mark, I gasped and closed my eyes.

"It's also okay"—his breath brushed against my clit—"to tease."

And then I felt the slightest pressure. Just a hint of his fangs. Not enough to break the skin, but definitely enough to have me sucking in a sharp breath.

"Gabriel—"

"No biting. I swear."

I nodded. The idea had been circulating in my head lately, but I wasn't sure I was ready. My loud thoughts were suddenly silenced when Gabriel got to work. The pressure of his mouth and tongue working in tandem brought on the fastest orgasm I'd ever experienced. One moment, I was fine. The next, my back bowed off the bed, and I was gasping for air.

"Mm," Gabriel murmured when I came back down. He climbed up my body and kissed me. "Just lovely."

I blushed, but before I could retort, he thrust his hips forward and slid inside me. He started to move, pumping slow and deep, his gaze holding mine the entire time. I cupped the back of his head and brought him closer for an equally deep kiss. Then I wrapped my legs around his hips and lifted my rear to grant him better access. Gabriel responded immediately, quickening his pace. My head fell back against the pillow and I closed my eyes, enjoying the ride. The feel of him inside me made me feel whole. Complete. I knew without a doubt that I would never tire of this.

"Harder," I pleaded. "Faster."

Gabriel happily acquiesced. And then, to prove that he was a sex god with vampiric strength, he shifted his balance to one arm so that he could use his other hand to make me climax again. I had to admit, the man had talent. Enough that it didn't take me long at all to shatter around him. The second my inner walls clamped down around him, Gabriel groaned and rode out his own orgasm. His head fell forward, the tips of his hair brushing my throat as he shuddered above me.

Yeah, this was the perfect way to revel in our win tonight. Nothing better than a little impromptu sex with the man of your dreams after beheading a demon. Who knew?

Smiling, I relaxed against the bed. Gabriel stretched out next to me, a satisfied grin spreading across his handsome face. He propped himself up on one elbow and looked down at me, his eyes shining with post-coital bliss.

"So, that was one way to celebrate our victory," he quipped.

I chuckled a bit breathlessly. "Hey, it's better than cake and balloons."

"Speak for yourself," Gabriel teased. "I quite like cake."

"Oh really? Doesn't rot your fangs out?"

He snorted.

"So, what now?" I asked, nestling against his side. "How do you think the coven and your father will react to us killing the demon?"

Gabriel's smile faded. "Hard to say. I'll call Elias and have him keep an eye on our dear ole dad in case he decides to retaliate. If he's truly the person behind all this, I'd imagine he's getting a little antsy. All his plans to kill me keep failing. Must be driving him batty."

I nodded, letting the weight of his words sink in. He

didn't think Adrian would give up, and honestly, neither did I. The man had gone to some extreme lengths to try to kill Gabriel. He was clearly determined to see this through. I feared whatever he pulled out of his hat next.

"It did feel good to be the bait that actually gets to kill the fish for once," I said, holding onto the positives. "Usually, the bait just gets eaten."

Gabriel chuckled quietly. "That's what happens when the fish underestimates the bait."

I grinned, recalling tonight's events. "Seeing the surprise on the demon's ugly face when I took its head off was oddly satisfying. But you're right. I don't think this is over. Not by a long shot." I snuggled closer to Gabriel only to find myself fighting off a yawn.

"Someone's getting sleepy," he observed.

"Mm. Orgasms tend to do that to a girl."

Gabriel rolled onto his back and pulled me closer. I nestled into the crook of his arm and closed my eyes.

"Rest, Maddie," he said. "We've had a long night, and tomorrow's bound to be just as long. We still have to deal with the coven and the Academy."

"I know, I know," I murmured. "I'll sleep for a bit, but only because you make such a great pillow."

"I aim to please," Gabriel replied softly.

"Oh, you definitely pleased me," I said, snickering.

Gabriel laughed, then hugged me close. Comforted by his presence, I shut off my brain. I would worry about our next step later. When my body wasn't so blissfully content.

~

I WOKE UP TO THE DULCET TONES OF MY MATE'S voice. Blinking away sleep, I found Gabriel sitting in a chair across the room, shirtless, a phone held to his ear. Even in the dim light, he looked like he'd just stepped out of an immortal GQ magazine.

"What new development?" Concern laced Gabriel's voice, tinged with his British accent that still drove me crazy in the best way.

"Our father's called a council meeting," Elias replied, his own accent echoing through the phone line.

Gabriel pushed to his feet, the light reflecting off his well-muscled chest. His eyes narrowed and his mouth pursed. "*My* council?"

"Yes, your council. He's trying to stir the pot, and you know what happens when you leave the kitchen unattended," Elias joked, but the seriousness of his

tone undercut his humor. *"Word has it he's been causing some unrest among your loyal followers. And since you aren't here to stop him..."*

"I've been a bit busy." Gabriel's voice deepened, a growl slipping into his words.

"Yes, well, the council has agreed to hear him out. They might just order you to come back home, you know. You do have a job here, after all, brother. And many are tired of hearing that you're in America. Myself included. It's challenging to consult with you, seeing as how you're in a different time zone."

A knot formed in my stomach as I sat up, clutching the bedsheets to my chest. How on earth had I not considered this little problem? Of *course* Gabriel would have to return to England. That was his place of power, his home. And it wasn't like he could just up and move here. He was the Vampire King, for crying out loud. He had a *throne* over there.

"Gabriel, you are the king. You have responsibilities here, duties you can't just ignore," Elias advised. *"Your council claims they haven't spoken to you in person in days. That's unacceptable."*

"I haven't forgotten, Elias," Gabriel said, glancing my way. Our eyes met, and I suddenly felt exposed, even though I wasn't the one on trial here. "My people understand why I've remained in America."

"Well, in the meantime, Adrian is doing a bang-up job sowing confusion and discontent."

Gabriel palmed his face and sighed, exasperated. "I'll deal with it."

"I must implore you to see reason. I understand you're smitten with your lovely lady wolf, but—"

"She's my mate," Gabriel cut him off, his voice short and clipped.

"My apologies," Elias immediately replied. *"My point is, if she's the reason you haven't returned home, may I suggest you bring her here? We can make arrangements and accommodate her here in England."*

A pit opened up in my stomach. England? That was a whole world away. I didn't want to leave the States. I had family here, my friends. I'd worked so hard to build all this up. I couldn't fathom losing it all now. But I also couldn't ask Gabriel to abandon everything for me. He belonged in England.

"Keep an eye on Adrian," Gabriel finally said, redirecting the conversation. "We need to prepare for whatever he's planning next. And in the meantime, I'll speak to my council and remind them who their king is."

"Ah, Gabe, they may remind you of the exact same thing. Be careful. You're walking a tightrope."

Gabriel's jaw clenched. "I'm always careful."

They ended the call, and Gabriel set his phone down on the bedside table. He turned to face me, his expression conflicted.

"England?" I repeated.

Gabriel sighed and slid into bed with me, his muscles flexing as he moved. "Let's not jump the gun. We have enough problems to sort out before we start borrowing new ones. No one is asking you to move to England."

Yet. I bit my lip. "But you can't move here."

He hesitated, then admitted, "No. Technically, my place as king is in England."

Staring into Gabriel's eyes, I realized our future wasn't as set in stone as I'd originally believed. How had I not realized that we'd have some big decisions to make? How had I not seen this as a problem?

Gabriel sighed, then reached up and cupped my cheek. "One problem at a time, luv, okay? Right now, we need to focus on the coven and the Academy. Once we've sorted those out, then we can tackle our geographical conundrum."

"You already realized this would be a problem," I whispered.

"It's crossed my mind a time or two."

Yet, I'd remained completely oblivious to it.

"Hey, as long as we're together, everything else will work out," he assured me, pulling me close.

I wanted to believe that. God, I really did. But the future stretched out before me right now looked quite different than the one I'd been picturing. I didn't want to lose everything I'd built, but I also refused to lose Gabriel.

"One step at a time," Gabriel repeated.

"Right," I murmured, even though uncertainty held my chest in a vice grip. "One step at a time."

17

"YES!" CAME A SHARP SHOUT FROM THE LIVING room.

I jolted up in bed, my gaze darting from Gabriel's prone form next to me to our closed bedroom door. I had no idea what time it was—though clearly the sun had already risen—but that was unmistakably Lucy's voice. I just hoped it wasn't a shout of...intimate ecstasy. Supernatural hearing was both a blessing and a curse—and overhearing my sister and her husband during passionate moments definitely hovered on the "curse" end of the spectrum. A feeling I was sure they shared with me.

"Maddie!" Lucy shouted.

Oh, thank god. Relief loosened my shoulders. If Lucy was screaming *my* name, odds were she and Sam weren't in the middle of, well, you know.

I scrambled out of bed and threw on some clothes, then hurried out into the living room. I found Lucy standing by the couch, triumph alight on her face, her phone still gripped in her hand. Sam stood next to her, his lips tugged into a celebratory grin as he stared at his wife.

"What is it?" I asked while tugging on a pair of socks.

"Good news. That was Cole," Lucy said. "He tracked down Elara's coven."

When she didn't immediately reveal the information, I lifted my hands and said, "And?"

"This is the bad news part," she said. "Elara is the high priestess of the Hallowed Moon Coven."

That literally meant nothing to me. I knew very little about the local covens. "Okay, and what's bad about that? Other than the tragic name."

"Well, according to Cole, they operate similarly to mercenaries. Dark magic for hire. It's not uncommon for covens to go that route—they have a service they can provide that others can't. But it's not ideal for us. I doubt they'll willingly sit down and engage in a semi-friendly chat that ends with me threatening them to smarten up or risk eradication."

Yeah, I didn't see that conversation going particularly well either.

"The upside is we've taken out their demon, so they've lost one of their key weapons," Sam said.

"Unfortunately, they're still quite powerful," I commented. I knew firsthand exactly how strong these ladies were. I'd faced the coven twice now, and both times nearly died. Real witches were nothing like the movies portrayed. The women were practically assassins, armed with immensely powerful magic.

"I'd still like to meet with Elara," Lucy continued. "Not only would it allow us to meet our enemy face-to-face, but I might be able to convince them to behave if they believed I had the weight of *all* the alphas standing behind me."

"And do you?" I asked.

"I haven't confirmed anything yet, but I have no doubts the alphas would stand behind me. *No one* wants to risk destroying the veil between the two dimensions. Not to mention, Maddie is a werewolf, lone or otherwise. The alphas take great offense to one of our own being targeted."

Seeing the veil come down was certainly *not* on my to-do list. Thankfully, the coven had only summoned the one demon—that we knew of—so it seemed unlikely that there was any risk to the veil. Yet.

"Now, they haven't attacked us since I put out word that I would be quite upset if any witches were to harm my family again," Lucy continued. "That gives me hope that I can get them to listen. However, the downside is, if we take the witches out of the equation, that may force the person behind all this to change tactics."

"Adrian," I said, correcting her. "That might force Adrian to change tactics."

"You don't know that for sure," Lucy said, pointing a finger at me. "And we can't just assume. We're still operating under the assumption that it could be anyone."

"So, what do we do?" I asked.

When Lucy didn't immediately respond, Sam spoke up, "We continue with our plan as is. I'm sure the coven will agree to meet with Lucy."

"And we have our meeting tonight with Ginny," I said, hope fluttering beneath my breast. The demon was dead, we had a coven name, and tonight we would secure yet another slayer on our side. Finally, we were making progress. Or so it felt. "Once we hear her full story, we can approach the Academy. They can't ignore our evidence."

Lucy nodded. "You guys need the Academy on your side. If there's corruption within its ranks, it needs to be rooted out."

"I just wish it was as easy as it sounds," I commented. "I'm confident that once we expose the rot within, the Academy will do everything they can to fix it. They didn't create this institution to murder innocents. They built it in pursuit of justice. This whole shadow sect problem goes against their founding principles."

"Which is why you need to be careful," Sam added. "It's dangerous to make allegations without concrete proof."

"We have concrete proof," I argued. "Gabriel is innocent. He's the perfect case study. Ginny and her situation will only strengthen our case. Her testimony might just be the linchpin we need."

"And you're sure she's willing to publicly go against the Academy?" Lucy asked.

I shrugged. "I'll find that out tonight. But she came to us about all this. So I don't see why she wouldn't be. Besides, worst case scenario, I can present her situation anonymously."

Before Lucy could respond, a sharp knock echoed through the living room. Lucy, Sam, and I all exchanged wary glances. It was nine in the morning, and my friends were all at home, tucked into their comfortable beds, as was my darling vampire mate. Besides, everyone we knew would just barge inside, no knocking required. This place was like a second home to them.

I approached the door, then glanced through the peephole. On the other side stood a woman who appeared to be in her late twenties, maybe early thirties. She hovered close to the door, a hood pulled over her head as though to obscure her face from sight.

That didn't bode well at all.

I scanned the rest of her, my gaze snagging on a crescent moon pendant resting at the hollow of her throat. Alarm bells rang in my head. Werewolves revered the moon, but we focused entirely on the full moon. Crescent moons *screamed* witchcraft to me.

Glancing at Sam and Lucy over my shoulder, I silently mouthed the word "witch," then resumed staring out the peephole.

The woman kept glancing toward the

surrounding trees, as though expecting someone to leap out at any second. I had a fair bit of experience with witches, enough to know that they loved to play siege.

Shit. Was this a trap? Another attack? My wolf rushed to the front of my mind, prepared to shift if necessary. My mate slept in this house, completely vulnerable. I'd been down this path once before. I hadn't liked it then, and I didn't like it now.

"What do you want?" I demanded through the door. No way would I open it to her. Not after my history with these women.

The woman jerked, like she hadn't expected me to shout through the door. She cast another glance toward the driveway, then cleared her throat. "Uh, hi. My name is Bethany." Her voice wavered, but she drew a deep breath and continued. "I know you have no reason to trust me, and I respect that, but I swear, I mean you no harm. I'm here because I need to speak with you. Please. It's urgent."

I exchanged yet another quick glance with Lucy and Sam, who had moved toward the door. Both exuded a dangerous aura, one that assured this Bethany would die if she so much as said the wrong thing.

"And why should I believe you?" I challenged, keeping my voice firm.

In all fairness, the witches I'd fought had never lied to me. In fact, they'd been pretty honest about wanting to kill me, if only to clear the path to Gabriel. I went on high alert then. Was that what this was? Another scheme of theirs? To find a way past my defenses to finally kill my mate?

Oh, hell no.

Had I been standing outside, I could have studied the woman's body language. Liars tended to reveal themselves fairly easily. But through the door, I couldn't pick up on much other than her witchy scent of clover and white sage.

"I'm not with the Hallowed Moon Coven," Bethany quickly stated, catching onto my source of apprehension. "But I do know about them. And I also know what you and your family have gone through recently at their hands. I'm...I'm from a different coven. One that only wishes to maintain peace and balance. We're not all mercenaries or demon summoners."

Lucy scoffed under her breath, expressing her dislike for this entire situation. Three werewolves, a slumbering vampire, and a witch knocking at our door? It sounded like the start of a really bad fairytale.

"Why should we trust you?" Lucy demanded, revealing her presence.

"I know nothing I say will convince you. You have no reason to trust witches, and I'm truly sorry for that. What can I do to help you with this? It's imperative that we speak. I carry no weapons—"

"You *are* a weapon," I bit out.

Bethany had the decency to wince, as though my words physically harmed her. "Please listen. I'm here because the veil is at risk. And my coven and I believe you are the only ones who can help us. If you allow me to speak with you, I promise no harm will come to you."

"But harm will come to us if we *don't* speak to you?" I asked.

"No." She lifted her hands as though to show me she was friendly. But I knew the damage those hands could do. "I just need you to hear me out. Once you have, I'll leave. I swear."

Lucy and I locked gazes. After a momentary pause, she shrugged.

As much as I hated it, I slowly turned the doorknob and opened the door just a crack. The witch took a slow step backward, her hands still held up.

"You have five minutes," I said. "But you aren't stepping a foot inside this house. Make one wrong move, and it'll be the last you make."

She bowed her head in respect and took another step back, giving us room to step out onto the front porch. The three of us moved as a single unit, proving we were a united front. I had to admit, the witch had some iron ovaries, considering she held her place and didn't cower at the sight of three threatening werewolves closing ranks on her.

When she lifted her head, the morning sun caught her moon pendant and started to softly glow, lending an ethereal aura to her appearance. The depth of her eyes, a honey shade of brown, shone with sincerity. She kept her movements slow and careful, to reassure us that she was friendly. That didn't stop me from studying every inch of her. Her hood covered her head, but I was fairly certain she was bald. And when she moved, I caught a few scant glimpses of tattoos.

"Thank you for giving me this chance," she said, keeping her distance from us and the door. "I won't take any more time than necessary."

Lucy crossed her arms, her eyes never leaving

Bethany's face. "Start talking."

She swallowed, then nodded. "My coven, the Luminous Crescent keeps mostly to ourselves. We focus on protection spells, energy balancing, and the like. Nothing sinister. We're aware of our sisters, who take payment in exchange for performing the dark arts, but we're more about nature and wholeness. However, we have our sources who keep an eye on our sister covens, and recently, we've heard some disturbing chatter."

"What sort of chatter?" Sam demanded, his alpha voice coming out to play.

Bethany's gaze darted to him. "If the talk is to be believed, the Hallowed Moon Coven plans to summon another demon tonight—to replace the one you killed. I don't have to tell you how dangerous that is. For everyone. Not just werewolves or vampires, but for humans as well."

I clenched my teeth.

I really hated this Hallowed Moon Coven. It was like they went out of their way to do anything and everything to make my life miserable. And it was all thanks to Adrian. I was sick of these games. Sick of being forced to clean up these messes. I just wanted this whole thing over and done with.

"Despite the differences between our people, my

coven and I believe in doing what's right. I might be a witch, but I'm also a resident of this state. The Hallowed Moon Coven is playing a dangerous game. They're risking our whole world by summoning demons. There's a reason we prohibit demon summoning. The dangers far outweigh the benefits."

"Why come to us?" I asked. "You're witches. Equally as powerful as them, I assume. So why bother coming to us to tell us about this?"

"Because you're the only ones we know of who have successfully killed a demon. If the Hallowed Moon Coven succeeds tonight, then you're our best shot at killing the creature before it can cause any harm."

"If they succeed, they'll have already harmed the veil," I told her. "You could have gone after the coven now."

She shook her head. "We aren't strong enough. They are a black magic coven. My sisters and I don't have training in that area. They would slaughter us."

"So you came here in order to persuade us to do your dirty work?" I sneered. "Why aren't I surprised?"

"If the Hallowed Moon Coven continues down this path, the whole world is in danger."

"Yeah, we got it, thanks," I muttered. Sighing, I

turned to Lucy, trusting Sam to watch my back. "Well?"

"We can't ignore this," she replied. "I need to reach out to the rest of the alphas. I think it's time for extreme measures. It's becoming too dangerous to let this coven live."

I sucked in a breath. "You want to kill the entire coven?"

"I don't see any other option," she replied.

I bit the inside of my lip and considered Lucy's suggestion. I was no stranger to killing witches. I'd killed multiple so far. But so far, every fight had been instigated by them. I'd never once hunted them down. And now, my sister was suggesting we do exactly that. On the one hand, this coven was *far* from innocent. Allowing them to live was far too dangerous. On the other hand, we had no idea if every witch in that coven was guilty. I hated that it'd come to this, but what choice did we have?

I didn't have an answer for that. Turning back to Bethany, I asked, "What time is this summoning supposedly happening?"

"It has to be when the moon is at peak illumination."

"Meaning?" I asked.

"Meaning a full moon," Lucy replied. "And

before you ask, yes, that's tonight."

"Uh-huh. I was looking more for a specific time though. Are we talking nine p.m.? Three a.m.? See what I mean?"

Bethany smiled. "My apologies. The ceremony will start at ten tonight."

"Okay, and where?"

She withdrew a slip of paper, creased at the center, from her pocket. On one side was an address on the outskirts of town. On the other was a phone number with Bethany's name written next to it.

I rubbed my eyes, suddenly exhausted. "We're supposed to meet Ginny at ten tonight."

"I assure you, this summoning is more important than any other meeting you might have," Bethany argued.

I shot her a sharp glare. Considering Ginny was helping us prove the Academy's corruption, and thereby exonerating Gabriel's name, *nothing* was more important than that to me. But I couldn't ignore this either.

"Jaden is the one who established the relationship with Ginny," Lucy said. "Send her and Josh to the meeting. The rest of us can handle the summoning."

"Good times," I mumbled.

"So, you'll do it then? Stop the summoning?" Bethany asked, hope brightening her voice.

My glare deepened. "I need to be *very* clear about something." When I had her undivided attention, I continued. "If this is a trap or if any shadiness takes place, any shenanigans whatsoever, your coven is next. I don't care if you're peaceful or not. Betray us, and I will unleash hell on you and yours. By the end, you'll be begging me to kill you."

She blinked, then nodded. "I swear, this isn't a trap. We have no reason to hurt you."

They had every reason. And we were taking a massive leap of faith here.

"Get lost," I growled before slipping back into the house with Lucy and Sam hot on my heels.

I glanced at the paper again, staring at the address. "I'm not going anywhere without Gabriel, so we'll leave after sunset. Lucy, text Anna and have them meet us here as soon as they can. We'll need all hands on deck for this one. I'll text Jaden and inform her about the change in plans."

Lucy nodded. "Already on it. I'll call in my pack as well. The coven isn't walking away from this tonight. We take them out. All of them. I'm through with this."

Yeah, so was I.

18

THE ENERGY IN THE ROOM WAS THICK WITH anticipation, the sort that came before a major mission. Someone—likely Sam—had transformed the dining room into an armory, laying out our weapons on the table. The selection ranged from stakes to daggers to swords, our usual tools of the trade. But the three gleaming 9mm pistols sitting at the table's edge demanded my attention. Anna had given me one, specifically outfitted with special witch-killing bullets, before our last showdown. Unfortunately, she'd only been able to secure one magazine prior to that encounter. Now, it seemed she'd managed to procure an additional two pistols, along with adequate ammunition.

At a quick count, there were at least sixty rounds. That could kill a lot of witches. Guilt still ate at me, but I had to admit Lucy was right. We couldn't allow these witches to live. The coven had become a major risk. Not just to my way of life but to everyone's. I didn't love the idea of committing murder, but these witches were simply too dangerous.

Gabriel strode into the room then, adjusting his sword sheath's straps—which, I had to admit, was straight-up hot. He gestured to his human guards, who would be joining us tonight. After a bit of back-and-forth, they'd unequivocally told their king that there was no way they would let him walk into a witch fight unprotected. Apparently, I didn't count as protection. While I didn't love the idea of Daniel tagging along, I saw their logic. Even though Gabriel was a pro swordsman, thanks to his many, *many* years of experience, their attendance meant we gained more fighters. Sounded like a win-win to me.

My mate came to a stop next to me and placed a light hand against the small of my back.

"Stay close to me tonight," I whispered. His

guards would protect him, I knew that. But I suffered from a little complex known as "I do things better." I wanted him with me where I could keep an eye on him at all times during the battle.

He reached out and brushed a loose strand of hair behind my ear. "Only if you do the same," he murmured back, sealing the promise with a gentle kiss.

I lingered for a moment longer, reveling in the feel of his lips against mine, then nodded.

Heading to the table, I grabbed a few extra stakes and slid them into the slots next to Sir-Stab-A-Lot—my trusty stake. Then I armed myself with a single dagger, my sword, and finally, the gun. I wasn't as good of a shot as Jaden, but seeing as how she wouldn't be there tonight, the responsibility fell to me.

"Alright, team," Lucy called, her voice—and stare—hard.

She paid a quick glance around the room, locking eyes with me, Sam, Chris, Gabriel, Anna, and Vlad. Team Try Hard. Jaden and Josh had their own mission tonight—meeting with Ginny and Benjamin. We absolutely could *not* miss that meeting, seeing as how Gabriel's freedom hinged on everything we learned from them. I hated that I couldn't be there, but Jaden and Josh could handle this interview themselves. I needed to be here, on witch duty.

"We all know what's at stake tonight," Lucy said. I refrained from making a pun—now wasn't the time. "We've killed one demon already. And now we have intel that claims the Hallowed Moon Coven intends to summon another tonight. We can't allow that to happen. I've spoken with the other alphas and they agree. So, now it's up to us. From what we sussed out, the Coven consists of thirteen members."

Because of course it did.

"It sounds like they need the entire coven to summon the demon tonight," Lucy continued. "My pack has already headed to the location with orders to wait for our arrival. We go in, clean house, kill the demon if necessary, and get out. We've alerted our contact on the police force about tonight's mission, and he'll do all he can to keep everything under wraps. Does anyone have any questions?"

No one spoke.

"Good."

Lucy nodded to me and I stepped forward. "Remember, we have the element of surprise tonight, provided Bethany's coven doesn't betray us. The Hallowed Moon Coven has no idea we're coming. Chris and I have firearm experience and will take one gun each. They're equipped with mercury bullets, specifically for killing witches. Who would like the third?"

"Sam and I will be in wolf form," Lucy said, "as will the rest of my pack."

Which left the vampires—all of whom preferred blades to guns.

I shot Gabriel a questioning glance. He, in turn, studied Vlad and Anna.

Instead, a hand raised in the back. "I'm trained in firearms."

My eyes widened, then immediately narrowed at the sight of Daniel. We didn't get along on the best of days. But he was one of the most vocal when it came to Gabriel's safety.

Pursing my lips, I looked at Gabriel, who nodded without hesitation.

"Fine." I scooped up the third firearm but paused before handing it over to him. "Shoot any of my friends and I'll eat you for dinner."

He blanched, likely remembering the sight of me in wolf form, my fangs the size of his fingers. Then I slapped the weapon into his open palm and returned to my friends.

"The only other thing we need to remember is to take the high priestess, Elara, alive. I have some questions for her, and if she's dead, she can't answer them."

Everyone nodded. How we would know which witch Elara was, I had no idea. But I figured we'd wing that. Maybe she'd be wearing a special hat with the words "high priestess" scrawled on it or something.

If only life were that simple.

"Okay, everyone. Let's head out. Gabriel and I will take Daniel and Ethan," I said, pointing at Gabriel's guards. "Chris?"

"I brought my own car," he said. "I'll follow behind."

I nodded. "Vlad, Anna?"

"We'll ride with Sam and Lucy."

I reached for the door, paused, then glanced back at my motley group of family and friends. "I expect to see each and every one of you back here tonight. We aren't going to lose anyone, right?"

"Right," a few muttered.

I shook my head. "I said, *right?*"

Laughing, my friends all shouted, "Right!"

Grinning, I opened the door and stepped out into the crisp night air, all the while praying everyone made it home safe and sound tonight.

Thirty minutes later, we arrived at the rendezvous point, a seemingly deserted patch of land surrounded by overgrown trees and dense foliage. Not a house or cabin in sight. Odd. I'd expected the coven to perform the summoning in a secluded warehouse or something, but they were completely exposed out here. Were they so confident that they felt no need to hide their antics? I mean, they were summoning a demon, for crying out loud. Yes, we were in the middle of nowhere, but that wouldn't stop someone from stumbling across the ritual. Hell, drones were so common these days. The risk was astronomical.

Gabriel and I climbed out of the vehicle and joined Lucy and Sam, who stood surrounded by her pack. Those in human form discussed strategy, while those behind them in wolf form pawed anxiously at the earth. It wasn't her entire pack, which spanned over a hundred members, but she hadn't needed everyone tonight. She'd called in only her most dominant wolves.

"From what Cole's been able to find out"—she pointed at her second in command—"all thirteen members of the coven have arrived. They're just beyond that treeline, hidden in a small clearing that's blocked from sight. Apparently they're surrounding some big old oak tree."

"I overheard them mention that they need the oldest tree. It gives them a power boost or something," Cole finished.

"Sure," I commented. I strained my eyes, trying to spot the coven through the shadows. "Makes sense." It did not, in fact, make sense to me. But I didn't understand the first thing about witches.

Chris approached, armed to the teeth. "How do you want to approach this?"

I gave another slow nod, then glanced at Lucy. "These are your people. You tell us."

She flashed me a brief, but thankful, smile. "I have a few wolves stationed in the trees keeping watch on the coven. If they knew we were here, my wolves would have alerted us. So we still have the element of surprise. We need to surround them so no one escapes. There's thirteen of them and thirty of us. This should be over quickly."

I sure hoped so. I'd faced these people before and had no desire to once again be on the receiving end of their magic.

"I'll give my people the order to take position. Then we approach. We need to find out if they've summoned the demon yet. Once we have that information, I'll signal my people and we'll attack." She glanced at me. "Are you sure you don't want to shift with us?"

I knew Anna could talk to us while in wolf form, but I didn't want to lose direct communication with Gabriel. Plus, shifting meant no witch-killing bullets for me. So, I shook my head.

"Okay," Lucy said, nodding. "This should only take a few minutes. I regret having to do this, but they've truly left us no option."

"And remember," I said. "We take the high priestess alive."

Sam and Lucy spared each other a single glance before shifting, along with the rest of her pack, before darting to the treeline to surround the coven. Once they were out of sight, I approached Gabriel and took his hand. I wasn't worried. We had the numbers. But I wanted this over and done with as soon as possible. They were summoning a demon, and therefore deserved to be put down like rabid dogs. The rationalization didn't make me feel any better.

A low hum emanated through the trees—a deep, foreboding sound that lifted the hairs on the back of my neck.

Gabriel squeezed my hand. "They're starting."

Which meant it was time to make our move. I released Gabriel's hand and drew my pistol, checking the safety and the ammunition.

"Ready?" I asked those of us who remained.

The sound of Chris's weapon being loaded was answer enough for me.

With a nod, I signaled us forward. Seeing as how we were all supernatural—save for Chris, though his training as a hunter made him nearly as stealthy—our footfalls were perfectly silent, carrying us toward the clearing without making any noise. I couldn't even hear the wolves creeping through the trees.

But with every step, the dreadful hum intensified, pulsing through the ground beneath our feet. We slipped into the trees, then approached the coven, who had positioned themselves in some strategic fashion I didn't understand around a massive white oak tree whose branches practically touched the sky.

The tree's leaves rustled in the breeze while half of the witches chanted in a haunting cadence. The rest focused their unnaturally intent gazes on what looked like an intricate circle. Encased within a ring of what looked like salt, symbols painstakingly etched into the ground glowed with a soft blue luminescence. At each cardinal point of the circle stood a small stone pillar inscribed with runes that matched the tattoos etched into their witchy flesh. In the center, a large black crystal sat upon a makeshift stage made of sticks and rocks. It seemed to absorb all the darkness, sucking the shadows into the crystal's core. It seemed safe to assume that *this* was the summoning circle they would use to call the demon.

Next to the black crystal stood a single witch, her arms cast out and her head thrown back. If I had to guess, that was Elara, the high priestess. Foreign words spilled from her lips, words that I'd never heard before, but I assumed it was demonic. That had to mean they hadn't completed the ceremony yet. Which hopefully meant the damn demon remained on its side of the veil. I didn't relish the thought of facing another so soon.

And it seemed I wasn't the only one.

Anna nudged me in the shoulder and gestured toward Lucy, who stalked through the foliage, her gaze intent on Elara. Sam crept alongside her, their every step synchronized. Lucy's wolves followed, edging closer, fanning out in formation around the circle. Their footfalls were soft, barely displacing the fallen leaves.

My hand gripped my gun and I readied myself.

The second the wolves made their move, so would we.

Then, just as the werewolves neared the edge of the clearing, a twig snapped beneath the weight of one wolf's paws. The sharp crack split the silence, and the chanting abruptly halted. The high priestess's eyes shot open, revealing a pair of otherworldly green eyes that illuminated the darkness.

The rest of the witches spun to face us, their robes billowing in the breeze. Without a word, they bolted toward Elara, crowding her within the summoning circle. If they thought they could keep her safe, they were in for a nasty surprise.

Lucy growled and together, she and Sam launched forward, initiating the attack. Her pack moved seamlessly behind her, their lips drawn back and fangs bared. But the instant the first wolf tried to breach the circle, it yelped in pain and leaped back from the now-smoking boundary. Two other wolves crashed into the boundary, only to collapse, screaming in pain.

Eerie laughter echoed through the clearing.

"Do you like it?" the high priestess demanded. "It's of my own making. A magical barrier infused with silver."

Lucy's hackles rose at the same time my eyes widened.

"Go on, try again," Elara cackled.

A thin line of smoke rose from the silver circle and the first injured wolf hobbled backward, unable to place any weight on his foot.

Fine. The werewolves might not be able to cross, but the vampires could. Change of plans. Time to level the playing field. I whirled around and snatched the guns from both Chris and Daniel. Chris immediately gripped the crossbow slung over his back and took aim, while Daniel drew one of his swords.

"Lucy, Sam!" I shouted.

Their attention turned to me and I gestured with the guns. They immediately shifted back, and once they stood on two feet, I lobbed the weapons across the clearing, both of which they snatched out of the air and immediately took aim. Were the situation not so dire, I might have burst out laughing at the sight of my sister and brother-in-law standing nude in the middle of a forest, aiming guns at a bunch of witches.

"Get close," I told Gabriel and Chris. "Destroy that circle so we can get inside in case a demon arrives."

Determination shone in Chris's eyes, and he gave me a sharp nod.

Lucy and Sam, now armed, spread out, their narrowed gazes locked on the witches.

The high priestess's smirk faded as she took in the scene. I had a feeling she didn't know about our specially concocted bullets. But I was all too happy to give her a lesson.

Chris, without any hesitation, loosed a bolt from his crossbow. Seeing as how he had perfect aim, it didn't surprise me when the bolt went right through one of the witch's throats. I'd told him they needed to speak to cast their magic, advice he must have taken to heart.

The other witches, who weren't currently choking on their own blood, started to chant. The one nearest me splayed out her hand, power coalescing in her palm. Now familiar with their fighting style, I waited for the moment the magic detonated, then ducked. The power sizzled over my head and slammed into another tree, splintering the bark. I straightened, raised my arm, and pulled the trigger.

My aim wasn't as perfect as Chris's, but I was no slouch either, as seen when the bullet landed right between her eyes.

Not as much fun when I could shoot back, was it?

Two down, eleven to go.

As if that was the cue, absolute chaos erupted. Anna, Vlad, Gabriel, Daniel, and Chris dove toward the circle. The silver circle didn't deter them, and they crossed it without any hesitation. Vlad, with his vampiric speed, had one witch pinned to the ground before she could even mutter a word. He delivered a swift blow, one that instantly ended her life.

Gabriel, who seemed to be everywhere at once, launched at another witch. He slashed with his sword, decapitating her with a grim efficiency. The grace and power he emanated had the high priestess hesitating, her focus torn between the assault and her summoning.

Outside the circle, the sharp report of gunfire echoed as Sam and Lucy took aim. They didn't make every shot, seeing as how neither had much experience with firearms, but they landed a few.

"Keep them away from the crystal!" the high priestess screamed in an attempt to rally her coven.

Chris took that moment to slam the butt of his crossbow into another witch's face just as they released a spell. The power slammed into Chris and took him to the ground. He gasped for air, his face pale as he clutched at his chest.

Yeah, I knew that feeling well.

"Gabriel!" I shouted. "The circle!" Then I fired another three shots, two of which landed and took out my targets.

Gabriel met my gaze, and he gave a brief nod of understanding before breaking away from his current opponent. My shout, however, drew the ire of two nearby witches. In tandem, they unleashed their magic, aiming for both me and Gabriel. While Gabriel managed to swerve behind one of the stone pillars just in time, shielding himself, I wasn't so lucky. The spell struck me, hitting me square in the chest—exactly where the demon had impaled me only two weeks prior.

Searing pain tore through me, reigniting my freshly healed wounds. The pain winded me, causing my knees to buckle and my vision to blur. Agony seared my every nerve ending, and I felt my heart stutter. The gun slipped from my fingers as I crashed to the ground, gasping for breath and clutching at my chest.

Distantly, I heard Gabriel shout my name. My head turned on the grass and I caught sight of him bolting toward me, fury blazing in his eyes.

Even in my agony, I managed to muster a raspy, "The...circle..."

Gabriel unleashed a furious growl, then pivoted his trajectory back toward the boundary. Using the full force of his supernatural speed and strength, he plunged his sword into the ground within the silver ring. A visible ripple of energy disrupted the barrier's steady glow. Cracks of light shot up into the air seconds before the once-luminous circle went dark.

The werewolves didn't need another invitation. With the barrier now gone, Lucy and Sam shifted and surged forward with the rest of the pack, joining the fray with renewed vigor. In a matter of moments, they had full control over the battlefield, with the witches now dangerously outnumbered.

Hands encircled my forearms and I lifted my head to find Gabriel now kneeling before me. He helped me stand, then pulled me into his chest.

"I'm fine," I wheezed.

Gabriel's hands remained firm on my arms, even as he held me against his chest. I tipped my head back and met his steely blue gaze. Every emotion, every unsaid word resonated between us. He finally released one of my arms and touched my chest.

"Damn witches," he growled, his voice a mix of relief and rage.

I didn't bother to agree with him. Instead, I leaned into his embrace, content to let Sam and Lucy finish this fight. I was so sick of witches and hoped I never saw another for as long as I lived.

An enraged shout pierced the night and I glanced up in time to find Lucy holding the black crystal above her head. With a heave, she slammed it down to the ground, and we all watched as it shattered into hundreds of tiny pieces. No more demon summoning for *that* crystal.

Or the coven, for that matter.

Only one witch remained standing—the high priestess. And Chris held her in a vice-like grip, a sharp dagger pressed to her throat. Daniel stood in front of her, clutching the two firearms that Sam and Lucy had dropped. Vlad stood next to him, his teeth shimmering in the moonlight. And all around her stood thirty werewolves, each slavering for a taste of witch.

With the immediate threat diminished, I turned back to Gabriel and caught sight of his triumphant smile.

"Shall we?" he asked, indicating our group of friends.

I nodded. We still had a high priestess to interrogate, after all.

19

I SQUARED MY SHOULDERS AND DREW A DEEP
breath, trying to expel the last of the pain that still
throbbed in my chest. The surrounding woods
hummed with an eerie post-battle stillness, broken
only by the soft whispers of the wind and the
rhythmic breaths of the pack.

Lucy moved to stand in front of the witch, her
posture taut and her teeth gritted. It'd been more
than a week since I'd stood in front of my first witch,
and still, she terrified me. The high priestess, bald
and imposing, looked more like a warrior than a

prisoner. Her scalp displayed the ominous, dark tattoos that encircled her entire head and vanished beneath her billowing robes. The symbols represented some glorious deity they revered. The witches burned them into their own flesh, a painful tribute to the gods they then used the tattoos to siphon power from. But it was her eyes, glowing with a defiant green fire, that truly unnerved me. I was used to glowing eyes—I'd seen them more than once in the mirror when looking at my own reflection—but Elara's were different. Older and far more powerful. The only thing holding her in check right now was our numbers. She knew, as well as we did, that we wouldn't let her so much as mutter an incantation before lopping her head off.

With Gabriel's hand locked securely around mine, we both approached the defiant witch. We had questions, and she had the answers. The hard part would be getting her to talk.

Chris repositioned his grip, digging the blade a little deeper into her flesh until a drop of ruby spilled over the metal.

"You know what we want," I began, my voice a bit weak from the last hit I took.

Those glowing eyes fixated on me and her smirk morphed into a full blown grin, one that showcased a mouth full of horrifyingly razor sharp teeth. I could only imagine she'd filed them. If I hadn't said it before, I'd say it now: Witches were terrifying.

"I owe you nothing, wolf," she drawled in a voice as sharp as her teeth.

My temper flared and I released Gabriel's hand and stepped forward, pressing into the high priestess's space. I gripped Chris's hand and pushed the blade deeper, spilling more blood.

The witch's eyelids didn't so much as flicker. Instead, her grin only widened. She reminded me of the damn demon. And didn't that thought just unnerve me. She stretched out her neck, giving me full access.

"Cut me more," she demanded. "My blood will feed the earth."

With my own leering grin, I leaned forward until our faces were a mere inch apart. "Why would I give your blood to the earth when I have three vampires here who would love to sink their teeth into you?"

If I wasn't mistaken, a flicker of fear danced in her eyes, one she quickly blinked away.

"Tell me who hired you," I demanded. "I want a name." I needed concrete proof that this all boiled down to Adrian.

Her lip curled. "And I want to skin you alive and

hang your pelt on my wall. I guess neither of us is getting what we want tonight."

A deep, threatening growl rumbled at my back.

"Speak to her like that again, witch, and I'll drink from your brain stem," Gabriel snarled.

"Nothing any of you say will convince me to give you the name. I fear *his* wrath more than I fear yours."

Frustration welled within me and I took a step back before I did something stupid like rip her head off. We needed answers. Decapitating her wouldn't help us accomplish that.

I massaged my temples in an attempt to stave off a blossoming headache. "Adrian," I breathed his name. "Is he the one who hired you? Gabriel's father?" Maybe if I showed her that we already knew who was behind all this, she would play ball.

The witch's glowing eyes locked on mine, as though searching for something, but her expression remained unreadable. She didn't respond, instead glancing at each of us one by one.

The tension in the clearing grew palpable, and her silence spoke louder than any confirmation she could have provided. I turned to Gabriel and saw my own frustration mirrored in his expression. His tight jaw and narrowed eyes spoke volumes. For all his controlled demeanor, the scent of his rage perfumed the clearing.

"Tell us!" Lucy snarled, her own eyes illuminating as her wolf started to slip free.

Elara held her tongue, the air around her thickening. When she grinned for a third time, it became distressingly clear that she had no intention of answering our questions.

I blew out a strained breath and turned away from her, rubbing my hands down my face. We'd come so far, accomplished so much. We'd killed their damn demon, and every witch they'd thrown at us. We'd obliterated Elara's entire coven, for crying out loud, thereby stopping them from summoning a second demon. And how were we rewarded?

With absolutely zilch.

No answers. No confirmation. Nothing but a witch too arrogant to speak. There had to be a way. I would never stoop to torturing someone—we were all better than that—but there *had* to be something.

A light bulb went off in my head and I whirled back around, staring at the witch with wide eyes. Maybe there *was* a way. Bethany and her coven could perhaps help us. I had no idea what exactly witches were capable of magic-wise, other than nearly killing me, but maybe there was something we could do to loosen the high priestess's tongue. A spell or something.

With a half-crooked grin, I nodded. "Fine."

I dug into my pocket and withdrew my phone. On the back of the slip of paper Bethany had given me with the address was her phone number—to call her and let her know when we were done.

"Let's see if the Luminous Crescent Coven can help us out here," I said.

Elara's eyes narrowed. I'd started typing in Bethany's phone number when a swift blur of movement caught my attention. I lifted my head in time to watch the high priestess, in an uncanny display of strength and agility, wrench her arm free from Chris's grip. Power flared from her tattoos, and in one fluid motion, she disarmed him and threw him to the ground.

I gasped and dove toward her, but I was too late.

With an inner strength I'd never seen from someone before, she turned the blade on herself and plunged it deep into her heart. I skidded to a stop, my mouth agape and eyes wide. Two stuttered breaths were all she managed before she toppled to the ground.

Dead.

And she'd taken her secrets with her.

THE RETURN TRIP TO LUCY'S HOUSE WAS somber. No one spoke, our thoughts weighed down by the gravity of the witch's death. I'd so hoped we'd get a name from her. Anything to help us confirm that Adrian was the mastermind behind all this. Now, that goal seemed almost impossible. Our only other option was the Academy. But I didn't expect much luck there either, considering those involved used pseudonyms, which was incredibly unhelpful.

When we finally reached Lucy's front door, the familiar aroma of our home greeted us—a mix of wood, leather, and a faint hint of cinnamon. Gabriel nudged the door open and we all filtered in, lost in a sort of trance.

Personally, I just wanted to slip into bed and call it a night.

We'd destroyed the coven and stopped a demon summoning—and yes, I considered those wins—but they weren't the wins I'd truly been aiming for. All I'd wanted was a name. Someone I could go after to put a stop to all this. I just wanted this all to end. I wanted to focus on my and Gabriel's happily ever after. I wanted to heal. I wanted to get back to my life. But there always seemed to be something standing in our way.

Sighing, I slipped my jacket off and hung it on the hook by the door. Lucy did the same, her face pallid. I wasn't the only one feeling a wee bit disgruntled. Even Chris's movements were robotic, his face blank as he removed his weaponry and outer garments.

"You all look like hell," came Jaden's voice.

I glanced up to find her and Josh seated on Lucy's plush couch. Hell, I hadn't even noticed them or their car when we arrived. That was how exhausted I was.

"We feel like it," Lucy replied with a tired sigh.

"It didn't go well?" Josh asked.

"It went well enough," I said. "We stopped the summoning. Demolished the coven."

"Okay," Jaden hedged. "Then why do you all look like someone just kicked your puppy?"

I shrugged, strode into the living room, then plopped down beside her. "The high priestess decided she preferred death to talking. So we weren't able to find out who wants Gabriel dead."

"Ah, that's not ideal. However, there's still lots to celebrate!" Jaden said, trying to cheer us up. "The coven is gone, right?"

I nodded.

"Well, that's one threat handled." She held up a hand. "High five!"

Laughing, I couldn't help but slap our hands together.

"And the demon?"

"No demon," I said.

"Even better!" She curled her fingers into a fist, and laughing harder, I knocked our knuckles together.

"That's all amazing," Jaden said, ever our cheerleader. "No reason to look all mopey. So you didn't find out the identity of the big bad. That's okay. Because guess what?"

"What?" I asked, trying to muster even five percent of her energy.

Jaden grinned, then glanced at Josh. The two beamed at us, as though they had the best news in the world.

"We got you a meeting with the Academy Council!" Jaden shouted, punching the air for emphasis.

The entire room fell silent. Jaden's enthusiasm infectiously buzzed through the room, even in our state of exhaustion. The words "Academy Council" ricocheted in my head, bringing with it a mixture of hope and anxiety. This was *exactly* what we needed.

"How on earth did you manage that?" Chris demanded, dropping into a chair across from us. He leaned on his thighs, his eyes wide as he stared at Jaden.

"It's all thanks to Ginny," Jaden began, a smirk playing on her lips. "After our little chat with her and Benjamin, things took an interesting turn."

"Tell us everything," I urged, now suddenly alert.

Jaden paid Josh another glance, and he nodded, smiling.

"Okay," Jaden said, clearly excited to regale us with her tale. "So, Ginny's contract was for Benjamin, right? But once she confronted him, Benjamin protested his innocence. The interesting part? He was her *fourth* vampire in a row to claim they were being framed. We've all had that happen before"—she winced, likely now wondering how many had actually been innocent—"but four was enough to give Ginny pause. Not to mention, he claimed he had proof."

Jaden turned to the side and fished a stack of papers out from her bag, spreading them on the coffee table. I leaned forward and studied them, taking in what looked like concert tickets, a hotel booking, and a car rental receipt.

"Benjamin was adamant that he wasn't anywhere near the killings when they took place."

"Wait," I said, holding up a hand. "Ginny's contract had that information?" Because Gabriel's hadn't.

"Yes!" Jaden exclaimed enthusiastically. "Weird, right? And do you wanna know something even weirder? Ginny couldn't find any proof of death for the victims listed in his contract. As far as she can tell, they never even existed. Anyway"—she waved a hand—"Benjamin was adamant that he was innocent, and told Ginny he could provide her with an alibi."

Lucy stepped toward the coffee table and scrutinized the evidence. "And Ginny believed him?"

Jaden shook her head. "Not at first. I mean, we're taught not to trust anyone on the sharp end of our stakes. But, like I said, this was the fourth time in a row that her mark had claimed someone was framing them. So she did her own digging. She verified his alibis, checked with eyewitnesses, spoke to those he claimed to have attended the concert with. Everything suggested that Benjamin was telling the truth. That was when she took it one step further and started investigating the so-called victims."

"Except there's no proof of their deaths," I concluded.

Jaden tapped her nose then pointed at me, clearly excited. She'd always loved a good mystery.

"Alright. So that's a solid case in support of Benjamin. Now, how did all this lead to you getting us a meeting with the Council?"

Jaden's eyes gleamed with pride. "That's where the twist comes in. Ginny is the niece of one of the council members—a woman named Lorraine."

Whoa. I sat back on the couch, flabbergasted. We finally had the name of one of the councilmembers. This was huge. No wonder Jaden was grinning like a fool.

"Ginny vouched for us?" I asked.

Josh chimed in, "It's more than that. Word has been spreading about our investigation. Other slayers have been voicing their concerns. Not just us and Ginny. There are quite a few of us now who believe that someone—or a bunch of someones—is taking bribes to kill vampires. *Any* vampire."

Jaden nodded. "Ginny handed us her evidence, along with a message from Lorraine to meet at the Academy tomorrow night at eight p.m." Jaden glanced at the closest clock. "Or rather, tonight at eight, since it's now after midnight. According to Ginny, they want to hear our side and understand what's been happening. But here's the kicker. They asked specifically for you, Maddie," Jaden said. Then she glanced at Gabriel. "And you."

I shot Gabriel a stunned look. "*Just* the two of us?"

"No," Jaden said. "Apparently, Lorraine said you could bring one more person. But they wanted to keep the meeting contained."

I wasn't sure how I felt about that. I swallowed hard, my thoughts a whirlwind. "Why just us?"

Gabriel ran a hand through his hair, his gaze never straying from mine. "It's strategic, I suppose. As a council, they'd want to hear from the primary players. Not the rabble-rousers. And with the threat being directly against me—the king of vampires—it makes sense to have me there. As for you, you've been involved since the very start. You're the source. The first person who'd suspected something was wrong."

I nodded, now understanding the logic.

"Who'll be your third?" Lucy asked.

Chris stepped forward. "Me."

I stared at him, unsure if Chris was the right

319

choice. But when I ran through the list, I wasn't sure if anyone else was better. I couldn't take Sam or Lucy. The council didn't know them, and I wasn't introducing more werewolves to the Academy. And I certainly wasn't bringing any more vampires than necessary into the Academy. That left Jaden, Josh, or Chris. And while we were all exceptional slayers, Chris wasn't just the best of the us, he was the best in the entire Academy.

"Are you sure about this?" I asked.

Gabriel frowned as he perused Chris. "He might actually work in our favor, given his prejudices. The council might take us more seriously, especially if they're aware of Chris's...sentiments about vampires."

"Uh, thanks?" Chris said. He rolled his eyes and faced me. "You know I've got your back. I may not like vampires, but even I have to admit, yours is... okay."

Laughter swept through the group.

"Alright then. Gabriel, Chris, and I will go to the Academy tomorrow night, and we'll set things straight. With Ginny's evidence and everything we've discovered, they can't ignore us."

I hoped.

God, did I hope.

TOGETHER, GABRIEL AND I SLIPPED INTO OUR bedroom and closed the door behind us. A comforting silence enveloped us, and with a contented sigh, I moved to the bed and sat on the edge. Gabriel did the same, his shoulder brushing mine. After the night's events, I just needed a moment to breathe and process.

A part of me couldn't believe that we'd eliminated the coven. I wanted to feel happy about that, but sadness was the only emotion I could muster. We'd ended thirteen lives tonight. I understood that it was necessary, due to their evil demon summoning ways, but I still hated that it'd come to this.

It was so hard to reconcile the person I'd become with the person I'd always thought I was. This had all started thanks to the corruption within the Academy. I'd wanted to prove that we, as slayers, weren't mindless killers, that we had a code we abide by. We only took out vampires proven guilty of murder. I'd firmly believed we were merely another arm of the law, protecting innocent humans from the ways of evil bloodsuckers.

I didn't feel like that same person anymore.

Something had changed.

And it'd changed tonight, with the death of the thirteen witches. Like I'd lost a bit of my innocence. Like I'd been dragged deeper into the paranormal world and I didn't quite know what to make of it.

Sighing, I glanced at Gabriel. He stared at the floor, as though the carpet might provide him some unspoken answers. With a weak smile, I nudged his side.

He looked up and met my gaze.

"Penny for your thoughts?" I asked.

His mouth quirked. Then he whipped a hand through his tousled hair before dropping it back down into his lap. "I was just thinking about everything that's happened over the last few weeks." He gave a soft laugh. "If someone had told me even half a year ago that *this* is what my life was to become, I would have called them mad. Demons, witches, and vampire slayers—"

"Oh my," I teased.

Amusement brightened Gabriel's face. "I'm used to vampire politics and schemes. But those seem almost tame now in comparison."

That made me laugh. "Glad we're keeping you on your toes."

"Mm." His eyes softened and he reached out to take my hands. "I certainly wouldn't have believed them if they told me I'd find another mate. Or that she would be a vampire slayer herself." He shook his head. "Finding another mate had never once crossed my mind. I wasn't even sure I wanted one after Camilla." He blew out an unnecessary breath, then tore his gaze from mine and stared across the room. "Nothing ever felt right with her. It felt like the universe was trying to force us together, like two magnets pushing away from each other. But with you..."

He fell silent, once again lost in his thoughts. I

reached out and took his hand, gently threading our fingers together.

"With me?" I urged.

A corner of his mouth lifted. "With you, everything feels natural. And right. And so very terrifying."

I cocked my head, frowning. "Terrifying how?"

Gabriel gazed at me thoughtfully, as though trying to figure out how to respond to my question. "When you jumped in front of that demon to protect me, it was like my world ended. I thought you were going to die, and for the first time in my long existence, I wanted to die too. I couldn't imagine a world without you in it. All the color had vanished, and merely existing hurt." He ran a hand over his chin. "Then tonight, when the witch hit you with that spell, I had that same flash of fear."

"Hey, I'm alright. I barely felt it."

He leveled me with a stare. "You felt it."

Yeah, I'd felt it.

"I'm just saying, all this is so new to me. And frightening. Camilla jumped in front of me too. Took the blow that was supposed to kill me. She died to save me. And I wasn't anywhere near as frightened with her as I was with you. With her, I was angry it'd happened. Furious that my mother could facilitate something like that. But with you, I wanted to destroy the entire world. Even if that meant destroying myself."

I drew in a slow breath, his words fanning a heat in my chest.

"I felt the same, you know," I finally admitted. "The day I learned that Chris held your contract, I was terrified. I didn't understand why then. I just knew I had to get to you and protect you. We didn't even know each other then. We'd met once." A blush burned my cheeks. "Kissed once. But somehow I knew that I had to save you. I couldn't imagine a world without you in it."

I leaned against Gabriel's side and rested my head on his shoulder. "Strange the direction our lives took, huh?"

He grunted a half-amused response.

"A few months ago, I never would have thought it possible that I could fall in"—I choked on my breath and stumbled over *that* specific word, grateful that I couldn't see his face right that second—"um, never would have imagined the Vampire King becoming so important to me."

I cursed myself silently once I finished speaking, scolding myself for not having the courage to finally admit, out loud, that I was in love with him. What was I waiting for? It wasn't like I had anything to fear. This was Gabriel, for crying out loud. My mate. The one person in the entire world who would never hurt me. I *knew* he cared deeply for me—he'd just admitted it. Even Josh suspected Gabriel loved me. But those words were so hard for me to get out. I'd never actually said them before. To anyone.

I wanted to. More than anything. I just couldn't make my mouth form the words. Fear held my lips and tongue hostage.

"There's something else you should know," Gabriel said, apparently oblivious to my internal struggles.

I adjusted my head so I could see his face. "Hmm?"

"I'm going to abdicate the throne. Step down."

Time came to a dead stop. I stared at him, waiting for the moment he cracked a joke. But that moment never came. I sat up and faced him. "What?"

Sighing, Gabriel took one of my hands and started running his thumb over my knuckles, as though to soothe himself. "I've been thinking about this a lot. I didn't want to say anything until I knew for sure. But I've been kidding myself. I've known since the moment I met you." He paused, then finally said, "You are the most important thing to me, Maddie. The crown, my home, all of that comes second. To you."

I sucked in a sharp breath, telling myself that I must have heard him wrong. "No, those can't come second. The crown—"

"Will continue without me," he said. "But I can't continue without you."

My breath caught in my throat and I rose onto my knees, gripping his hands tightly. "What are you saying?"

"I'm saying I want to be with *you*. I want to be wherever you are. If you want to stay here with your family, then this"—he waved a hand around the room —"is where I want to be. Where I *will* be. You're all that matters to me, Maddie. And I refuse to lose you."

"But your people—"

"Will survive without me. Elias can take the throne. He'd hate it, but I have faith he'd do a worthy job. I can advise him as needed."

I blinked, trying to process his words. "I-I can't ask you to give up your kingdom for me."

He tucked a stray strand of hair behind my ear, his cool touch sending shivers down my spine. "You didn't ask, Maddie. This is my choice. My decision. I took the throne to save Anna and Vlad's lives, but I never truly wanted it. The only reason I was even in line for it was because Genevieve adopted me. I was born a poor lad, raised in an even poorer abbey. But you've shown me what it feels like to be truly alive again. And yes, I know," he said, holding up a hand when I started to interrupt. "I'm not alive, blah, blah, blah."

I gave a quiet, albeit shocked, laugh.

He cupped my cheeks and drew me near, resting his forehead against mine. "You're the one bright spot in my eternal existence. You're something I can't —*won't*—give up. I love you. I need you. And I refuse to lose you."

His words hit me like a bulldozer, and I wasn't able to stop the tears from slipping down my cheeks. He'd said it. He'd said the *actual* words. My whole life, I'd been told I was worthless and unimportant. That no one would ever love me. Want me. *Choose* me. Not like this. And with three small words, he'd just blown my entire existence to smithereens.

Frowning, Gabriel thumbed away my tears, his gaze searching mine. "What's wrong? Why are you crying?"

A knot tightened in my chest, my emotions threatening to overwhelm me. "Because no one has ever made me feel this way before. No one has ever put me first. I grew up in a system where they constantly showed me that I wasn't enough. Always passed over, always on the outside looking in."

Gabriel's eyes darkened. "You absolutely are enough," he growled. "I can't change your upbringing, but I can spend the rest of my existence proving to you just how perfect you are."

Oh god, he was gonna turn me into a weepy, sobbing mess if he kept this up.

"Every moment I've spent with you has made me feel whole," he said. Then, with a wink, he added, "Even when you had me chained to that pitiful couch of yours."

I snorted a laugh, then wiped the tears from my cheeks.

"Before that, I felt like I was merely existing. But with you, life is bright. Clear. Vivid. And I'm not stupid enough to give all that away for a stupid crown."

"I could move with you. To England," I suggested. "I could do that."

Gabriel chuckled, then shook his head. "You could. But I don't want you to. I know you want to stay close to your sister and her family and your friends. I know how much family means to you. And how hard and painful it would be for you walk away from them. It isn't painful for me to walk away from the crown. Not in the slightest. So we're not going to even consider that option."

"We're not?" I asked teasingly.

"Nope. We're not."

I lifted my teary gaze and held his. I needed to look him in the eyes for what I wanted to say next. Wanted him to know I meant it. Butterflies the size of bats flapped around in my stomach, but I told myself to calm down. There was nothing to fear. Gabriel had just proven that to me.

"I..." I drew a deep breath and mustered all my courage. "I love you."

Gabriel gave me the sweetest smile. And instead of pretending my words meant nothing—which I knew he would never do, but my brain wasn't exactly forming logical thoughts right now—he leaned in and kissed me. He brushed his lips against mine, softly, tenderly. The warmth of his touch chased away my lingering fears, and instead, bolstered me.

I sucked in a sharp breath and climbed into his lap, plunging my fingers through his silky locks. Gabriel's arms came around my back and he held me so tight that a human might have protested. Luckily, I wasn't as fragile.

Breaking the kiss, Gabriel leaned back and stared into my eyes. "I've waited so long to hear you say that."

I couldn't help but snicker. "So long? We've only known each other a few weeks."

"Sure, luv. But it feels like I've been waiting forever."

Pulling me close, he kissed me again, and I savored every second of it. We still had so much to face together, but together, I knew we could accomplish anything.

21

THE NEXT NIGHT, AT EIGHT P.M. ON THE BUTTON, we stood in front of the Academy in downtown Jackson. Once upon a time, I'd felt nothing but pride whenever I stepped through the front doors. Even under the silvery glow of the moon, it exuded an aura of authority and prestige. But now, my emotions ranked somewhere between sadness and disappointment. I'd given so much of my life to this organization, only to learn about the corruption steeped within. Hopefully, after tonight, that would become a thing of the past, and we could return to our regularly scheduled programming. I loved my job. I loved slaying vampires. But only if they were actually guilty.

I pulled my coat tighter around me in an attempt to stave off the early March chill and the spring breeze that whistled through the surrounding buildings. Gabriel, being a vampire himself, seemed unaffected—the lucky jerk. His tall and elegant form moved with its usual grace, his eyes scanning our surroundings. Next to him, Chris, with his broad shoulders and stern expression, radiated determination. He was just as resolute as I was to fix this entire situation. It was why I'd chosen him to come with. Well, that and the hope that his and my reputations combined would lend us some credibility.

"I can't believe we're about to meet with the council," Chris murmured.

"I don't think we left them much of a choice," I replied. "With everything we've discovered, they'd look guilty if they ignored it. We've more than proven the corruption. They can't *not* address it."

"Do we have everything?" Chris asked.

I patted the inside of my jacket, where I'd tucked all the relevant papers Josh and Jaden had given us. "Ginny's testimony, along with Benjamin's proof of alibi." Then I glanced at Gabriel. "Are you ready for this?"

"Of course. I have nothing to hide," he stated.

At least he was confident. I wanted to believe we had nothing to worry about, but my gut said otherwise. We already knew one of the council members was guilty of taking bribes. But there were four other members. What if we'd overlooked one? Were we leading Gabriel to his demise like a lamb to slaughter? My wolf didn't love that idea at all, and a low growl rumbled deep in my throat, one that drew the attention of both men beside me.

Gabriel merely raised a brow, but the half-crooked smile told me he knew exactly what had rattled my wolf. Chris, however, seemed alarmed. Fair enough. He wasn't used to hanging around werewolves.

"Sorry," I muttered, waving a dismissive hand. "It's a werewolf thing."

Chris looked a little taken aback. "It is?"

I almost laughed at his expression. "Yeah. We're a territorial lot, and I'm taking my mate into the viper's den, so to speak. My wolf isn't happy about any of this."

"Okay," he murmured. "But might I suggest

getting all that under control? You don't want the council learning you're a werewolf, right?"

"I know," I told him. "Don't worry. I got this."

Chris didn't look as convinced as I sounded.

I calmed my wolf, then faced Gabriel. "How should we play this?"

"We go in calm and collected," he said. "The most important thing is to keep our emotions under check, regardless of our feelings. The more emotional people become, the less others tend to listen. We *need* them to listen. We need to present the facts. Give them all the information we've gathered. They need to know we're here to help root out the corruption, not threaten or dismantle the organization."

"That all sounds wonderful, but don't forget, we're also here to clear your name," I said.

Gabriel's smile returned, warm and reassuring. "I knew there was a reason I loved you."

I chuckled, my cheeks heating. Hearing him causally throw those words around almost made everything we'd been through worth it.

"Come on then, lovebirds," Chris said.

Together, the three of us approached the main entrance. The automatic glass doors slid open, revealing a spacious lobby with minimalist décor.

Chris and I had walked through these doors many times, but it'd never felt quite like this. Almost like we'd been summoned to the principal's office.

From the depths of the lobby, a tall, regal-looking woman with jet-black hair approached us. Her posture was impeccable, her gait confident, and there was an air of authority about her. As she neared, her piercing green eyes sized us up, her focus especially lingering on Gabriel.

My whole body tensed and I barely managed to restrain a growl. I did *not* like the way she looked at my mate, as though he was something for her to eat, as opposed to kill.

Something pinched my arm and I tore my gaze away to find Chris standing next to me with a silent warning glare. Right. Now wasn't the time to let my werewolf take control. It didn't matter how the woman looked at Gabriel. Not right now, anyway.

"You must be Madison and Chris," the woman said, her voice resonant but not unkind. "We've heard wonderful things about you two."

"Thanks," I replied, my voice a touch deeper than I'd intended. "Just call me Maddie."

She dipped her head, then turned to Gabriel, her gaze once again taking in every inch of him. "And you must be Gabriel, the King of Vampires. We're all keen to meet you. Welcome."

Gabriel merely nodded, maintaining his composed demeanor.

"I'm Councilwoman Lorraine," she continued. "And I'll be escorting you into the meeting."

So this was Ginny's aunt then, and the reason we were here. "Thank you, Councilwoman," I said, trying to sound as diplomatic as possible. "We appreciate you granting us this meeting."

Lorraine nodded. "Given the nature of your claims and the evidence you've purportedly gathered, the council believes this is a matter of utmost importance."

Mm. Yes. I was sure they did.

I shared a brief glance with Chris and Gabriel before responding. "We certainly are of the same opinion. And we're hopeful that once you've laid everything out, the truth will become clear."

Lorraine gave another slow nod, her gaze darting to the bulge inside my jacket.

"It's just papers," I told her in case she thought I was carrying a weapon. I mean, I was. But the council didn't need to know that.

"Ah. Well, we're eager to see what you've brought forward. Follow me, please."

With that, she led us down a wide corridor. As we walked, a low hum of conversation emanated from the room straight ahead of us. As we neared it, Lorraine paused and looked back at us. "Remember, the council is here to listen. Present your evidence, and speak your truth. We're all here in search of the same thing: justice."

Gabriel met her gaze evenly. "That's all we want too, Councilwoman."

I took a deep breath, steeling myself for the confrontation ahead. This was our chance, our moment to expose the corruption, clear Gabriel's name, and return honor to an institution I'd once held in the highest regard. We couldn't fail here tonight.

Lorraine threw open the boardroom doors and gestured us inside. Gabriel and I entered first, with Chris hot on our heels. The room was expansive, with a massive table in the center made of sleek black marble. Large glass windows framed one wall, giving us an eyeful of Jackson. The other walls were adorned with portraits of council members—both past and present.

Seated around the table were the remaining four council members.

As we approached, Lorraine gestured to them.

"Allow me to introduce you to the rest of the council. This is Harold," she said, pointing to a middle-aged man with silver streaks in his neatly combed hair. His eyes, sharp and analytical, studied us intently.

"Next, we have Elaine," Lorraine continued. Elaine was a beautiful woman with striking red hair that cascaded over her shoulders. Her green eyes glinted with intelligence and curiosity.

"To her right is Damien," she indicated to a younger-looking man with dark skin and a bald head.

"And finally, Sylvia," Lorraine continued. Sylvia was an elderly woman, her face lined with wisdom and experience. She'd tied her silver hair back, and her piercing blue eyes sparkled with life.

I nodded to each of them, trying to get a read on who might be the corrupted member. Jaden and Josh hadn't been able to discover that information specifically. Truly, it could be any of the five, and at first glance, I had no way of guessing.

Gabriel, ever the diplomat, extended his hand in greeting, which Harold and Elaine accepted. Damien gave a curt nod, and Sylvia just observed with a faint, inscrutable smile.

When the four council members glanced at me and Chris, I squared my shoulders and lifted my chin. I refused to let them cow me. I was one of their best slayers *and* a werewolf to boot. These five, while backed by the power of the Academy, were human. If they tried anything, Gabriel and I could massacre them in under a minute.

I wasn't worried.

Not at all.

The trained slayer in me took a moment to peruse our surroundings. The boardroom seemed typical. A massive table surrounded by chairs and another set of doors behind the five council members. I strained my senses but heard nothing coming from behind them. No hint of any other heartbeats, no whispered breaths, nothing but silence.

Just us and the council here tonight.

Relieved, I turned my focus back to the meeting.

Lorraine took her seat at the table, then gestured at us. "Now that the introductions are out of the way, let's get to the matter at hand. Maddie, Chris—please present your findings."

I took a deep breath and centered my thoughts. This was our moment, and the weight of the situation bore down on my shoulders. The council's reaction, for better or worse, would dictate the future, not only of the Academy but of the city as well.

"Okay, so here's the thing—" I started.

Chris cleared his throat and shot me a telling glance.

Heat burned my cheeks and I closed my eyes, once again centering myself. Right. I needed to speak clearly.

"Um." I drew in a steadying breath and imagined how Lucy or Anna would behave in a situation like this. I considered all the crime dramas I'd watched over the years and channeled my inner lawyer. "Over the course of the last few weeks, we've discovered some things that concern the very foundation of our organization, and it's crucial we address them immediately."

I shot Chris a quick glance from my periphery and caught his slight nod.

Okay. I was on the right track here.

I dug into my jacket and pulled out the stack of papers. "This is a sworn statement from one of our fellow slayers, Virginia 'Ginny' Lefebvre. Recently, she began noticing discrepancies in her assignments. Her last three marks all vehemently claimed their innocence. Now, this isn't unheard of. We've all faced marks who lie and beg our forgiveness and claim they're innocent"—to which I was now wondering how many were telling the truth—"but when Ginny's most recent target, Benjamin, provided her an alibi for his supposed crime, Ginny took it upon herself to dig a little deeper into this situation. Upon hearing talk from other slayers regarding my own issues with a similar matter, Ginny reached out to us. With Benjamin's alibi, it was clear the charges were false."

I slid the concert tickets across the table. "These are tickets for a concert Benjamin attended miles away from Jackson. Prior to meeting with us, Ginny examined his alibi and corroborated his whereabouts. She spoke with hotel guests and employees who saw him, we have evidence of his credit card being used to purchase blood, along with the hotel, and confirmation that he was the one to pick up and drop off the rental car in both locations. Upon further investigation, Ginny substantiated that this was a personal vendetta from a former business associate who approached the Academy to place a bounty on his head. Unfortunately, we couldn't figure out which Academy employee took the payment for the contract."

Sylvia leaned forward, examining the tickets and reading Ginny's statement. Beside her, Harold's brow furrowed as he studied me, his sharp eyes assessing every detail.

Elaine sat back in her chair and folded her hands in her lap. "One false accusation does not suggest our organization is corrupt."

"We don't believe the entire organization is corrupt," I told her. "But there *is* corruption within." I motioned to Gabriel, who stood tall beside me. "Gabriel, the Vampire King, stands accused of murder." I pulled out another paper, the one with his portrait, and smoothed it out on the table. "If you look closely, you'll see that the bounty lists murder as the charge, but gives no indication as to who he supposedly killed. Nor does it offer us any further information. Due to this, we've had no means of proving he's innocent. However, if the Academy could give us the name of his victim and the date of the supposed murder, we could provide it. Being that he's the king, Gabriel is never without his guard. I'm confident he'd be able to provide a perfectly acceptable alibi."

Elaine lifted a hand. "If he's unable to prove he didn't commit the crime, then how can we trust he didn't commit it?"

Frustration boiled beneath the surface, and I thought back to Anna's words when we first discussed this. "In the human legal system, evidence is required for conviction. That's why we have an

Investigations department within the Academy. But it doesn't seem like anyone actually conducted an investigation. When we dug deeper, we unearthed even more unsettling information. Vera was the officer who issued Chris the bounty on Gabriel. When we questioned Vera, she revealed that she received the bounty from her boss, Liam. And Liam revealed that he received the bounty from his boss, Claire. Claire works in Reparations and according to her, she has been taking bribes from anyone who can pay enough. From what we learned, there are quite a few people in this 'system' and it's anonymous to protect those involved. Our entire method allows for personal vendettas and bribes to dictate bounties rather than actual violations. There're too many hands in the pot."

Damien sat forward, his eyes filled with incredulity. "Are you suggesting that the Academy has targeted vampires for personal motives rather than actual transgressions?"

"Exactly," Chris said, confirming our stance.

The five council members sat back in stark silence. I studied each and every one of them, reading their body language for any who might be guilty. But no one revealed themselves.

"There's more," I said. "During our

investigation, we were given reason to suspect that"
—I drew a deep breath and blurted out the words I
never thought I'd have to say—"one of *you* are
involved in all this."

The room went quiet, but I watched as the
council members exchanged glances. What if we
were wrong? What if it wasn't just one but *all* of
them? What if the corruption was so deeply rooted
that we'd missed the signs?

Lorraine, her posture rigid, addressed me
directly, "These are not light claims, Maddie. To
suggest that one amongst us might be complicit is
grave indeed."

"I understand that. My goal was to expose the
corruption within the Academy once we learned
about it. We've done so, revealing Claire and the
bounties and the system she belongs to."

"Yes, but where's the evidence suggesting one of
us may be involved?" Sylvia demanded.

"We don't have concrete evidence to directly
implicate a council member," I admitted.

"We didn't come here to throw wild
accusations," Gabriel said, offering me assistance,
"but to inform you of the possibility so you can look
into the matter internally. It isn't the job of your
slayers to police your council or to eliminate

corrupted members. Now the responsibility falls on you to handle your organization."

Damien raised an eyebrow, clearly skeptical. "So you present us an accusation without evidence and expect us to...what? Distrust each other?"

Harold, who had been silent until now, spoke up, "It's not about distrust, Damien. It's about awareness and vigilance. If there's even a whisper of such allegations, it's our responsibility to handle it. In any way we deem necessary."

Damien paused and stared at Harold. Then two seemed to share a silent conversation before Damien nodded.

"Very well," Damien said. "All in favor?"

Five hands shot up, shocking me. *All* agreed to look into the corruption? But wouldn't the one corrupt member argue against it? Understandably, doing so would likely reveal their identity, but it seemed odd to me that they would so willingly agree to look into the corruption if it threatened their position within the council.

"Good. Then we're agreed," Harold said. He leaned forward and rapped his knuckles against the table.

My brows rose. Was that supposed to be like a judge's gavel type thing? Was he effectively dismissing us? Before I could ask what that was supposed to mean, the double doors behind us began to creak open, revealing a group of shadowy figures. A dozen figures stepped inside, and as they moved into the light, their pale skin and lack of heartbeats betrayed their vampiric nature.

Understanding dawned and I swore under my breath. No wonder I hadn't heard anyone behind those doors. But in all fairness, I hadn't expected to see *vampires* in the Academy. And certainly not in cahoots with the council. How blind we had been. It wasn't *one* corrupt member. It was all five. Including Ginny's aunt.

We were idiots.

Chris's hand moved to the weapon at his side, but it was Gabriel's sharp curse that made my heart race. His focus was intent on the leader of the group, who strode across the room toward us.

"Hello, Adrian," Gabriel snarled.

Adrian? My eyes widened as my whole body tensed. *This* was Adrian? Gabriel's father? But wasn't he supposed to be in England? Wasn't Elias supposed to be watching him? Why had no one warned us that he was he here?

I quickly sized up the towering figure before me, from his imposing height to his broad shoulders and sharp features. Given the way others had described him—the boozing and whoring—I'd pictured someone less...formidable. But standing before me was a behemoth of a vampire, one who exuded a menacing aura.

Part of me wanted to congratulate myself for correctly guessing Adrian's involvement. But that feeling faded fast, especially when he turned his dark gaze on me and flashed his fangs.

Adrian stalked toward us, his hands clasped behind his back.

Chris didn't utter a word, but I felt his solid presence beside me. If it came down to a fight, I wasn't sure it was one we could win, but I was grateful to have Chris on our side. If anyone could help us, it would be him.

Adrian came to a stop just in front of Gabriel and leaned in, their faces mere inches apart. Hatred burned deep in Adrian's eyes, and his lips seemed frozen in a permanent sneer.

"If it were up to me, I'd end your miserable existence right here," Adrian said. "Unfortunately for me, there's someone else who wants to see you first."

Wait. What? Someone *else* wanted to see Gabriel? Who? And why? Did Adrian have a partner in all this? We'd been so focused on him that the idea of multiple puppet masters had never once crossed my mind.

Gabriel gritted his jaw and held his chin high. "I'm disappointed in you, Father."

Fury rippled across Adrian's face, but he didn't reply. Instead, faster than my eyes could track, he whipped out what looked like a syringe and stabbed Gabriel in the neck.

I screamed Gabriel's name, the sound of his deep gasp burning fear through my veins. Reacting instinctively, I sucker-punched Adrian in the face, his nose rupturing in a fountain of blood. He staggered back with a curse, and I grabbed Gabriel just as he started to fall.

We toppled to the ground with him sprawled in my lap. I stared down at him, watching as his skin grew impossibly, and frighteningly, pale. His veins darkened, like spiderwebbing crawling beneath his flesh. But it was his body convulsing in my arms that had my heart racing.

"Holy water," Gabriel rasped, struggling to speak as his body writhed in agony on the floor.

Horror ripped through me. I plucked the syringe from his neck and held it to my nose, sniffing it. Holy water was innocuous to mortals but deadly for vampires, which was why we treated our stakes in it.

Gabriel's entire body gave one last spasm before his eyes rolled into the back of his head and he fell still.

"Gabriel?" I cried, cupping his face and holding him close.

Vampires didn't breathe. Their hearts didn't beat. So I had no means of measuring whether or not he was alive.

"Gabriel!" I screamed.

He didn't respond.

Hate and ire and fury built within me until I could barely stand it. I lifted my head and stared at Adrian. He stood among the other vampires, hands cupped over his gushing nose, but he still managed to sneer at me.

"Her too," he muttered through his fingers.

Oh, hell no. He wouldn't lay a finger on me.

I gently lowered Gabriel's head, then slowly rose to my feet. If Adrian wanted a fight, he'd get one. Because no way was I letting him leave here with Gabriel. Or me. I reached into my jacket and drew Sir-Stab-A-Lot.

Adrian's gaze dropped to my hand and he laughed. "Allow me to remind you that you're currently surrounded by a dozen vampires," he said. "There's no escape this time. Not to mention..." He pointed behind me. I stole a quick glance back to find five vampires surrounding Chris. He was good, but I wasn't sure he was good enough to fight off that many vampires at once. Not to mention the other seven surrounding me and Adrian.

"Let me make this clear for you. You fight, he dies." He jerked his head toward Chris. "Then he dies." He pointed at Gabriel. "Then you die. Are you willing to lose them both? Drop the stake."

I ground my teeth, my grip tightening around Sir-Stab-A-Lot. My fingers itched to drive my stake into Adrian's heart. But when I weighed the odds, they weren't great. There were too many of them. Even if I shifted, I couldn't save both Chris and Gabriel, and I certainly couldn't take on a dozen vampires by myself. Adrian hadn't killed Gabriel yet because he apparently needed to take him somewhere—to *someone*. If I fought, I would be signing all three of our death certificates, but if I played along, Gabriel and I would live to fight another day. And so would Chris.

I couldn't win this fight. Yet.

Releasing a shaky breath, I forced myself to meet Adrian's stare. "Alright," I whispered, dropping my stake. "You win." Best to wait until they were unsuspecting, for a moment of weakness, and attack then.

He flashed a victorious grin. "Smart girl."

A growl vibrated through my chest. My wolf did *not* like this plan. But we couldn't fight and expect to win. Sometimes surrendering was the only option.

Adrian nodded to someone behind me. Before I could react, a vampire appeared next to me and injected a sharp needle into *my* neck. Panic flared the instant my nose detected the all-too-familiar metallic scent of silver.

My eyes briefly widened, then I choked out a gasp and staggered backward. How did he know I was a werewolf? Who told him? Agony instantly erupted within my body, like every inch of me was on fire. My vision blurred, and my legs buckled. I fell, dropping helplessly to my back while struggling for breath. For werewolves, silver wasn't just incapacitating, it was also lethal in large doses.

The last thing I heard was Chris shouting my name before everything faded to black.

22

THE FIRST SENSATION I REGISTERED, AS consciousness nudged at me, was the cold hardness beneath my body. My eyes fluttered open, my vision blurry and unreliable. Pain, in the form of a single lightbulb dangling above me, speared my eyes. I raised an unsteady hand and shielded myself from the light, all while trying to make sense of my surroundings. When my vision steadied, the reality of my situation hit me with a gut-twisting thud.

Lorraine, Harold, Sylvia, Edgar, and Damien. Five names I would never forget. Five names now added to my shit list. They'd betrayed us. Handed us over to Adrian and his lackeys without so much as batting an eyelash.

I'd been worried about the corruption turning me into a murderer.

I wasn't so worried about that anymore.

Because when I got out of here, I'd slaughter all of them.

But I couldn't focus on that right now. I needed to focus on surviving this—whatever *this* was.

I had no idea how long I'd been out, or how I'd ended up here. The last memory I had was of the searing pain that'd coursed through my veins, setting every nerve ending ablaze, when one of Adrian's vampires injected me full of silver. Even now, my muscles protested any movement I made, and my skin felt like it had been flayed, every inch of it sensitive, tender. In hindsight, I was lucky to have survived. Silver was incredibly lethal to werewolves. And I had a feeling Adrian hadn't been too careful about the amount he'd pumped into me.

With trembling fingers, I reached up to my neck, feeling for a wound or a mark, but found nothing. The injection point had healed. But how long had I been out? And where were Gabriel and Chris?

I rubbed my eyes with the heels of my palms and

sat up, taking in my surroundings. Bars... Panic rippled through me. They'd caged me like a wild animal. A cage that sat in a cold, grey basement with stone walls and no windows. In fact, the only point of entry seemed to be the single door at the top of a short flight of wooden stairs.

An eerie silence hung around, the place seemed desolate, abandoned. I listened hard, trying to pick up on any sounds or signs of life, but found nothing. It was dead silent, which chilled me to the bone.

This place screamed horror movie.

I climbed to my feet, then froze when I caught sight of a second cage jutted up against mine.

"Gabriel!" I shouted.

His cage was a mirror to mine, bars of cold iron fashioned into a prison. I rushed toward the bars and gripped them hard. He lay inside his own cage, unconscious, his face pallid against the dark curls falling across his forehead. He didn't so much as twitch at the sound of my voice, and I had no idea what to make of that. Adrian had pumped him full of holy water, which was equally as dangerous to vampires as silver was to werewolves. Maybe he hadn't recuperated yet? Or maybe it was daytime? I had no way of gauging the time.

Clutching the bars, I shook them hard, a wave of

anger fueling my strength. They rattled but held firm against my assault.

"Come on!" I shouted, pulling with every bit of strength I possessed.

When they didn't relent, I attempted to squeeze between. Unfortunately, my captors had seemingly prepared for that too. The bars were too narrow, even for my thin frame.

A growl built in my chest and erupted from my lips. I turned away from the bars and coaxed myself into a few deep breaths. Losing control wasn't an option right now. I needed to *think*. There had to be a way out of this. I just needed to *think*.

Except, I couldn't think of anything beyond Gabriel.

My attention kept drifting back to him, while I silently begged him to wake up.

"Okay," I whispered to myself. "You can do this. You can figure this out. It's just the two of you. Chris isn't here. Maybe they let him go, and *if* they did, he would have gone to the others for help." I refused to consider any other outcome.

And when we didn't return home, Lucy would unleash hell to find me. She'd scour the entire city and tear anyone who got in her way to shreds.

Unless we weren't in the city anymore?

That thought stopped me and allowed a sliver of fear to creep in. I truly had *no* way of knowing.

No, I couldn't let fear take hold. I just needed to come up with a plan and a way out of this iron-barred hell. Except, every second that ticked by felt like a cruel reminder of my helplessness.

But I refused to sit here and play the victim. They had *no idea* who they were keeping in this cage. Eventually, someone would come for us. And when they did, they'd find out they needed something a hell of a longer stronger to keep me caged.

The door was clearly the only way in or out. So, I had to assume that was where Adrian and his goons would come through. It was only the only means of escape for me and Gabriel. Not that I was even ready to start contemplating that part yet. I still had to find a way out of this damn cage first.

I wasn't the kind of werewolf to accept captivity. And it certainly wasn't in my nature to remain imprisoned and helpless. I *would* find a way out. I believed that to my very core. I would show Adrian why it was a bad idea to cage a wolf.

Quickly stripping, I let my wolf take over. The transition came so easy to me now that I barely felt it. Or perhaps my mind was just on *other* things. Like my unconscious mate. Once I stood on four legs, I pulled back to the furthest edge of the cage, then charged forward, ramming my oversized shoulder into the bars.

The entire cage shook and rumbled its displeasure with me, but it didn't so much as give an inch. Growling under my breath, I backed up as far as possible in the cramped space and charged again. And again. And again. I didn't stop, not even when my shoulder and knees buckled. I simply picked myself up and tried again. And again. I wouldn't quit until I destroyed this fucking cage.

I. Had. To. Get. Us. Out. Of. Here.

I refused to accept any other scenario.

The sound of my frantic ramming against the bars echoed through the silent basement. Each collision sent a torrent of pain down my spine, but also fueled my resolve. I would not give up.

"Maddie..."

I halted in my tracks and whirled around at the sound of the familiar, but weak, voice.

With barely any thought, I shifted, transforming back into human form. Covered in sweat, I rushed toward the two sides of our cages closest together, then knelt nearest to Gabriel. He turned his head toward me, but his eyes were barely open, his lips a faded pink. I'd never seen a vampire look so sickly before. It also told me the sun hadn't risen yet. If it had, Gabriel's condition would have improved.

"Gabriel," I whispered, my voice trembling. I reached through my bars and then his, but the distance between us was too great, and I couldn't reach him. My hand fell a few feet away from him.

With a strained breath, Gabriel rose onto his elbows and dragged himself closer, not stopping until he could touch the bars. Our hands came together, and tears pricked my eyes. He was so cold. Colder than the metal bars separating us. He managed a weak smile, then brought my hand to his lips and kissed it.

"Save your energy, luv," he rasped, his every word seeming to drain the energy from him.

I shook my head vehemently. "I can't do nothing. I don't know what they have planned for us, but it can't be good. I don't intend for us to be here when they return. We have to get out."

He tried to muster a smile, but it came out looking more like a grimace. "I know. But you're draining yourself. And it isn't working."

He couldn't possibly know that. Maybe one more hit was all this cage needed.

I pressed my forehead against the cold bars

separating us and fought back more tears. "I can't sit here and wait for someone to rescue us." I wasn't built that way. From my experience, no one ever came for you. If you needed saving, you had to do it yourself. And that was exactly what I intended to do.

Gabriel gave a slow nod, his eyes fluttering closed.

"No, stay with me," I begged, my voice breaking. "You need to help me get us out of this. You can't expect me to save your ass."

His lips twitched into a weak smile. "Love you."

Before I could reply, the door above the stairs swung open, and a bright beam of light illuminated the bottom of the stairs. Fear welled within me and I reacted instinctively, shifting into my wolf form. I felt stronger on four legs and with fangs.

"...wants him incapacitated," someone said before they stepped into the light. "Just until *he* arrives."

My lips curled up and I braved a step toward the front bars. If they so much as got within reach, I'd tear their asses apart.

Two figures descended the wooden stairs, one carrying a tray with what looked like two syringes on top. At the scent of silver and holy water, I unleashed a menacing growl that shook every inch of me.

The two men jolted to a stop at the bottom of the stairs, their surprised expressions almost comical.

"She wasn't supposed to be awake yet," the one on the right said. I studied him, memorizing his blond hair, green eyes, and the dusting of freckles forever immortalized on his pale cheeks.

"Who cares? We'll deal with her after," the one on the left said. My head turned and I took in everything about him too, down to his pungent stench.

Green eyes watched me as he moved toward Gabriel's cage. The other unlocked it, and together, they stepped inside. Rage boiled within me and I lunged in their direction, smashing into the bars. I knew *exactly* what they were going to do, and I would *kill* them before they so much as touched Gabriel again.

"Knock it off!" the one with the syringe shouted at me. "Or I'll double his dose."

His words burned through my enraged haze and I fell still. But I didn't once tear my eyes off them.

"That's unnerving as hell," the first guy muttered, his gaze dropping mine.

The other grabbed Gabriel's chin and turned his head to the side. Then, without even the slightest hesitation, stabbed the syringe into Gabriel's neck and pressed down on the plunger. With a choking gasp, Gabriel's back bowed off the floor, his hands clawing at his throat. He struck the one on the left, but it was barely hard enough to throw him off balance. His skin paled and his veins darkened, but it was the sight of his eyes rolling back that brought a pitiful whine from my throat.

The one who'd injected Gabriel lifted his head and sneered in my direction. "We're supposed to dose her again too, but hell if I'm getting into a cage with a raging werewolf."

His companion nodded vigorously. "Let's see if Adrian has any brilliant ideas."

They quickly left Gabriel's cage, pausing to lock it again—much to my dismay—then hurried to the stairs, not taking their eyes off me once. I growled a warning and a promise that this wasn't over, then they disappeared from my sight, once again enclosing us in darkness.

I immediately shifted back and hurried toward the bars, snatching up Gabriel's hand. He didn't so much as flutter an eyelash or twitch. I held his hand, my heart racing in my chest. I had no idea what prolonged exposure to holy water would do to a vampire, but I had to imagine it wasn't anything good.

"I'll get us out here," I promised Gabriel, even though he couldn't hear me. I gripped his hand and lifted it to the bars, holding it as close as I could. "I'll do whatever I have to do to get us out here." It wasn't an empty vow or a pretty promise. It was a binding oath.

I would save us.

I had to. I couldn't let Gabriel die down here. We'd just found each other, and I refused to let anyone take him away from me.

EPILOGUE

Almost dying sucks.

But you want to know what sucks more?

Watching someone you love almost die.

I've said it once, and I'll say it again: The universe has a sick sense of humor. To give me Gabriel and then try to steal him away so soon afterward? That's fucking cruel.

If my life were a movie, this is the part where suspenseful music would play dramatically in the background while our plucky hero and heroine face their darkest moment yet. On the upside, we cut off a demon's head and sent a coven of witches packing. They won't be causing any more trouble. Check and double-check.

But oh, the plot thickens. The Academy Council decided to show its true colors, revealing their connection to Adrian. Father of the year, he's not. I mean, injecting his own son with holy water and me with liquid silver? Bold move, asshat.

One I intend to make him pay for.

I have every intention of making Adrian—and this esteemed *"he"* everyone keeps chatting about—regret the day they decided to harm Gabriel.

They better get ready. When I come tearing out this cage, I'll rip out the throats of anyone standing in my way. Because I have something far stronger than fear fueling me—revenge. The kind that's best served cold.

The universe may have a sick sense of humor, but it met its match with us. We're not your regular fairytale characters—we write our own endings. And trust me, the bad guys won't be smirking for long.

After all, they say love conquers all. And we've got that in spades. With my vampire king at my side, and a vendetta that's grown fiercer with every twist in this tale, our story is far from over.

HITCHED TO THE VAMPIRE KING SNEAK PEEK

We had to get out of here. Escape wasn't just a pipe dream; it was a damn necessity. I'd promised Gabriel I would save us, and I couldn't—*wouldn't*—fail.

I paced the short length of my cage, my paws silent against the cold cement floor. I'd maintained wolf form since Adrian and his goons dumped us here, and not because I was trying to make some sort of fashion statement. My fur, my fangs, and my hulking size gave me an edge my human form seriously lacked. The guards refused to enter my cage because, in their words, "I was a walking nightmare."

They weren't wrong.

My version of playing fetch was a little more violent than a golden retriever's. And I'd be lying if I said I hadn't fantasized once or twice about redecorating my cage with my guard's guts. I *ached* to sink my fangs into them, rip out their throats, and laugh while they died. Perhaps that sounded a wee bit...insane. But honestly, revenge fantasies were the only thing keeping me going right now.

I stopped pacing and forced myself to look at the *other* cage next to mine. The one that contained my mate.

Time had lost all meaning since Adrian's ambush. The only means I had to measure it in this godforsaken place was by counting the number of injections given to Gabriel. Five times now, I'd helplessly stood by and watched as the guards pushed holy water into his veins. Each time, my heart screamed in silent terror. The last time I let a snarl slip, they'd promised to double his dose. The threat was enough to muzzle me. I wouldn't be the cause of his added suffering.

Gabriel lay motionless, his once formidable presence reduced to a ghostly stillness that gripped my heart with icy fear. His veins stood out like black spiderwebs beneath his abnormally pallid skin. Every time I looked at him, a fresh wave of anguish ripped through me. Seeing him like this, so close to death's precipice, made me want to scream into the void.

The problem with vampires was they technically weren't alive. When they were out cold, there was no means to measure their stats. No breathing, no fluttering pulse, no comforting heartbeat, nothing but a cold stillness that threatened to drive me insane.

I'd never been so terrified in my entire life.

The fear choked me. It paralyzed and broke me.

I'd promised to get us out of here, except I didn't know how. I'd thrown myself against the bars over and over until my shoulder screamed in protest, but they didn't budge. Not even a dent. And the floor might have been a mile thick for all the good my claws did.

I was strong, but strength wasn't enough. Adrian had prepared for that—the bastard.

Somehow, he'd known I was a werewolf. I hadn't quite puzzled that one out yet. Then again, Gabriel's vampire council knew about me. They knew we were mates. They knew I'd kidnapped him. Perhaps they'd merely spread word about the king's new *paramour*.

He'd built these cages with me in mind. *Me*. He'd made them to withstand my brute strength.

I stared at Gabriel, a spark of insight flickering to

life amidst my chaotic and desperate thoughts. Gabriel was just as strong as me. But he had a strength I didn't have—a *power*.

Compulsion.

I sucked in a breath, my gaze jumped to the stairwell. At the top sat a door, and our only way out. Beyond that door stood the guards. I could hear them chatting amongst themselves.

The guards held the key to our cages. A key I very much needed.

My focus shot back to Gabriel.

I wasn't the one who would save us. Gabriel was. Slight problem with that plan, of course. He wasn't conscious enough to use his power. He'd told me once he needed to maintain eye contact while compelling someone. Which means I needed him awake in order to implement my weakly-developed plan.

The guards would administer another dose of holy water soon. I couldn't allow that to happen. Gabriel needed to heal, and fast. To accomplish that, I only saw one solution: blood.

My blood.

The very thought sent a shiver down my spine. I had a firm no-biting rule. A rule that, truthfully, I'd been wavering on recently. Ever since Gabriel taught me about the eternal kiss. There'd been a few moments before all this where I'd wondered...where his fangs had tempted me. But those had been passionate moments.

This was different and quite dangerous.

Gabriel was near-death. Weak. Starved. If I let him feed from me, would he have the strength to stop before he drained me dry?

And did I care if he didn't?

I glanced at Gabriel's limp form, hope swelling beneath my breast. Feeding would help him regain his strength. And werewolf blood was far more potent than human. With my blood coursing through his veins, we might stand a chance—provided I survived. I knew the risk, I just didn't care. Fear for my own life paled in comparison to the thought of losing him. Without my blood, he wouldn't have the strength to fight off the guards, to compel them to free us.

Just like that, I made my decision. Strange how easily it came to me now.

Frighteningly calm, I stalked across the cage and approached the bars separating us. I quickly shifted, then crouched low. My gaze dropped to my bare wrist where my pulse thrummed beneath my flesh, a stark reminder of the life force coursing through my veins.

"Gabriel," I whispered, my voice cracking. "If you can hear me, you need to drink. For both of us."

Bracing myself for what I was about to do, I squared my shoulders and brought my arm to my mouth. I hesitated for a split second, the gravity of what I was about to do weighing heavily on me. A second later, I bit down, the sharp pain barely registering over the roar of adrenaline in my ears.

Blood welled from the puncture wounds, the crimson droplets contrasting against my pale skin. A metallic scent filled the air and I silently cursed, my attention darting to the door. Two vampires stood on the other side—our constant guard. If they caught a whiff of blood, they'd come running.

When no one came running, I sighed in relief, then slipped my hand through the bars. I lowered my wrist to Gabriel's lips, praying the scent of my blood would reach him even in his unconscious state.

"Gabriel, please," I whispered. "You need to wake up and feed."

I studied his face intently, searching for any signs of life, any twitch or flutter of eyelids. *Any* sign that my plan would work.

"Come on, Gabriel. Fight," I quietly urged. "My blood will heal you. Then you can save us."

Movement brushed against my wrist and I had to bite my tongue to keep from crying out. His lips parted and his mouth sealed around my bite. I felt the scrape of his fangs, then winced when they punctured my flesh. I wanted to sob with relief. His vampiric nature couldn't resist the call of fresh blood.

Quickly tiring, I slumped against the unforgiving metal bars, allowing them to bear my weight while Gabriel fed ravenously from my wrist. The transformation beneath his skin was swift. Color and life chased the deathly pallor from his face, and erased the webbing of dark veins.

His fingers curled around my arm, strength surging in his grip, and his fangs pierced deeper. A jolt of pain shot through me, and I nearly screamed. Only the terror of us drawing unwanted attention kept me silent.

Gabriel kept drinking, drawing on the essence of my life, pulling himself back from the brink of death. With every swallow, he seemed to grow stronger, and relief spiraled through me, one that quickly dissipated when the world started to sway. Everything seemed to blur around me, the edges of the vision growing dark.

I lay my head against the bars and closed my eyes. Things were getting murky. But just as the darkness threatened to steal me away, I sensed a change. Gabriel's grip loosened and his swallowing slowed. A few heartbeats later, his eyes opened, revealing the stormy depth of his gaze, now clear and conscious.

A weak smile tugged at my lips as our gazes locked, a silent acknowledgement passing between us. Gabriel released my wrist, his lips parting from my skin with the gentlest of kisses.

"Maddie..." he whispered.

I pulled my arm back into my own cage, then laid down on the cool cement floor. I just needed a moment to gather myself.

"Play dead," I slurred. "Then compel them to give you the key."

I rested my head on the floor and closed my eyes. I just needed a minute or two to recuperate. I'd be fine. But before another word could pass my lips, sleep claimed me.

ABOUT THE AUTHOR

Kinsley Adams is a thirty-something-year-old author who stopped counting when she turned twenty-five. When she isn't writing uproariously hilarious romantic comedies, she's raising her womb-gremlin with the hopes that he might one day become the world's first Supreme Leader (and yes, *Debbie*, that's a Star Wars joke). You can find her and her books online at kinsleyadams.com.

If you enjoyed this book, please leave a review! Your support and feedback are greatly appreciated. And be sure to sign up for Kinsley's newsletter at kinsleyadams.com/newsletter for updates on new releases, sales, and more!

ALSO BY KINSLEY ADAMS

www.ingramcontent.com/pod-product-compliance
Lightning Source LLC
Chambersburg PA
CBHW020257030726

47499CB00001B/236